The Call of Zulina

Other Books by Kay Marshall Strom

Forgotten Girls: Stories of Hope & Courage

The Second-Half Adventure: Don't Just Retire—Use Your Time, Resources & Skills to Change the World

In the Presence of the Poor: The Passion of Dr. Vijayam

Once Blind: The Story of John Newton

Harvest of Hope: Stories of Life-Changing Gifts

Quiet Moments for Grandmothers

Daughters of Hope: Stories of Witness and Courage in the Face of Persecution, with Michele Rickett

Hand in Hand: Devotions for the Later (and Lately) Married, with Daniel E. Kline

The Savvy Couple's Guide to Marrying after 35, with Daniel E. Kline

The Cancer Survival Guide

Ordinary People, Extraordinary Faith, with Joni Eareckson Tada

A Caregivers Survival Guide

You Can Afford the Wedding of Your Dreams

Seeking Christ: A Christian Woman's Guide to Personal Wholeness and Spiritual Maturity

The Complete Adoption Handbook, with Douglas Donnelly

Making Friends With Your Father

Making Friends With Your Mother

Mothers and Daughters Together: We Can Work it Out

Perfect in His Eyes: A Women's Workshop on Self-Esteem

Women In Crisis: A Handbook For People Helpers

In The Name of Submission: A Painful Look at Wife Battering

Chosen Families: Is Adoption for You?

John Newton: The Angry Sailor

Special Women in the Bible

THE CALL OF ZULINA

Book One of the Grace in Africa Series

by

Kay Marshall Strom

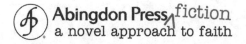
Abingdon Press fiction
a novel approach to faith

The Call of Zulina

ISBN-13: 978-1-4267-0069-9

Published by Abingdon Press, P. O. Box 801, Nashville, TN 37202
www.abingdonpress.com

Published in association with the Books & Such Literary Agency,
Janet Kobobel Grant, 52 Mission Circle, Suite 122, PMB 170, Santa
Rosa, CA 95409-5370, www.booksandsuch.biz.

Cover design by Anderson Design Group, Nashville, TN
Cover illustration by Taaron Parsons

Library of Congress Cataloging-in-Publication Data

Strom, Kay Marshall, 1943-
    The call of Zulina / Kay Marshall Strom.
      p. cm. ~ (Grace in Africa ; bk. 1)
    ISBN 978-1-4267-0069-9 (alk. paper)
    1. Women~Africa, West~Fiction. 2. Slave trade~Fiction. 3. Slave
insurrections~Fiction. 4. Africa, West~History~To 1884~Fiction. I.
Title.
    PS3619.T773C35 2009
    813'.6~dc22

                                        2009014253

Printed in the United States of America

2 3 4 5 6 7 8 9 10 / 14 13 12 11 10 09

Acknowledgements

My deep appreciation to my dear friend Rene Mbongo who first took me to Goree Island in Senegal and stood with silent dignity as I walked through the horrible reality of one of the launching points for millions upon millions of slaves shipped to the plantations of the New World, including America. The fictitious Zulina is modeled after the slave house there.

I also recognize John Newton, slave ship captain turned abolitionist and author of the hymn Amazing Grace. It was while writing his biography that I learned of the English/African couple who inspired the characters of Joseph Winslow and Lingongo.

Thank you to my husband, Dan Kline, my chief encourager, main editor and critic, and my best friend.

1

West Africa, 1787

Hot, dry harmattan winds swept across the African savanna and awakened the yellow-brown sand, whipping it up with wild gusts that swirled and soared high into the air. The sandy clouds that blew in with the first shards of daybreak to shroud the dawn in grit refused to release their grip, and by late afternoon a thick layer of dust coated the entire landscape. Irritated goats paused in their search for edible blades of grass to stomp and shake themselves, and the children who herded them scratched at the itchy grit in their own eyes and hair. On the road, donkeys turned their heads away from the sandy wind and refused to pull their loads. Impatient masters swiped at their own faces as they whipped at the donkeys' flanks, but all that accomplished was to send still more billows of dust into the air.

Sand whistled through banana leaves thatched atop clusters of mud huts in villages, and it settled over the decks of ships as they rocked idly at anchor in the harbor. Even at what was mockingly called "the London house," with its ostentatious glass windows locked tight and European bolts securing its imported doors, gritty wind found a way under and between and beneath and into.

Twenty-year-old Grace Winslow, who had claimed the plumpest of the upholstered parlor chairs for herself, shifted from one uncomfortable position to another and sighed deeply. She reached out slender fingers and brushed a newly settled layer of sand from the intricate lace trim on her new silk taffeta dress and resigned herself to the day.

"The ancestors are angry," proclaimed Lingongo, Grace's mother, from her imposing position beside the rattling window shutters. Silky soft *kente* cloth flowed over her in a kaleidoscope of handwoven color, framing her fierce beauty. Lingongo made a proud point of her refusal to sit on her husband's English furniture—except when it was to her advantage to do so.

"Ancestors! Sech foolishness!" Joseph Winslow snorted . . . but only under his breath. "Wind jist be wind and nothin' but wind."

"Maybe the ancestors don't want me to marry a snake," Grace ventured.

No one could argue that the first harmattan of the season had roared through on the very day Jasper Hathaway first came to court her. He had swept through the front door and into the parlor in a blustering whirlwind of sand, his fleshy face streaked with sweat and his starched collar askew. He stayed on and on for the entire afternoon. Only when it became obvious that no one intended to invite him to eat supper with the family did he finally heft himself out of Joseph's favorite chair and bid a reluctant farewell. When the door finally shut behind him and Grace's father had thrown the bolt into place, Lingongo had turned to her daughter and warned, "Snake at your feet, a stick at your hand. So the wise men say. Keep a stick in your hand, Grace. You will need it with that snake at your feet."

Surely, Grace had thought, *that will be that. Never again will I have to endure such an agonizing afternoon.* And yet, at her parents' insistence, here she sat.

"Perhaps it angers the ancestors that white men insist on settling in a country where they do not belong," Lingongo said, her black eyes fixed hard on her husband.

But Joseph was in no mood for arguments. Not this day. So, turning to his daughter, he said, "Ye looks good, darlin'." And he meant it too. He fairly beamed at Grace, bedecked as she was in the new dress he had personally obtained for just this occasion. The latest fashion from the shops of London, Captain Bass assured him when the captain unwrapped the package and then carefully unfolded and laid out the frock he had secured in London on Winslow's behalf. Captain Bass said it again when he presented the shop's bill of goods, with the price marked out and double the amount scribbled in ("To account fer all me trouble," Bass explained).

In the end, Joseph had been forced to turn over two of his prize breeding slaves to pay for the dress. But, Joseph consoled himself, it would be well worth his investment to get a son-in-law with extensive landholdings, not to mention endless access to slaves. A son-in-law with enough wealth to flash about, to impress the entire Gold Coast of Africa and no doubt dazzle the company officers in London, too . . . well, such a bloke merited the calculated investment he had made in his daughter.

"Ye looks almost like a true English lass, me darlin'," Joseph exuded. "Yes, ye very nearly does."

Grace sighed. In her entire life, she had met only one true English lass. Charlotte Stevens was her name. And if Grace Winslow knew anything, she knew she looked nothing like Charlotte Stevens. Small and dainty, with skin so pale one could almost see through it—that was Charlotte. The she-ghost, the slaves called her. Charlotte's hair was almost white, like an old woman's—very thin and straight. In every way, she was the opposite of Grace. Tall and willowy, with black eyes and thick

8

dark hair that glinted auburn in the sunlight, Grace was a silky mocha blend of her African mother and her English father.

Charlotte's father ran a slave-trading business down the coast. Grace had never been there, although she had seen Mr. Stevens on a number of occasions when he came to see her father on business matters. Charlotte never accompanied him, though. She and her mother mostly lived in England and visited Africa only two months every other year. The few times Grace and Charlotte had occasion to be in each other's company, Charlotte had treated Grace as though she were one of her father's slaves. Never once had she even called Grace by her given name.

"Mr. 'Athaway—now there's as fine an Englishman as ye could 'ope to find, Daughter," Joseph Winslow continued. "English 'ouse 'e 'as too. Even finer'n ours, if ye kin believe it. An' 'e 'as 'oldin's all up and down the coast, 'e 'as—"

"I don't like Mr. Hathaway," Grace interrupted.

"You do not have to like him. You only have to marry him," Lingongo replied. "You are a woman, Grace. Tonight, you will tell the Englishman what he wants to hear. After you are married, take what he has to give and then make your life what you want it to be."

Grace stole a look at her father. A deep flush scorched his mottled cheeks and burned all the way up to his thinning shock of red hair. Embarrassed for him, she quickly looked away.

Outside, the wind grabbed up the aroma of Mama Muco's cooking and swept it into the parlor. It was not the usual vegetable porridge, or even frying fish and plantains. No, this was the rich, deep fragrance of roasting meat. Forgetting his humiliation, Joseph blissfully closed his eyes and sucked in the tantalizing fragrance. A smile touched the edges of his thin, pale lips, and he murmured, "Mmmmm . . . good English food. That's wot it be!"

Lingongo's flawless cocoa face glistened with impatience and her dark eyes flashed. "Where is Mr. Hathaway?" she demanded. "He keeps us waiting on purpose!"

Grace and her parents had endured one another's company for almost an hour by the time Jasper Hathaway finally blustered in, full of complaints and self-importance and, of course, a tremendous appetite. He talked all through dinner, not even bothering to pause as he stuffed his mouth with roasted meat, steamed sweet potatoes, and thick slices of mango.

"... so I sent detailed instructions by the next ship to London inquiring about my various and sundry holdings," Hathaway said. Little pieces of sweet potato fell from his mouth and settled onto his blue satin waistcoat. "I should have gone myself. It is the only way to get things done right. But I do so hate the long sea journey. I am not of your kind, Joseph."

Here he stopped his fork long enough to cast his host a look of pity.

"Aye," Joseph said. "Sea air. 'Tis wot keeps me lungs clean and me 'ide tough!"

"No, no!" Hathaway said with a dismissive wave of his fork. "That isn't it at all. I mean, you can be away for a year at a time and no one misses you. That is, your work in Africa does not suffer in the least in your absence. Not so with a true businessman such as myself. Why, if I were to be away so long—"

Grace stopped listening. The truth was, she had absolutely no interest in anything Mr. Hathaway had to say. And as for his demeanor, she found that absolutely disgusting. So she allowed her mind to move her away from the table and nestle her down in the mango grove, to settle her in her favorite spot where the wind rippled through the branches above her and she could lose herself in books. There, Grace could leave Africa and travel to wonderful places around the world. One day, she promised herself, she would see all those places for real—London and Paris and Lisbon and Alicante . . . the mysterious cities of the Orient . . . yes, even the New World. Oh, just to be outside her parents' walled-in compound!

". . . a business agreement, of course," Mr. Hathaway was saying. "And as a husband . . . well, as I am quite sure you know, I have a good deal to offer your daughter. A very good deal, indeed!"

Mr. Hathaway glanced at Grace and flashed a leering smirk. With a start and a shudder, Grace jerked her attention back to the table.

"Now once again I have come to your house—and under miserable conditions, I might add—for the sole purpose of seeing and of permitting myself to be seen," Mr. Hathaway continued, his voice tinged with pompous irritation. "If there is to be a marriage, as I have been led to believe, I insist that we talk terms immediately. Of course, the business of Zulina will be a necessary part of those terms."

Outside, the trees groaned in the howling wind. Suddenly, a great jackfruit, scorched hard by the sun, smashed through the shuttered window and crashed onto the table. It shattered the hand-painted English platter and sent roasted meat juices spewing across the linen tablecloth. Grace screamed and jumped to her feet and then stared in horror as a dark stain spread down the front of her new dress.

"This is not the time to discuss such things," Lingongo pronounced. "The ancestors are much too displeased. We will talk another time."

"Now see here—" Mr. Hathaway blustered.

"Another time!" Lingongo repeated. Her tone made it clear the discussion was over.

Jasper Hathaway judiciously turned his attention to his

waistcoat. The close-fitting satin garment might be the latest fashion in Europe, but Hathaway's fleshy body proved too much for it, dangerously straining the seams. Sighing deeply, he tossed fashion to the wind. He undid the buttons and freed his ample stomach.

"The ancestors are invisible, Lingongo," Jasper Hathaway stated as if to a not-too-bright child. "They have already collected what was due them in their own lifetime. Now they have nothing more to say. You need not fear the ancestors." Shifting his gaze to Joseph, he added, "Fear the living, present threats to your well-being, my dear lady, not powerless shadows from the past."

Joseph Winslow flinched and paled.

At long last, Mr. Hathaway, jovial and flushed in his flapping waistcoat, and far too familiar toward Grace, sent for his carriage and bid his farewells. Yet even as his carriage clattered down the cobblestone lane toward the front gate, he leaned out the window and called back, "I will not be patient for long, Winslow. Time is running out. And as for Zulina—" The rest of his words swirled away in the harmattan winds.

As soon as the door was closed and bolted, Grace announced, "I refuse to marry Mr. Hathaway!"

Joseph Winslow stopped still. Never in his twenty-one years with Lingongo had he dared speak to her in such a way. Oh, he had wanted to. How many times he had wanted to! But the most he had risked was a mumbled opinion under his breath. Nor had Grace openly contradicted her mother before. But the harmattan winds blew harder than ever. They rattled the shutters and sent jackfruit clattering down onto the roof. And when such a wind blows, anything can happen.

"And just who are you to tell me what you will and will not do?" Lingongo challenged.

"It's my life, Mother, and I . . . I—"

I will what? Grace thought with a sudden jolt of despair. Undoubtedly, the same question occurred to her mother because a mocking sneer curved Lingongo's mouth into a twisted grin, and all Grace's bravery failed her.

"Do you really think I will allow you to stay here forever, playing the part of a useless idler?" Lingongo demanded. "Why should you live like a princess when you bring absolutely nothing to my house? Even a princess must do her part, Grace. *Especially* a princess."

Grace opened her mouth to answer, but Lingongo wasn't finished. Her voice dripped with bitterness as she said, "You, with your washed-out skin and the color of rust in your hair! You, with your English clothes and English ways and English talk. Oh, yes, Grace, you *will* marry Mr. Hathaway. You *will* marry the snake. You will because I command it of you!"

2

"**M**ama Muco?" Grace called softly. She poked her head through the doorway of the inside kitchen, her ruined dress rumpled over her arm. "Mama?"

No answer.

Grace dropped her dress down on a chair in the empty inside kitchen and headed out to the low entryway. The outside African oven still burned hot from breakfast.

"Mama Muco?" Grace called out a bit louder. "I need your help!"

Still no answer.

Grace followed along the entryway all the way to where it opened onto the stone courtyard. There she stopped and shaded her eyes against the blast of swirling sand. Something wasn't right. Then in the shadows she saw Mama Muco on her hands and knees, scrubbing hard at the courtyard stones.

"Mama?" Grace asked in confusion. "What are you doing?"

Muco paid her no mind.

Grace, hands on her hips, positioned herself directly in front of Muco. "Mama Muco!" she demanded. "Talk to me!"

Mama Muco, her face grim, tipped her bucket over and poured soapy water across the stones. With a silent vengeance, she renewed her scrubbing.

"What is all this?" Grace asked, pointing to the dark stains splattered around her feet.

"Blood," Mama said.

Blood? On the courtyard stones? Why, Lingongo would never allow such a thing. No. She would. . . .

And then in a flash, everything became horrifyingly clear. Dinner last night. The tender roasted meat laid out so generously before the insatiable Jasper Hathaway.

Grace fell to her knees and shrieked, "Bondo!"

Mama, her hair flying wild, rose to her feet and flung her black arms wide. "I told her I would not do it," she said in a voice pulsing with controlled fury. "No, I said, not Grace's own gazelle. I will not put it to the knife, I said. Not even for fear of the whip, will I do that."

Bondo! Her dear pet! Grace covered her face and dissolved into wracking sobs. So great was her distress that she never noticed the shadow pass in front of her and stop.

"So I did what my slave refused to do."

Lingongo stood over her.

"Stop that this instant! I will not have such foolishness at my house!"

Choked with grief and shaking with rage, Grace stood up before her mother's crushing presence. But when Grace opened her mouth, her words tumbled over each other, and the best she could manage was to stammer out a tangled, "How ever could you dare to . . ." and "You had no right . . ." and "It isn't fair . . . !" Always it was the same. Grace, overwhelmed with passion. Grace, mute with fury. Grace, helpless before her mother.

Poor Bondo. Back when the monsoon rains flooded the fields, Grace had dared defy her mother and splash out to sit in the relative shelter offered by the canopy of mango trees. A flash of black and brown—that's what first caught her attention. But as she looked more intently, she saw a flicker of white. When she crept close, she found a tiny gazelle trembling in pain and paralyzed with terror. Too injured to run away, it cowered in the trees, resigned to its fate. Grace reached out and picked it up.

"Attacked by a caracal is what I guess," Mama Muco had said when Grace carried the injured animal to her. Though how so little a one could possibly have survived such an attack even Mama couldn't imagine. "Sometimes a creature is just supposed to live," she said. "No way to explain it except that's the way God wants it to be."

"How do you suppose the gazelle got over the wall?" Grace asked.

"It did it because it had to," Mama told her. "No wall is high enough to block out cold, hard desperation."

At Mama Muco's direction, Grace had run back out into the pouring rain to gather fruit from the ghariti tree while Mama built up a fire in the African oven. Then under Mama's supervision, Grace had boiled the oil out of the fruit to make a healing poultice that she tenderly pasted onto the gazelle's wounds. Bondo survived, and with no more to show for his ordeal than a lame leg. And as the gazelle healed, he also grew tame. Grace could grab a handful of fresh millet from the storage huts, and Bondo would walk up to her and nibble the grain from her hand.

Now, as Grace glared at Lingongo, she demanded through trembling lips and clenched teeth, "Why, Mother?"

Lingongo's eyebrows arched in mock amazement. "Why? A true daughter of Africa would never ask such a question. That creature was weak and useless. Surely, even you know that. It was put on this earth to be a gazelle and nothing more. A gazelle does not make a good plaything. But it does make an impressive dinner for an honored guest." Turning to Mama, she added, "Roasted to perfection, Muco. I thank you and pass along compliments from our guest."

Mama Muco, her jaw clenched tight, glared at Lingongo.

"So, you see, Grace, nothing is completely worthless, despite how it may appear," Lingongo continued. "It is all a question of how it is put to use. Remember that lesson, Daughter. It will serve you well."

3

Blinded by tears and spurred on by fury, Grace sprang from the courtyard and sprinted across Mama Muco's kitchen garden. She bounded through the squash and jumped over the calabash gourds, then ran past the millet fields and out into the barren land beyond.

The last of the sweet potatoes had already been dug from the fields closest to the house. In the distance, Grace saw a line of slaves working the field with hoes. Perhaps because she knew how much it infuriated her mother when she talked to slaves, she walked directly toward them. Old men . . . lame men . . . young boys . . . women. Not prize workers, any of them, which was precisely why they made up the majority of the slaves at their compound. Except for planting time and harvest, Joseph Winslow saw no reason to work valuable young men in his fields when he could sell them to the slave ships at inflated prices. That was why Grace immediately noticed the muscular young slave at the head of the line who was doing twice the work of anyone else. When she got closer, she saw something that snatched her breath away—this muscular young slave had just half an ear on his right side.

"Yao!" Grace gasped.

Slaves came and slaves went. In the busy season, many worked the fields. Harvest time, too—always strong young slaves aplenty then. Soon they disappeared, though, and Grace never saw them again. But Yao . . . she had spent her childhood with him. He had grown up working in her father's fields, and to Lingongo's dismay, the two of them had devised all types of ways to play together. One day, as they climbed the ghariti trees, just when Yao was pointing out the village path to his mother's house, Lingongo happened by. Immediately, her whip had knocked the boy out of the tree. How Yao had howled! When he took his hand away from the side of his head, it was covered with blood and half his right ear was gone.

After that, Grace didn't see Yao again. For months she mourned the loss of her playmate, but she was not allowed to so much as mention his name.

That was years ago. Now, here he was, back working in the fields—tall and proud, and not at all like the child she had run and played with.

Grace made her way toward the line of slaves, all of them swinging their heavy hoes up over their heads and then heaving them down onto the dry dirt clods, all chopping in rhythm. She stopped behind Yao.

"You are with slaves," Yao said without breaking rhythm. "Your mother will not be pleased."

"She doesn't know I'm here," Grace said.

Yao's hoe thudded down. A gust of wind snatched up the freshly chopped dirt and tossed it high into the air. His head didn't move, but his eyes shifted toward a stand of trees off to the side of the field.

"Does anything happen here that your mother does not know?" he asked.

Grace followed Yao's eyes. The overseer—a slave named

Tuako, though Joseph Winslow called him Tuke—stretched himself in the late afternoon shade and gazed back at her. An immense feeling of despair washed over Grace. No, not one thing did happen without Lingongo's knowledge. Not one. Fighting back tears, she surveyed the sandpapered land before her. Hopelessness was never clearer than when viewed through a cloud of blowing sand.

"The harmattan winds . . . ," she began. "Some say they tell of dangers."

"*Bubuanhunu,*" Yao said in rhythm with the chopping of his hoe. "Dangers too many to count. They hide in the places you least expect."

Dangers, yes! Grace wanted to scream. *On our own courtyard!* But instead she blustered, "Well, maybe I won't be waiting for dangers to come to me! Maybe I'll leave this place. Maybe I'll follow the road down into town, or perhaps I'll board a ship and sail across the sea to England."

"No. You will not," Yao said.

Chop. Chop. Chop.

"And just how do you know what I will or will not do!" Grace demanded.

"You will not leave this place because you are a slave here," Yao said.

"I am no slave!"

"A slave is exactly what you are."

Chop. Chop. Chop.

"You are the slave, not me!" Grace shot back.

What a thing for Yao to say! Angry and perplexed, Grace glared hard at him: his back, crisscrossed with scars from Lingongo's whip . . . his ankle, bolted into an iron manacle . . . Yao's entire black body glistening with sweat. He swung the heavy hoe all day long, even in the sweltering noonday sun. Nothing like

Grace's family. Oh, no. They all sat inside when the sun was high and entertained guests with food cooked by their slaves, and then they rested and sipped cool drinks and waited for the air to cool. But Yao, he worked through the blistering heat, and he would go right on working until the sun sank into the sea—even longer if his master desired it. That was what slaves did.

"You make no sense at all," Grace protested. "Just look at you!" She pointed to the scar on Yao's shoulder where her father's branding iron had seared the Winslow property mark into his flesh. "Right there! Anyone can see it's you who are the slave!"

"The weak only make the strong stronger," Yao replied.

Chop. Chop. Chop.

"What is that supposed to mean?" Grace asked impatiently.

Tuke called out to Yao, and Yao put down his hoe and moved to the outer edge of the field. He hefted a barrel of oil onto his shoulder. As Grace watched in sullen silence, Yao toted the barrel over to a pile of dry vines, tipped it on end, and thoroughly doused the vines. Though it took some doing, Tuke managed to strike a flint, and Yao set an oil-soaked rope against the spark. When it flared, he tossed it onto the pile. With a whoosh and a roar, flames leaped into the air. Grace let out a cry and jumped back, but Yao did not flinch.

"You belong to my parents!" Grace insisted. "So *you* are the slave, Yao! You, and not me!"

For the first time that day, Yao actually looked at Grace. The quiet control of his voice didn't come close to matching the fierce flames reflected in the depths of his black eyes.

"I belong to your parents? How is that different from you?" he asked.

Grace stared at him. She wanted to explain . . . to argue . . . to prove her case. But the winds whipped the fire into a roaring field of flames, and its heat beat her back.

"The road divides, and each of us chooses our own way," Yao said. "You will stay a captive here forever because you need all this. I need nothing but my wits, and so I will not stay. I will go to the place of my choosing, and then I will—"

The roar of the fire swallowed Yao's words. Grace jumped away, frightened and confused. Tuke called out orders, and the slaves bunched together. In the gathering dusk, Grace could no longer see Yao.

"Will what?" Grace called. "What will you do?"

But no one answered.

Because she had nowhere else to go, Grace walked back to the house. Not through the vegetable garden, though. She refused to look at those stains on the courtyard stones again. Instead, she went around the garden, all the way out to the cobblestone road and then up the path that had carried Jasper Hathaway's carriage away the night before.

When Grace opened the front door, Lingongo met her with simmering rage. "This is *my* house!" she informed her daughter before Grace could shut the door behind her. "*My* compound! Everything here and everyone in it belongs to *me*! I can and I will do exactly as I please with any one of them."

Grace stole a glance at her father, who nervously busied himself shuffling through a stack of papers. He physically flinched as though he had been hit in the face. Grace said nothing. Nor did she look her mother in the eye. But Lingongo had hit her mark, and she knew it.

"I paid dearly for what I have," Lingongo added. "If I must live in this English house, at least it will be mine."

"Me darlin'—" Joseph began in what he meant as a conciliatory voice, although it came out as more of a wheedling whine.

"And you, Grace Winslow. Why did I ever expect more of you?" Lingongo pronounced. "However you may look, your heart is English!"

Grace said nothing. She turned and walked up the stairs and then closed the door behind her. From the corner window she could gaze across the wide expanse of Winslow land. Grace knew every square foot of it—every corner, every field, and every tree. She knew the slave shacks, too, although Lingongo had strictly forbidden her to go there. Even when she was a little child, the groves surrounding those shacks had been her favorite place to hide. The musical jumble of tongues as the slaves called out to one another had so fascinated her that despite the threat of Lingongo's whip, she would hunker down among the trees and listen for hours on end. In time, the languages began to sort themselves out in her ear. Then to Grace's delight, she found she could understand words, only a few at first, but as she grew bold enough to venture among the slaves, more and more words shaped into meaning. Now she could understand most of the slave languages. She was even able to speak many of them.

But while Grace was intimately acquainted with just about everything on her parents' land, she knew next to nothing beyond the stone wall that cut off the Winslow compound from the rest of the world. That wall—as thick as two men standing beside each other shoulder to shoulder and higher than the head of the tallest slave—had two gates, both of which were kept bolted and locked. Only Lingongo and Joseph had keys. The back gate, which opened out to the flat savanna and stretched endlessly eastward toward Africa's inland plains, was overgrown and rusty with disuse. Everyone used the front gate—the one out to the road that led uphill to the villages in one direction and downhill to the sea in the other. Even now a wagon rumbled up that road and stopped beside the storage shed.

"'Ere now, Yao!" Joseph called out from down below. "Load 'em all!"

Grace watched as Yao jumped down from the wagon and set to work emptying out the entire store of cassava and groundnuts from the storage shed. He loaded them into the wagon and then piled in freshly dug sweet potatoes, taking care to fill every empty space.

"Git started early in the mornin'," Joseph said. "Give yersef time at the baobab tree. They's always traders there lookin' to buy."

It was so dark now that Grace could no longer see either of them.

"An' don't be rushin' 'em buyers, neither," Joseph ordered. "Ye won't 'ave so much to carry to market."

As the fully loaded wagon clattered toward the gate, Grace closed the window and sank down on her bed. *"The road divides . . . each of us chooses our own way."* That's what Yao had said to her. He was going to choose a way for himself. She was sure of it. What about her? She could choose her way too!

The baobab tree! I can meet him there.

Yes, Yao would see her waiting at the baobab tree. He would take her to town with him, and she would be away from the compound forever—away from Lingongo and away from Joseph Winslow. And away from Jasper Hathaway. The whole world would be open to her. She could go to the harbor and find Charlotte Stevens's father. Those wonderful places she had always dreamed about—she could see them all!

Grace opened her door into a dark and quiet house. "Mama," she called in an urgent whisper. "Mama Muco, I need you!"

4

Far up the road outside Joseph Winslow's stone wall, past where it winds into a narrow village footpath, dawn broke over a clutch of mud huts. It awakened fathers and mothers and children and grandparents and aunts and uncles and cousins because they all slept together under ever-expanding roofs of banana leaves. Already, blowing dust sanded the savanna countryside. Just the day before, village men had filled the storage huts with harvested millet, which was why wild pigs snuffled and grunted around in such determined exasperation. For them, the millet harvest usually meant full stomachs. But this year the villagers outsmarted the wild pigs. They piled sharp-thorned acacia bushes in front of the entrances to the storage huts. It worked. The pigs' snorted displeasure was proof of that.

By the time the sun was fully awake, the comfortable crackle of cooking fires arose from in front of every hut, and on each fire, a pot of millet bubbled. Already the men drifted together, their bows and arrows and slingshots and digging sticks in hand, restless to head to the bush. There were edible roots to dig up and tender wild plants to pull and frogs to catch and lizards to bring home, all to toss into the stew pots. Perhaps someone would even catch a larger animal, which would mean a feast for the entire village. By the time the sun was hot enough to bake the earth, each family's porridge would be thick and tasty. Everyone would fill a calabash and then stake out a place in the shade to enjoy the day's big meal. And for the families of the most fortunate hunters, a special treat—a handful of beetles to toss into the dying coals to toast up deliciously crisp and crunchy.

Just outside the village gates, a group of monkeys chattered and scolded, demanding a handout. But no one paid them the least mind.

Several women gathered up the sticks and branches their children had collected and tied them all into huge head loads to make them easier to carry to the market to sell as firewood. Other women wrapped up gourds, or beeswax and honey, or even eggs they had gathered. Anything they could sell, they could carry to town on their heads. Older women prepared to spend the day in the village weaving cloth as they minded the little ones.

Speedy girls settled their water pots on their heads and waited for the slower ones to catch up so they could all go together to fetch water. They ignored the boys who chased each other to the goat pens.

"Tread softly on the ground so as not to disturb the ancestors who lie under it," the village elder admonished the rambunctious boys from his place under the great baobab tree around which the village had been built. Because the young respected the wisdom of the old, the boys immediately stopped yelling and walked reverently the rest of the way.

The elder sat alone under the baobab tree. Some days, he had no business at all. It was, after all, a peaceful village, and his job was to settle any differences that came up. When a difference was brought to him, he always began the same way—by chanting, "We are one. We are of one opinion. We love each other."

Another day had begun. One more day in the comfortable familiarity of what had happened every other day that anyone in the village could remember.

As the men headed for the bush, their eyes to the ground where the frogs and lizards hid . . . as the women turned down the path toward the next village, and the next, and the next, and then finally to the marketplace . . . as the giggling girls adjusted empty water pots on their heads . . . as the boys tugged at the staked gate of the goat pen . . . as just another day began in the village, men from a distant tribe swarmed out from their hiding places and encircled the villagers. They entangled them in great nets, like flies trapped by human spiders.

The village men were strong and brave. They did their best to put arrows in their bows and stones in their slingshots and to take aim at their captors, but what good are such weapons against the white man's fearsome firesticks? An ear-blasting roar and a man fell to the ground. He lay still, looking as though a lion had pounced on him and tore parts of him away. Then another roar and the villager's brother fell beside him. Still the village men fought. But what could they do? The strangers charged them with clubs and beat them unconscious.

Before the women could comprehend what was happening, strange arms grabbed them and forced them to the ground. Then ropes wound around their necks. If they struggled, they choked until they couldn't breathe, and so they stopped the struggle. Instinctively, the girls ran to their mothers, but when they did, the strangers snatched them up one by one. Perhaps the boys could have escaped into the bush if they hadn't been so confused that they hesitated too long. When they finally did flee, they ran right into the strangers' arms.

By the time the sun had moved overhead, when the villagers should have been taking their calabashes of porridge to their favorite shady places to enjoy a delicious meal, the men, women, and children stood in a long line—hands tightly bound and a rope tied around each neck—all lashed together into a line of misery. The strangers looked at the sobbing children and heard the mothers' whispered words of comfort, and they shouted for the villagers to be quiet and start to walk. And not to dare stop. Or to be too slow. And to demonstrate that they meant business, they aimed a white man's firestick at the young boy who sobbed at the end of the line, and they made it roar. The boy fell down dead.

And so the line started to move—awkward and slow at first. But as the *slattee's* fighting men's lashes slashed across one back after another, the villagers' feet managed to pick up a rhythm, and the line of people disappeared down the road. Hopelessness faded into a cloud of blowing sand.

All that remained in the village were bubbling pots of porridge, a handful of stunned old women who had started out the day weaving cloth but now were left to comfort a flock of sobbing babies, and one toothless elder who wept alone under the baobab tree as he begged the ancestors for help. But before he begged, he chanted, "We are one. We are of one opinion. We love each other."

Because that was the way he always began.

5

Before dawn cast its first streaks of pink across the sky, Grace pulled her bird-wing blue cotton day dress from the bottom of the pile of clothes heaped in front of her empty wardrobe and slipped it over her head. Mama Muco's usually certain fingers fumbled with the buttons up the back, and Grace brushed out her skirt and straightened the bodice.

"Yes, I suppose this dress will do," Grace said.

"The road is just on the other side of the wall," Mama instructed. "Follow it down to the baobab tree."

Grace tugged at the ends of the puffed-out sleeves. "I hate these silly things!" she complained. "Does anyone outside the wall wear English clothes?"

"Makes no matter," Mama said. "English clothes is all you got."

That was true. Joseph made sure of it. And this dress was by far the best of her choices. The pale yellow gossamer frock with lace appliqués? That silly thing immediately wilted in the African sun. And the silk brocade waistcoat decorated with rosettes? The first time she wore it, buttoned up over her green linen skirt and high-collared shirt with ruffled cuffs, the slaves had actually covered their faces and laughed at her! No, the day dress would have to do.

"Wagons and animals and people on foot, they all gather under the great spirit tree," Mama said. "You certain about Yao?"

Grace grabbed up a handful of her skirt and examined the fabric. "These silvery filigreed ferns woven into the background. Do you think people will notice?"

"No, Child," Mama answered with a sigh. "No one will know how much that cloth cost your father, except for every white man who ever walked into this house and was forced to listen to his boasting."

The wind snatched up the screeches and buzzes and chirps and yips of the savanna, whipped them together with the echoes of moaning cries and then stirred them into a cacophony that soared into the air and gusted through the window of Grace's bedchamber. She cocked her head and listened. For as long as she could remember, those cries had prowled with the wind and haunted her dreams. As a child, she had trembled at the ghostly sounds.

"Wind," her father always said in response to her cries. "Jist the wind. Only a fool is afeared o' the wind."

Lingongo had a different answer: "Warning from the ancestors. They are unhappy. Their howling means trouble is on the way."

Grace knew better than to mention the cries to Mama. Their sound always upset her. The only answer she gave to Grace's questions was, "Do not ask, Child. You be better not to know."

Grace stepped into dark blue embroidered kidskin slippers, then she followed Mama who was making her silent way down the stairs.

Long into the night Grace lay awake, thinking. *Slave to my mother. Slave to my father. And soon, slave to Mr. Hathaway. No, that I will not be!*

Whatever was beyond the wall had to be better. And surely whoever was out there could be no worse than Mr. Hathaway.

Joseph Winslow was a sea captain, although he seldom went to sea anymore. Grace knew he was an important man— important, but not respected. *Admiral* Joseph Winslow: that's what he insisted people call him. And he truly did not seem to notice people's bemusement when they visited the *admiral* in his London house. Glass windows, the house had, and heavy carved furniture shipped over from London—fancy brocade upholstery and richly colored carpets.

When the hidden snickers and rib-poking jokes grew too obvious, Joseph shrugged his shoulders and said, "They's jealous o' me good fortune, is wot!"

On the rare occasions when Grace accompanied her parents to a party or rode in the wagon with her father to the market, he seemed oblivious to the mocking salutes and whispered ridicule his company produced.

As for Lingongo, although she constantly referred to herself as a princess, never once had Grace seen any of her mother's people. Oh, she had heard many tales of gold and riches. Certainly, Lingongo proudly draped herself in luxurious royal clothes. Grace heard stories of Lingongo's father, the great king, who with a single word had the power of life and death over entire villages. But other than slaves, Lingongo was the only African whom Grace had seen at the London house.

Across the inside kitchen, through the entryway, and on to the outside kitchen, Grace followed Mama Muco's sure steps. At every turn, she braced herself for the slash of Lingongo's voice, but the call of birds awakening in the trees and her and Mama's soft footfalls were the only sounds.

When Mama stepped onto the courtyard, Grace glanced down in spite of herself. Not one spot remained on the newly scrubbed stones. Mama hurried across the courtyard until she reached the gravel road. But then she stopped and grasped Grace's hands in her own. Those large, calloused hands that had wiped away Grace's baby tears and rocked her fever-wracked body. Those scarred hands that had more than once stopped Lingongo's whip from ripping into Grace.

"Please, won't you come with me?" Grace begged.

"I am a slave, Grace," Mama said. "You are not. Find Yao. He will take you away."

"Mama—"

"Your Bondo . . . I did not do it. I would not. She brought him to me already prepared for the oven," Mama said.

Blinded by tears, Grace kissed Mama on the cheek and took off running across the mint patch in the far corner of Mama's garden and toward the scorched field. The African savanna was dry and barren, yet cadres of slaves managed to coax fields of sweet potatoes and groundnuts and cassavas from the reluctant soil. Groves of trees peppered the compound grounds as well— papayas and mangoes, jackfruit and cashews.

When Grace reached the blackened earth where she last saw Yao, she paused, shaded her eyes, and squinted out to the east. The rising sun silhouetted clouds of mosquitoes swarming black against a silvery yellow sky. Suddenly, a great bird plunged from overhead and rent the morning with its shrill screech. So close did it pass that Grace could feel the rush of wings on her face. But before she could react, the bird swooped back into the sky, its freshly caught breakfast clutched in its claws.

So fast. So unexpected.

Watch out for mosquitoes, but fail to see the attack claws.

"*Bubuanhunu*," Grace breathed. "Dangers where you least expect them."

Grace lifted her skirt and plunged forward. Past the cassava fields, past the cashew trees, past the goat pens she ran. Her heart pounded and her breath came in ragged gasps, but desperation urged her on. At long last, Grace caught a glimpse of the wall stark against the morning sky. Good. That meant she couldn't be far from the grove of ghariti trees.

From the time she was very small, Grace had clambered up the rough trunk of the tallest of those trees, the one that grew at the far corner of the wall near the front gate. From that perch on a sturdy branch she could gaze at the outside world. Hidden in the canopy of leaves, she had spent many hours plotting a future for herself on the other side of the wall. That tree was the place of dreams. It was the place of hope.

More than once over the years Joseph had threatened to cut down those trees, but Lingongo forbade it. "It would anger the ancestors," she insisted. "Then we would see no end to our troubles." And so the grove stayed.

By the time Grace reached the shaded canopy of ghariti leaves, she was thoroughly exhausted. But already the sun was rising in the sky. Soon Mama Muco would climb the stairs to Grace's bedchamber with a basin of hot washing water. She would make an excuse for Grace's morning delay—say she was pouting, perhaps, and refused to leave her room. But soon Lingongo would know. It could be that she already knew. Grace brushed her weariness aside and searched out the tree pressed hardest against the wall.

The tree had grown since Grace's childhood climbing days. Now one gnarled branch twisted all the way over the top of the wall. Despite her cumbersome dress, Grace sought out footholds in the deep bark fissures. But she was no longer the tough-skinned child who used to shinny so easily up the trees. The rough tree trunk gouged her tender hands and ripped at her skirt.

A proper English lass! Grace laughed to herself. What would Charlotte Stevens think if she could see her hanging on this tree like an overgrown tomboy? And in a fine English morning frock, too, which Joseph Winslow would quickly inform Charlotte was extremely expensive because of the silvery fili-greed ferns woven into the fabric?

Proper English lass, indeed!

An English lass with not the first idea of how to be English. An African who didn't know Africa. A lady whom no one would ever see as a lady.

But not a slave. No, not a slave!

Slowly, cautiously, Grace eased herself onto the branch that hung over the wall. She inched her way out—a little more, then a little more—until the branch sagged under her weight. Stretching her body out as far as she could, she gripped the branch with both hands and continued to edge forward.

With a splintering crack, the limb suddenly broke loose. Grace had no choice but to leap. She landed on top of the wall on her hands and knees. Cautiously, she peeked over to the other side and saw to her alarm that the wall was high . . . much higher than she had expected. And there was no tree on the other side to help her down, either.

From her perch on top, Grace saw that the path didn't come up to the wall the way she had imagined it would. In fact, quite a wide expanse of thick brush lay between the two. Not a bad thing actually, since a number of people were already on the pathway heading for town. Were she to leap down directly into the middle of them, she would attract attention, which was the last thing she wanted to do.

"Good-bye Mother," Grace said with determination. "Good-bye, Father."

She moved to the edge of the wall. "And Mama Muco. Oh, Mama, how I hate to say good-bye to you!"

Then she closed her eyes and jumped.

6

Grace landed in a swath of dusty grass between the wall and the path. Quickly, she jumped to her feet and brushed the dirt and dry grass from her clothes. She adjusted her bonnet, which had been knocked askew by her undignified landing. Then with all the confidence she could muster, she turned her steps down the rutted dirt path and headed for the road that ran past the giant baobab tree.

Women balancing head loads . . . men walking together in twos and threes . . . people calling out morning greetings to one another. Grace looked straight ahead and hurried along the pockmarked road among them. She attracted more than a few curious stares, but most people seemed more interested in their own business than in her.

Surely, I'm getting close, Grace thought as the sun climbed overhead and the path veered away from the compound wall. *Maybe over—*

"Good morning, Grace!"

Grace gasped and jerked around.

"Is anything wrong, my dear?" It was Jasper Hathaway. He had come up behind her with no more sound than a stealthy leopard stalking unsuspecting prey.

"Why . . . no . . . Mr. Hathaway," Grace stammered as she stepped back from the grinning trader. Too eagerly he reached out his plump hands to her. Flashy diamonds on his fingers caught the morning light and sparkled blue and yellow and red. Grace couldn't help noticing that already, even though the sun had not nearly reached its zenith, he was sweating profusely in his too-tight-around-the-collar ruffled shirt, ready-to-pop-at-the-stomach frock coat, and white silk stockings on feet stuffed into buckled black shoes.

"You just startled me . . . sir," Grace said.

"I do apologize," Mr. Hathaway replied with an exaggerated bow. "But, my dear, you really must leave off the undue formality and call me Jasper."

He smiled much too broadly for Grace's liking. In her opinion, Mr. Hathaway did everything much too broadly. While he sat at her parents' dinner table, filling his vast stomach with her pet gazelle, he made a point of showing off his two gold teeth. Now as he smiled, they flashed and glittered in the early morning sunlight. If only he knew how grotesque they appeared to Grace.

"What might you be doing out alone this fine morning?" Mr. Hathaway asked. "Am I correct to guess that you were on your way to visit me?" Once again that leer of a grin spread across his face.

"Um . . . no . . . I have business to which I must attend," Grace stammered.

"Business?" Mr. Hathaway raised his bushy eyebrows at so unexpected an answer. "So lovely a young lady as yourself?" Then a shrewd look crossed his jowly face, and he slipped his fat arm around Grace's waist in a most unwelcome way. "With me as your husband, my dear, you would never have to worry your pretty head about business again. You could lie in your feather bed until noon with slaves to wait on you, and I would take care of every business matter. I know you would like that, now, wouldn't you?"

Grace stepped aside. "If you will excuse me, Mr. Hathaway, I must be on my way," she said a bit more curtly than she had intended.

"Jasper. You must call me Jas—"

But Grace didn't wait for him to finish. She turned away abruptly and hurried down the road. As Jasper Hathaway watched her go, a flash of anger erased his cloying gaze and his face hardened in a resolute glare.

"We will be together soon enough," he called after her. "Soon enough, my lovely lass."

A chill ran through Grace at the stony tone of his voice. Without looking back, she broke into a run.

When Jasper Hathaway called out again—louder this time—a tinge of threat skulked through his voice. "And then you won't turn your back on me, Grace Winslow. No, you will not. Not ever again!"

What had been a simple path worn through the tall savanna grass by the tread of endless feet stopped just ahead at the gigantic baobab tree. That tree was the center to which the wide road led, as well as all the smaller paths. And it was also the point from which all roads began. Magnificent the great tree certainly was, although not many would describe it as beautiful. Completely leafless, as it was most of the year, it appeared to have been plucked out of the ground by a cosmic giant and stuffed back in upside down. That was because the baobab's branches looked to be a system of scraggly roots jutting off an enormous taproot.

"A spirit tree is what it is," Mama Muco had told Grace when the girl asked about it on her way back from a rare trip to the market with her father. "Power rests in its branches, and majesty in its great trunk."

Great trunk, yes. So huge that twenty men could stand together inside it.

Not that a baobab tree was unique in western Africa. Many dotted the grasslands, each one revered for its healing properties. Villagers gathered the seeds and leaves and made all types of medicines from them. If the stories were to be believed, many baobab trees possessed special powers. But only the trunk of this one tree, the largest and oldest and most revered of all, was the hallowed resting place of ancient chiefs. Only this one was said to be the dwelling place of the guardian spirits. Only this one was a great and powerful spirit tree.

"Show respect for the ancestors who have walked before you and for the spirits you cannot see," Mama Muco taught Grace. "But do not worship a tree. And do not worship anything that lives in a tree. There is only one God, and his name is Jehovah."

In Grace's bedchamber at night, when the house was quiet and she and Mama were alone, Mama told Grace many stories about Jehovah God and about his Son, whose name was Jesus.

"Are those the stories of your people?" Grace asked Mama.

"No," Mama Muco said. "They are true stories for all people. A man came to our village with a black Holy Book, and the stories were in there."

Those days with Mama Muco seemed so long ago. It was Mama who had cared for Grace. Mama who had taught her. Mama who had protected her. Oh, if only Mama were here now!

Dark-skinned men gripping clutches of birds pushed past Grace. Women set aside their head loads of firewood and baskets of cola nuts and shook the grit from the lengths of cloth that covered their bodies. Grace stepped off the road and pulled uncomfortably at her tightly buttoned bodice. No more a quiet morning, market day around the baobab tree had grown into a harmony of chatter and squawks and the clap of eager feet on the hard ground.

Clusters of two or three people moved together into ever larger groups in front of wagons fully loaded for the market that lined the side of the road. Grace looked at each wagon for some identifying mark, but they all seemed much the same with their loads of groundnuts and cassavas and sweet potatoes. It was impossible to tell whether one of them belonged to her father. So she turned her attention to the men. Hurrying from one group to the next, she searched each young man's face for a glimpse of Yao's sharp nose and the distinctive tuft of tight black hair on his chin.

"Oh, Yao, please be here! *Please!*" Grace pleaded under her breath.

For the first time that day, a knot of fear tightened in her stomach. It never occurred to her that she might miss Yao. Connecting with him was her whole plan. It wasn't as if she could march into town and look up a . . . a friend.

On the far side of the baobab tree, the main road made a sharp right turn and then led on down to town. Surely, that was the route Yao would take to the market. Perhaps he decided that this day he wouldn't stop at the tree. Or maybe he was delayed, and to save time, he went straight to town. Or it could be that he was early and had already come and gone. Grace might have missed him. Of course, in this crowd . . .

As she frantically searched every face, Grace struggled to fight back tears. So many people! More than a few with sharp noses, and even some with hair on their chins. But none with half an ear on the right side. None of them was Yao.

When Grace had whispered her plan to Mama Muco, Mama asked, "You told Yao you would be there, Child?" And because it all seemed so right, Grace immediately responded, "Yes! Oh, yes!" But the truth was she never actually talked to him at all.

What difference did it make now? Grace refused to allow herself to consider the possibility that Yao had found a way out without her. If he was not at the baobab tree, she would follow the road to town and find him at the market. One thought did stop her cold, however. The wide road that led to the market also led to Jasper Hathaway. And if it led to him, it would undoubtedly lead her—firmly gripped in his fat arm—right back up the road and back through the gate in the stone wall. Back to Joseph Winslow. Back to Lingongo.

Still, what choice did she have? Grace looked up at the other road—the narrow, rock-strewn trail that wound slightly uphill. That road led to Zulina. She could see its sprawling edge from the front upstairs window of the London house.

All of her life, Grace had lived in the shadow of the ancient, sprawling fortress. And all of her life Zulina had been shrouded in ominous wonder. "It's so big," she once said to her father. "Can I go up there sometime?"

"Ye go up an' ye won't never come down again," Joseph Winslow had threatened darkly. Then he added: "An' no one'll be goin' up to fetch ye back, neither!"

Whenever she asked Mama Muco about Zulina, Mama shut her up quickly. "It's a bad, bad place," Mama said. "A girl like you's got no business looking at it or talking about it. I won't listen to any more about that wicked place."

The wind chose the moment of Grace's quandary to rouse itself and blast up to the fortress. It grabbed up haunting cries and dreadful moans, whipped them into a furious howl, and roared them back down in a whirlwind. Under the baobab tree, business stopped and everyone fell silent. Although most people kept their eyes averted, a few, in spite of themselves, glanced up at Zulina. A chill crept down Grace's back and sent a violent shiver through her.

"Well now, look at ye! Could ye be the admiral's gal?" a young sailor called out from his loitering spot in the shade of a lashed-bamboo goat pen across the road.

Startled out of her trance, Grace looked to see who could be talking to her. A greasy-haired sailor with a foolish grin, dressed in the rough pantaloons and blouse of a common English seaman, swaggered over. He couldn't have been more than two or three years older than she. Right behind him was his mate, a tall, skinny lad with a gaunt face badly in need of a shave and eyes that looked Grace over in a manner more befitting a barmaid.

"I said, could ye be Admiral Winslow's gal?" the greasy-haired sailor persisted.

"Yes," Grace mumbled, stepping away from the two.

"Me's Tom and this 'ere's Reggie," the sailor continued. "We sailed with yer father once on a time. On 'is ship, we was. 'E talked about ye and yer African mother."

Tom grinned, as though he expected Grace to welcome them as old friends. She said nothing.

"What's 'a matter with ye?" snapped Reggie. He was distinctly unpleasant, and the vicious scar across his left cheek did nothing to encourage Grace's confidence. "Too good fer the likes of us, is ye?"

Grace opened her mouth, but since she could think of nothing to say, she shut it again.

Reggie looked her up and down. "Jist look at ye," he spat with disdain. "'Eathen Negro, dressed fancy and pretendin' to be white!"

Tom pushed Reggie aside and bowed low to Grace. "Come, now, cain't ye let two gentl'men escort ye to town?"

"Good day," Grace mumbled, unable to disguise her uneasiness. Her eyes darted anxiously down the road to town and then back up the way she had just come.

"Come, m'lady . . . ," Tom began.

"M'lady!" Reggie sneered. He spat on the ground. "She ain't no lady! And she shore ain't too good fer me. I'll 'ave 'er if I wants 'er, I will! And I won't be askin' 'er fer permission, neither!"

Reggie reached out and grabbed hold of Grace. But Grace darted sideways and tore loose from his grasp. All Reggie had to show for his effort was a handful of ripped blue pocket spangled with silvery filigreed ferns.

But Grace was not free yet. To her dismay, Tom had positioned himself in the middle of the road between her and town. Her only choice was to turn around and sprint back up the very path down which she had just come.

No! she determined. *I will not go back home! I will not go back to being a slave!*

With no time to think, Grace made a dash for the narrow road that wound up the hill—the road to Zulina.

7

As the stubborn sun blazed overhead, searing the African plains and sizzling the water in the harbor, a battered ship with the name *Dem Tulp* painted across her hull in peeling blue letters limped in from the wind-whipped sea and dropped anchor at the foot of Zulina fortress. Seven crewmen were still alive, three of them well enough to make their way without assistance into the longboat that rushed to their rescue. One of these was the captain, Pieter DeGroot.

Just three weeks and three days earlier, DeGroot, a lanky giant of a Dutchman, had sailed from Zulina with a crew of twenty-seven men and a cargo of 258 Africans bound for the slave markets of the New World. The plan was to stop first at the island of Antigua, then, if the price for slaves wasn't to the captain's liking, he would sail on to Charleston, South Carolina, in the Americas where riches were assured. Before DeGroot could get the order out of his mouth to raise the ship's anchor, an old priest wearily puffed his way onto the deck to bless the journey. Pieter would have greatly preferred that someone other than a papist perform the ritual, but it was the custom at this particular slave house to allow the old priest to do the honors, a leftover legacy of Zulina's Portuguese past.

Being a peaceable man not prone to push his own way, Pieter DeGroot swallowed his objection and made no argument.

"May God's hand be on this vessel and on all who sail aboard her," the priest had intoned. "May the winds be calm, and may God protect these seamen from attacks by the treacherous heathen on board. In the name of the Father, the Son, and the Holy Ghost. Amen."

It was the same blessing the priest had no doubt said hundreds of times before—perhaps even thousands. When the priest made the sign of the cross, Pieter winced. He couldn't help himself.

While the old man wove his way back to dry ground, the harmattan winds rose up out of nowhere, whipping priestly robes around knobby priestly knees and swirling gritty sand across the ship's deck.

"Sign o' the devil, it be!" toothless seaman Jack Barnes had hissed.

"You mean, a breath of relief from the searing heat," Captain DeGroot snapped. "You should all give thanks to the good Lord for that wind."

If there was one thing Pieter detested more than the business at hand, it was the foolish superstitions of the sea. Still, truth be told, an uneasy foreboding gnawed deep within him too. Already he wished he had not given in to the promise of slave riches and had chosen to fill the hold of his ship with bales of cotton, with fine silk from China, or with beeswax or Indian spices or rare African wood—with anything in the world except the men, women, and little children who lay crammed below decks moaning in terror and misery. It was Captain DeGroot's first voyage on a slave ship, and the wails and shrieks of human agony ripped through him, piercing his soul.

"Them cries won't bother ye a-tall once ye gits yer money fer the Africans at the slave market!" Joseph Winslow had called out jovially. With a laugh and a wink and a friendly thump on the back, Winslow had bid the new captain farewell. "Cain't never make yersef sech good money wi' trade goods," he added. "Ye'll be back. I guar'ntee it—ye'll be back!"

Well, Captain DeGroot was back at Zulina, all right, but not for more slaves to trade. Things had not gone at all as he had intended. First came the attack of jungle fever. Before he was even out of African waters, half his crew was sick with raging fevers and shaking fits. As if that weren't enough, the captives clamped their jaws shut and refused to eat. Within days, the first ones began to die. In desperation, Pieter herded all the Africans up on deck in the belief that airing them out in the sunshine would increase their appetites. How could he have known that they would promptly heave themselves over the railing? That they would rather drown in the sea than take their chances aboard his ship? His crew panicked. In an effort to force the captives to stop killing themselves, the crewmen turned their guns on them. That's when the Africans fought back. Well, why shouldn't they? They had absolutely nothing to lose.

"What a tragedy," Pieter murmured numbly as he stumbled over the uneven ramp planks, blinded by swirling sand. "What a waste. What a terrible, terrible waste." Again and again he repeated this lament, and every time he said it, he shook his head in shocked disbelief.

When he returned to Zulina fortress, Pieter DeGroot didn't talk to Joseph Winslow because the owner of the slave fortress was nowhere to be seen. But *Dem Tulp*, Pieter's wreck of a ship, certainly attracted plenty of attention from the assortment of crew members of the other ships anchored in the harbor. They seemed to have little to do but hang around the docks, and every one of them was eager to toss a bit of advice Pieter's way.

"Too soft, ye was," one old captain stated bluntly. "Pack 'em Africans in tight and chain 'em hard to each other. And don't never let 'em up on deck. 'Tis the onliest way to do it. If they refuses to eat, force their mouths open with a stick and poke the gruel down their throats. Ain't a choice they gits to make. They's yer property, and they does what ye tells 'em to do!"

The others nodded in unanimous agreement.

"Wrong crew, *señor*, that was *su problema*." It was Capitán Alfonso DeSalvo who offered this bit of advice. He was captain of a Spanish ship preparing to set sail for Barbados. "You must make *los Africanos duros*–make them tough. *Sí*, some maybe become troublemakers. But *es importante* that you make them *duros*. That way they no curl up and die. They be no good to you *muertos, señor*. You get paid no *dinero* for dead men."

The African sun blistered Pieter's fair skin, and the dry wind cracked his lips until they bled. Endless clouds of voracious mosquitoes poked through his clothes and punctured his arms and legs until they were raw. And the tortured moans and wails of captives locked in Zulina's cells never let up their cries of misery. Those cries framed the background of every one of Captain DeGroot's days and nights at Zulina. As one day passed, and then another and another, and as the days stretched into weeks, he could bear it no more. He absolutely could not bear it one more day.

"Does anyone have a ship leaving Africa?" Pieter begged one captain after another. "I'll fill any crew position. I'll go anywhere and I'll do anything. Just get me far away from this cursed land."

But one after another, the captains shook their heads.

"Ships ain't filled with slaves yet," each one said. "Ain't

enough good Africans fer us to make a profit at the slave markets."

Still, Pieter DeGroot continued to plead.

"Times is hard," he was told. "Traders is havin' to go farther inland to find good cargo. Ye'll jist have to be patient like the rest of us."

By the time Pieter finally made contact with Joseph Winslow, his patience was in tatters. "What about all the people you have chained up inside the fortress?" he demanded. "Why can't you fill up a ship with them? Then at least one ship could be on its way."

Winslow shook his head. "No, no. Most o' 'em slaves ain't fer sellin'," he insisted. "Them's me breeders."

Pieter stared at him. "Your breeders?"

"Me most valu'ble 'uns—me very best. Big an' strong an' 'ealthy, they is. I keeps 'em fer me own use. Ye knows." Joseph grinned and winked.

Pieter stared uncomprehendingly.

"Ye ain't been a slaver long, 'as ye?" Joseph said. It was a statement, not a question.

Pieter shook his head.

Joseph sighed and continued. "Breeders. They's the ones wot lets us grow the most valu'ble slaves right 'ere at Zulina. They's our own and they's our best. It's 'ow we gits top price fer our special slaves."

"And you never sell the . . . the breeders?" Pieter spit out the word as though it was bitter on his tongue.

"If'n I does, me lad, ye kin be sure 'tis fer a good 'igh price. And I don't take nothin' but gold fer 'em, neither!"

Joseph Winslow and Lingongo didn't summon Captain Pieter DeGroot to their compound and allow him to settle himself onto their comfortably upholstered mahogany chairs in the London house. Nor did they invite him to pull himself up to their imported English dining table with the carved legs and ask him to share dinner with them. And they certainly did not introduce him to their most valuable asset—their eligible daughter, Grace. The disgraced captain of one single wrecked ship? A Dutchman who humiliated himself by begging for employment as a common sailor in exchange for passage home? Obviously, he was not a man of financial means and not one with any valuable contacts or social standing. As for his attitude about the slave trade, that, too, left a great deal to be desired. So there could be no possible reason for the owners of the powerful Zulina slave fortress to waste their time, energy, and quality food on the likes of Pieter DeGroot. Mercy, no!

So Pieter took his meals in the fortress galley with the assortment of other seamen of various ranks whose ships lay anchored at Zulina—and on occasion with Capitán Alfonso DeSalvo, even though Englishmen did their best to keep a respectable distance from Spanish captains. One time, although Joseph Winslow scolded him soundly afterward, Pieter even ate with the African trustees.

"Slaves, they be!" Winslow chided. "Good workers, I grant ye. Me right 'ands, they is. But still, they jist be slaves! At Zulina, we eats wi' our own kind. Ye'd do well to keep that in mind."

Selected from among the captured African people, trustees were indeed slaves, albeit freed from their chains, awarded privileges, and allowed to live much better than their fellow captives. Sometimes, after they had proved themselves, they were allowed to carry muskets. All they had to do to earn such generous benefits was to work as traitors against their own people.

"If we don't do it, others will do it to us," a trustee named Adisa responded defensively to Pieter's pointed question about his complicity with the white traders.

"We still be in Africa," another, called Badu, pointed out. "And as you can see, we still be living."

Pieter had to admit that he did have a point.

The very next day after Pieter's discussion with the trustees, the day after he shared a loaf of bread and a pot of porridge with them, two newly arrived captives—a young woman and her mother—attempted to run away from Zulina. It was foolishly hopeless to be sure; the women were chained together at the neck. Pieter's dinner partners saw them go, and both hollered for the two women to stop. But when the trustees yelled out to them, the women's eyes glazed over and their mouths fell open. Desperation consumed them, and with a jerky urgency they sprinted in a frantic bid for freedom. Adisa raised his musket, aimed, and fired. The older woman crumpled. But the younger one kept running, dragging her mother along behind her, still chained to her neck. Then Badu took aim and fired. That time the daughter fell.

Pieter DeGroot did not eat dinner that evening. He went straight to the small cell-like room that Joseph Winslow allowed him to use as he awaited passage home. He climbed onto his bunk, pulled his knees up to his chest, and wrapped the rough blanket tightly around his shaking body.

Why would a man raise a gun and shoot someone so like himself? What would make someone take the life of a person who had done absolutely nothing to hurt him? To kill another whose plight he could not help but feel from his very own experience? Someone whose desperation he had to know and understand full well? What would make a man do such a thing?

Fear, Pieter reasoned. A man might kill out of fear. Especially fear for his survival.

Power. Oh, yes, there was no limit to what human beings would do in their quest for power.

And revenge. Certainly, revenge could drive a human being to kill another in cold blood. How well Pieter knew that.

Fear, power, and revenge. Pieter could think of nothing else that would drive a sane person to raise a gun and shoot another like himself. Trouble was, every one of those three existed within the stone walls of Zulina, all in desperate abundance—desperate, hopeless abundance.

Yes, that was it! Desperation. Hopeless desperation. That, above all else, could drive a person to unimaginable actions.

Pieter looked around at the stone walls of Zulina.

But what of those stone walls? What of a slave fortress, with locked cells and manacles and chains? What would drive civilized, God-fearing people to risk their lives to sail around the world, to pronounce a whole civilization less than human, to wrap them in chains and beat them, to turn them against their own people, and then to utterly destroy them and wipe out their way of life? What could so steal the hearts and souls from people who were otherwise good and loving and decent and just?

The dream of riches.

Pieter grew up in comfortable circumstances in the Dutch countryside, the youngest child and third son of a prosperous landowner. Although he had wanted for nothing physically, he had always known his was not an enviable birth position. From his earliest days, his father made it clear to him that he would inherit none of the family's land. Neither would Pieter's middle brother or either of his two sisters. Everything would go to his oldest brother, the strutting bully Andreas.

"It's not that Andreas is the best of all my children, nor is he the most loved," his father had explained matter-of-factly in answer to Pieter's protests. "It's just the way things must be. Otherwise, our ancestral land would be broken up into ever smaller and smaller parcels. Within a couple of generations, no one would have enough to support a family anymore. The land must be kept together. In order to do that, it must pass intact to only one child—and by law that is the firstborn son. It is the way the land came to me, and it is how it will go to Andreas. There is no other way."

The second son, Pieter's brother Jacob, chose a life of service to God and became a preacher. At his father's urging, Pieter went to sea.

Spices and fine silk, cotton and rare woods—such was the cargo Pieter had collected from around the world on his previous voyages. But at every port he heard sailors brag about the fabulous riches to be made in the booming slave trade. And all that talk got him to thinking: *Just two or three profitable voyages, and I could buy a nice piece of land of my own. A green veldt on the Dutch countryside all for myself. I could marry me a wife and raise a family. Then I would have something to leave to a son of my own, or to divide up between my sons, the way a good father should.*

Decent men had always done unspeakable things for material gain. And they were capable of astonishing explanations for their actions, all beautifully crafted in civilized Christian words. In time, they actually came to believe their justifications.

Despite the sweltering room and the woolen blanket, Pieter DeGroot shook uncontrollably as the wind roared outside.

8

Joseph Winslow's two-story London house, painted stark white with bright red window shutters, looked as out of place on the parched African savanna as Grace Winslow looked picking her way along the dusty road in a blue English day dress, a bonnet on her head, and embroidered kidskin slippers on her feet.

"Me 'ouse ain't African," her father always pointed out to visitors, as though anyone would have reason to think otherwise. "'Tis a real and true English place, it is. Glass in the windas too!"

He may have to live in Africa, Joseph Winslow had decided long ago, but by God, he would live like a proper Englishman. He was especially proud of the opulent library and its assortment of leather-bound books, and of his study, where brocade drapes set off intricate wainscoted walls and deep-set bookshelves. No visitor managed to make it out of the house without admiring those decorative touches of European extravagance. It had cost Joseph far too much money to miss an opportunity to prompt envy among his neighbors.

Usually, however, it was from his study and not the library that Joseph had the leisure to pull the greatest praise from his guests. For, years earlier, Grace had claimed the library as her own. Most days that was where she could be found, sitting cross-legged in a corner, surrounded by the books her father had brought back from his travels—books for prestige and for her. Truth be known, Joseph could barely read a sentence, though he made a show of pretending otherwise. Not so Grace, who from the tender age of six had the benefit of a tutor.

Joseph Winslow's intention to build himself a fat and protected future by raising a well-bred English gentleman son was not to be. What he got was a half-breed daughter. But the day Lingongo held the baby up to the light, looked behind her tiny ears, and pronounced that her skin would be "English," Joseph decided he might yet have a chance to grasp the the comfortable, respected life he craved. He would raise an English lass, one who would be snatched up by a well-bred and well-attached English gentleman.

On this day, however, the books remained neatly stacked on the library shelves. But then on this day many things were not as usual in the London house. No pot of vegetable stew bubbled over the kitchen fire. Nor did Mama Muco sing the songs of her people, the way she usually did while she halfheartedly waged her endless battle against the gritty dust that Joseph Winslow cursed whenever he discovered it in the carved crevices of his fancy furniture. Mama delayed the discovery that Grace was missing just as long as she possibly could. When Lingongo found her daughter's bedchamber empty, Mama made a point of looking in the library. Then she insisted that Grace was surely wandering through the garden practicing birdcalls, or maybe ducking through the fields distracting the slaves from their work. Of course, Grace was none of those places.

No, things were not as usual. Not at all. And the strangest thing of all was that after the original flurry of searches and blames and accusations, Lingongo and Joseph refused to speak of the matter.

Lingongo marched through the parlor and into the study where her husband sat surrounded by his maps and sea charts. He pulled a map up close to his weak eyes so that he could examine it more closely, and when his wife entered, he didn't even bother to look up.

"Joseph!" Lingongo accused. "The shed remains empty! Where are the muskets and pistols you bragged about to Jasper Hathaway? I see only one barrel of gunpowder as well. Where are all the others you said we had?"

"Storage crates up in the fortress is full to overflowin'," Joseph answered without taking his eyes off the map. "Got us powder an' guns aplenty. We ain't needin' to cart more down 'ere."

"How do you know what is in the storeroom up there?" Lingongo challenged. "Your favorite slaves are the only ones who know about the fortress these days. Now you spend your time at the docks throwing dice and playing cards—and losing *my* gold! Bring those guns and powder here to the compound where I can see them. I want to know you are not losing them to our enemies in your gambling games."

"Enemies, is it then!" Joseph answered in a barely controlled voice. The color rose in his mottled cheeks. He picked up a magnifying glass and lifted it to his eye. "Them trustees is hand-picked by mesef, Woman. I's the boss and they's me workers. They does the work and I tells 'em wot to do. That's 'ow it is."

"And who makes certain they do what you tell them to?" Lingongo retorted. "Only a fool would trust his business to slaves."

Carefully, methodically, Joseph laid down the magnifying glass. Then he folded his map, taking care to place it precisely on the right-hand corner of his desk. He picked up the glass again and with the tail of his shirt, he polished it before he set it back down on top of the map. Only then, with everything in order and perfectly positioned on his desk, did he lean back in his chair and look up at his wife.

"Gunpowder be dangerous, Woman," he said. "Why ye so all-fired set on pilin' it up 'ere behind our 'ouse? Come a fire, we all be blowed to bits o' nothin'. Let 'em trustees watch over it like they's s'posed to. It blows up at the fortress, it be slaves wot's dead an' not us."

"You are a lazy simpleton!" Lingongo hissed. She had long since given up any attempt to disguise her disdain for her husband. "Those trustees of yours would turn on you the minute they got the chance. Zulina is yours only as long as you rule it with a strong hand. Only as long as you force the slaves to cower before you. And cower they do not."

Joseph winced, but he refused to back down. Not this time. Instead, he shoved his chair back, stood up to his full height, and stepped forward to face his wife. "Me trustees is faithful to me 'cause they respects me," he said. "But if'n ye sees it different, then ye jist march yersef up there an' take charge. Ain't no one stoppin' ye."

Lingongo's clenched jaw quivered and her eyes flashed with fury. An African could not take charge of a slave fortress. She knew it and so did he. Otherwise, Lingongo would have taken over long ago. Otherwise, her father never would have needed Joseph Winslow in the first place.

But then Joseph's uncommon bravado began to crumble. Lingongo towered over him by a good four inches, and he felt every bit the way he looked—small and flabby and pale and blotchy-cheeked. When he had first laid eyes on her, he was fit, and his tanned arms were roped with muscles. But the years had worn heavy on Joseph Winslow. His shoulders slumped, and his washed-out, rheumy eyes darted away from Lingongo's steady glare. He never could stand up to his powerful woman. They both knew it.

"The ships'll be fillin' up soon," Joseph said, taking a step back and assuming a more conciliatory tone. "We'll be tradin' 'em muskets off so's we kin ship slaves out agin. So they's really no need to bring the firepower down 'ere, me dear."

Lingongo said nothing.

Joseph pulled his eyes away from her piercing glare. But immediately, against his will, he looked back up at her . . . and he waited.

When Lingongo finally spoke, her voice no longer burned with the anger and disdain to which Joseph had grown accustomed. "Word came to me from my father," she said. "Strength is with the *sika'gua*. The spirits of the ancestors indicate that it is time to prepare for war with the kingdoms of Oyo and Allada. Once the fighting starts, other nations will bring on wars of their own. With so many kingdoms battling, more than enough captives will be available to us. Then the ships will be full, especially if we have the most valuable trade goods—muskets and gunpowder."

Now Lingongo had Joseph's full attention.

"You must gather up all the firepower you can from the ships as they come in to the harbor. Offer the other captains all the cloth and beads and metal bars you have. Be shrewd in your trades, my husband. Make them think they are getting the best of you. Only we know about the wars. And only you and I know what will bring the best exchange once the fighting starts. When that happens, we will have what is of real value right here in our storeroom. Right here in back of our own house, where no one else can reach it. Then we will be able to set the price however high we want it."

Joseph ran his hand through his unruly mop of red hair. War between the African kingdoms. In the slave trade, nothing could be better than that. However the battle went, slave traders were the winners. The warring sides captured each other, and both sides sold their captives to the traders. Lingongo was right. In times of war, the most valuable medium for barter was arms and gunpowder. So if he owned all the munitions . . .

For a man who craved respect, Joseph Winslow put up with a great deal from the proud and demanding Lingongo. It angered and humiliated him to be ridiculed and mocked and held in contempt by his own woman. And not just any woman, but an African woman!

"'Tis a good plan," Joseph said with a hint of a grudge in his voice tempered by more than a touch of caution. "We kin do this, Woman, ye and me."

Despite all, they made a good pair, Joseph Winslow and his African wife. In a business sort of way, that is. If he could just settle this marriage affair with Mr. Hathaway, Joseph's life would be in a very good place. Hathaway's wealth would be most welcome in the Winslow coffers—most welcome, indeed.

The problem with Lingongo was that she would not hold her sharp tongue. Not even in the company of men. Not even before other men of the sea—other white men. It was downright disgraceful, is what it was.

9

Lingongo studied her husband's knit brow, and she knew his thoughts exactly. Yes, yes, yes . . . Captain Joseph Winslow had given up so much to live in Africa, and his wife did not show him proper respect.

Well, why should she respect him?

It was because of him that she was imprisoned in this ridiculous pretend white man's world, locked inside stone walls. She—Lingongo!—born a princess, the first daughter of the greatest ruler of the greatest nation on the Gold Coast of Africa. She, who had caught the eyes of men of wealth and power long before she reached an age appropriate to be given in marriage. She, who had every right to expect a life of luxury, who possessed a whole room filled with beautiful handwoven *kente* robes available to her every day because every day for her was a joyous royal occasion. She, who had so much gold jewelry in her chests that were she to fully adorn herself, she would require three servants to support her arms and her head. She, who had every right to expect to marry royalty and live out her life in pride and supreme comfort.

Because Lingongo was born a princess, respect, reverence, and strength were her due. And as the eldest and favorite of her father's many daughters, she had every right to expect to one day be declared the *ohemmea* and to share his royal power.

It was when the beautiful Lingongo's prospects for a life of royal luxury were at their height that her father, the great king whose feet rested upon *sika'gua*—the Golden Stool of power—called her to him.

"Prepare for a wedding ceremony, my daughter," he said.

Oh, the excitement! It was no secret that of all his children, Lingongo was the favorite of her father. What a wonderful union this was sure to be!

"Tomorrow you will marry an English sea captain," her father said. "His name is Joseph Winslow. After the wedding, you will leave my house and this village, and you will go to live with your husband in his house."

Because she knew she was her father's favorite, and because she knew that he would endure from her what he would endure from no other person, Lingongo dared to argue with the unapproachable king.

"I will not marry a white man!" she protested.

"But you will," her father said, not unkindly but with the decisive voice of authority that told her he was the king and she would be unwise to argue further. "You will marry him because I need you to do so. It is not enough for a princess to look beautiful, Lingongo. She must also serve her people. And with the war drums beating, no one can serve this kingdom now as well as you, my daughter."

Always, Lingongo had been the strong one—the one among all her sisters and brothers with an iron will that could not be bent. Perhaps that was why the great king chose her to seal the deal with the man who now controlled Zulina, the man through whose hands every bit of firepower in that area of Africa must pass. The one who alone could ensure who would possess the might and power of the area. And fortuitously, the one who—were he married to Princess Lingongo—would never have the strength or the will to rise up against him.

"I would rather die than endure such a marriage!" Lingongo cried. "Do not force me, Father, or I will kill myself!"

But the agreement had already been made. By the time Lingongo was informed of it, muskets and gunpowder were on their way to her father's storehouse.

"The marriage will take place tomorrow," the king said. "You do not have to like the Englishman, my daughter. You need only be a worthy princess to me and to your people."

Lingongo said no more. For twenty-five years, she had not liked the Englishman. But for twenty-five years, she had been a worthy princess.

Bowing to his daughter's pleas, the great king made arrangements for her to remain in his house until Joseph Winslow built and furnished his London house—two years, since so much of it arrived in sailing ships from England. But once it was completed, Lingongo's father sent his daughter to live with her husband. A cadre of slaves accompanied her that day, all bearing gifts of fine furniture (which Joseph Winslow spurned), gold jewelry (which he never saw), and fine royal cloth (which was all Lingongo ever wore from that day forward). Lingongo accepted the gifts, and she served her people well. But she did not forgive her father for exchanging her for power and wealth.

Never again could Lingongo walk proudly and hold her head high among her people. No longer did she or any children she might bear have a place in the royal line of a noble people. Never would she forget what her marriage had cost her. And never would she let Joseph Winslow forget—not for a day, not for one single minute.

Yet Joseph was far from the complete fool his wife took him to be. Although he was loath to admit it, he was well aware of where he would be without her—just another English sea captain on a slave ship, battling for survival against the treacherous sea and against the volatile crew and unpredictable human cargo packed aboard. Maybe not even that. With his love of the dice, and the abundance of rum he required to keep his fingers nimble, he needed no one to remind him that his losses in the back rooms and beside the docks were far greater than his sporadic and meager winnings.

Except on one fortuitous day. Joseph Winslow was a brash and confident young seaman back then, who loved a good game of lanterloo sharpened with a tankard of rum. In swaggered a certain boisterous captain by the name of Nathaniel Barbabella who immediately fell under the spell of the carved ivory lanterloo fish that Joseph slapped down on the table before him. With a tankard in one hand, Barbabella snatched up the dice in the other. He gave them a good shake and then tossed them across the table. Flushed with drink, he stayed in the game round after round, the stakes doubling with each play. Next morning, when the rum had worn off, Joseph Winslow announced that he was now the proud owner of Barbabella's ship along with its cargo packed full with firearms and gunpowder. In response, the distraught captain flung himself into the ocean and drowned. The very next day, Joseph Winslow received a summons to appear before the great African ruler.

Joseph had not planned to marry. No, no. He intended to live a carefree life, earning just enough on his slave voyages to keep him in gambling money, and then sailing off in time to escape the consequences of any possible misdeeds. But the African king did not ask Joseph his plans. The king stated his own will and declared that it be done.

Oh, yes, Joseph understood his position in the partnership. Lingongo was certain of that. Much was not to his liking. She was certain of that as well. Yet Lingongo brought alliances along with her, and she brought Joseph vital information—such as the news of the upcoming wars among the African kingdoms.

It was only because of her father's great influence in personal matters, and because of Lingongo's great influence with her father, that Joseph had been able to secure Zulina as his own. Owned by Joseph and controlled by Lingongo, that's what the slave fortress was. For, as both of them well knew, she was the only reason he could gather up the gold that fed his ever-growing hunger for a fling of the dice and the all-night sprees of lanterloo accompanied by his growing taste for rum.

Lingongo looked back at her husband. His eyes were on her. Just as she knew what he was thinking, he knew exactly what was in her mind. They had been together too long. Yes, they did need each other. Although neither would admit it out loud.

"No one anchored at Zulina is offerin' muskets o' pistols o' gunpowder fer sale," Joseph said.

Lingongo's eyes flashed with irritation. "Of course, no one offers it to you. But if you were to show them you had gold, then you would find it for sale. Everything is for sale if you are willing to pay the price."

Her husband, owner of the largest, most powerful slave-trading compound on the Slave Coast! Yet the riffraff that sailed white man's death ships into Africa dared to argue and dispute with him as though they were his equal. And all because of her foolish husband's penchant for making bets on cards and drinking rum as he rolled the dice.

"But, me darlin', they is no gold fer payin' 'em," Joseph said.

"Find Jasper Hathaway. If he wants to marry Grace, his loyalty should lie with us. Tell him if he wants to be the husband of your daughter, he must lend you the money you need. Then use it to buy the firearms."

"No, I won't do it!" Joseph said. But he hastened to add, "Anyway, it ain't fer sure 'e'll even . . ."

"Do it!" Lingongo snapped. Then slipping back into her conspiratorial tone, she cautioned, "But do not tell him anything about the upcoming wars, Husband. That is only for the two of us to know."

Giving their daughter to Jasper Hathaway as his wife was one thing. Trusting him with the secrets of their business was quite another.

"Them muskets and powder'll be in our storeroom tomorrow, me darlin'," Joseph promised.

He was out the door and on his way across the courtyard when Lingongo called out, "The slaves who bring it—after they finish their work, they must die."

10

Blowing grit dusted the sun-baked road as Grace picked her way through the rocks and the clumps of dead grass. Clouds of sand shrouded the sun in a yellow-brown haze. Grace paused to catch her breath, then she lifted the hem of her skirt and wiped at her perspiration-soaked forehead.

It was not the suffocating sun that distressed her so or even the endlessly blowing sand. It was the desperate, wailing moans—as though the very stones of Zulina fortress were crying out in agony.

Why did I ever set my feet on this accursed road? Grace moaned to herself.

Because she'd had no choice. Because it was either this way or back to her mother's house and then to Jasper Hathaway. And so what if people are unhappy up there? People are unhappy everywhere.

"Such foolishness!" Grace scolded out loud.

Lingongo's words! Grace had to look around to make certain her mother wasn't following her. She wasn't, of course, but her words certainly were.

"*You are a fool, Grace! Just like your father!*" That's what Lingongo always said. "*You and Joseph Winslow, two of a kind!*"

Well, maybe Grace did do some foolish things. But she never could understand why her mother always added that last part. Grace and her father, two of a kind? They were nothing alike. Her skin was the color of rich cocoa cream with just the barest hint of fire in her black hair. Why, anyone could see she was much more like her African mother than her English father. But Lingongo never seemed to see anything of her own people in Grace. Certainly not even a touch of African royalty. She was too busy pointing out the weaknesses of Grace's inferior English half.

No! Grace told herself. *I am not a fool. And I will not be one now! I can still turn around and go back to the baobab tree. I can wait for Yao, however long it takes.*

But when Grace turned to retrace her steps, she froze. Far down the zig-zagging road, she could just make out a line of people trudging up behind her.

A search caravan! Grace decided. *Mother must have sent them to catch me and force me back home!*

Grace turned and bolted up the road. But in her haste, she lost her footing and slipped on the loose rocks, landing on her hands and knees. Quickly, she scrambled to her feet and sprang forward, only to stumble again.

Go! Grace ordered herself. *Run!*

She must focus on the road ahead. She knew that. Yet she couldn't resist the temptation to grab a quick glance over her shoulder. When she did, she saw to her dismay that the line of people was closer.

Panic consumed Grace, muddling her thoughts and throwing her into confusion. *Forward! Forward! Faster! Faster!* It was all she could think as she plunged ahead. But dark blue embroidered kidskin slippers were never intended for such a road. Nor was a long day dress with a billowing skirt. Grace's feet slipped on the rocks and she stumbled on the uneven road, heavily pockmarked by footsteps dug into the thick mud during the rainy season.

Tears of frustration and despair flooded Grace's eyes. It was no use. She couldn't outrun her pursuers. And even if she could . . . Grace wiped her sleeve across her face. For the first time she dared look up at the fortress that loomed ahead. An enormous structure it was, hostile and foreboding.

Hide! That's what she must do. *But where?* On her left was a barren incline that dropped precipitously over the side. On the right, a rock-strewn embankment rose up steeply with absolutely nothing to offer cover. Frantically, Grace ran to her left and peered over the edge. Nothing below but a clump of acacia bushes bristling with inch-long thorns.

"*Joam!*"

A voice. And on the road just below her!

Slap, slap, slap.

Grace recognized that sound—bare feet on hard ground. She had no more time to think. Scrambling over the rocky side, she slid down the steep embankment. She braced herself against the pricks and gashes of the sharp thorns and stomped out a small nest for herself in the thornbushes, then she forced her bruised body into the refuge.

Everything fell silent. Even the wind stilled for a few moments, suspending the swirling cries in the air.

Cautiously, Grace inched forward and peered out from her hiding place. Far below, the Winslow compound that Lingongo so proudly claimed as her own stretched out across the vast grasslands. Grace scanned the landscape for her father's stone wall. Strange that as imposing as that wall was, it wasn't the first thing she saw. No, the first thing she saw was a large stand of tamarind trees just like the ones that grew beside the slave quarters—the ones in which she and Yao used to play.

Once again Grace's eyes burned with tears for what used to be. Or maybe for what never really was.

Shuffling feet and rattling chains yanked Grace out of her reverie. She couldn't see anyone, but when a sharp cry rang out, she shoved herself more deeply into her thorny refuge. Just below the spot where Grace slid over the side, the road made a sharp turn. Once the line of people rounded that curve, they would again be in her line of sight. Grace caught her breath and waited.

Within moments, the first man trudged around the bend. In spite of herself, Grace let out a strangled gasp. It was no search party! The man below her was an African. His hands were tied and his feet chained. He was a slave. There was no doubt about that. But . . . what was that on his neck? Grace stretched forward to get a better view.

A collar! The man was locked into a rough wooden collar about three feet long. As she watched, another man rounded the bend. The other end of the first man's collar was locked around that second man's neck. The two Africans were yoked together, like a pair of oxen plowing a field.

As Grace stared, yet another person came around the bend. Then another and another and another. Not all were locked in neck collars. Some were shackled with long, loose chains. But all were bound, and all were lashed at the wrist and ankle. And all, tied together at the neck, were fastened into one long rope train.

Eleven . . . twelve . . . thirteen . . .

Grace tried to count the people as they emerged around the bend. It was hard because the line swayed and stumbled as though the train of captives had walked and walked until they could hardly pick up one leg after the other and still keep moving. Yet they didn't dare slow down, Grace could see that.

Unchained Africans with guns and spears moved back and forth along the straggly human train, prodding and threatening anyone who lagged.

One woman had a baby tied to her back with a dirty cloth, and she kept falling farther and farther behind the man in front of her. Finally, the rope attaching the woman to the man was pulled so taut it looked as if it might strangle both of them. An African man wearing a white man's shirt ran over and jabbed repeatedly at the slow woman with his spear. She roused herself and, gasping and straining, managed to drag forward a bit more quickly.

Grace forced her eyes away from the struggling woman and looked down the line—a young boy who could not yet be in his tenth year . . . a woman ripe with child . . . two young girls clutching their bound hands and sobbing . . . several strong young men who stared straight ahead. All were tied together. One after the other, they stumbled along in the rope train.

Then she saw him. Before she could catch herself, Grace let out a strangled gasp and cried out loud, "Yao!"

He was the last person in line. His neck was locked into the back end of a wooden collar, his ankles tethered in chains. And his hands were lashed together behind his back.

"Lingongo!" Grace spat accusingly through clenched teeth.

The guard in the white man's shirt swung around and searched the incline, and then he fixed his gaze straight at Grace's hiding place. She shrank further into her acacia nest and pulled her head down as low under the thorny branches as possible. Lacy leaves of gray-green dipped down and danced in front of her face.

The African man took a step toward her hiding place and paused to survey the underbrush.

Grace hardly trusted herself to breathe.

Foolish, just like Lingongo always says I am! Grace cried silently. *Why, oh, why did I say her name out loud?*

Slowly, the guard moved forward, stomping down the grass in his path until he was so close that Grace could see beads of sweat glistening on his blue-black forehead. All he had to do was lower his eyes, and he would stare straight into her face. Grace willed herself to stop the trembling that had started in her legs and moved up to her arms. If she didn't, she would cause the entire thornbush to quake.

A sudden shriek jerked the man's attention back to the rope line of people. The woman with the baby tied to her back had fallen. Her little one tumbled loose and now hung upside down with his head on the ground. It was he who shrieked so piteously.

"Up!" black-man-in-white-man's-shirt ordered as he ran back. He jabbed at the fallen woman, all the while ordering, "Up! Up! Up!"

The woman grabbed for her baby with her bound hands and tried to rise, but she kept stumbling and falling back down. She couldn't get her footing because the human train never slowed its pace. Every time she seemed about to get back on her feet, the moving line yanked her down again.

Forgetting the black man in the white man's shirt, Grace stretched forward.

The man in front of the woman kept walking, and the woman behind her stared straight ahead as she lifted one foot after the other. They dragged the woman along between them. Grace could see the woman's mouth moving as she continued to grab for her screaming baby. Then the baby was silent. After that, the woman stopped trying. Still the line didn't stop.

"Won't anyone help?" Grace breathed through her tears. This time no one heard her. Misery swallowed up her words.

Then Yao shuffled past her hiding place. Grace could see fresh whip slashes crisscrossing his already deeply scarred back. Yet he held his head high. Even chained and beaten, he walked with pride.

Grace covered her mouth with her hand to stifle her anguish.

Long after the captives had passed out of sight, after the hot wind had swallowed up the sound of their footsteps, Grace trembled among the acacia thorns.

To come up this forbidden road had never been her intent. Yet it would be useless to go back to the baobab tree now. If she returned to the place where the roads met, which one would she take? She had hoped to get aboard a ship and leave Africa, but that was before she climbed over the wall—before she saw this other side. Now she knew she could never make it to London by herself. Even if she did, how could she manage in a place she knew only through books? Charlotte Stevens? She wouldn't speak to Grace in Africa, so why would she help her on the other side of the ocean? Grace would be even more of a stranger there than she was here. She didn't belong in Africa, and she certainly would not belong in London.

No. The only possible way to go was up. Frightening and unknown though it was, this road was the one that led to Yao. Yes, he was bound and in chains, but Grace had seen his face, and it was not the face of a slave. Besides, Yao had sworn to her that he would find a way out!

With new resolve, Grace pulled herself free of the sharp acacia thorns. Scratched and bleeding, she scrambled up the embankment and set her sights on Zulina.

11

On a cloudless morning, the rising sun cast fiery embers across the deep blue of the Atlantic Ocean. The spectacular dawn filled Pieter DeGroot with a great sense of renewed hope, for at long last he was ready to sail from Zulina's accursed harbor. Lucas Bass, the one-eyed, black-tempered captain of the notorious slaver *The Raven*, was not the person he would have chosen as a sailing mate. But then he didn't have the luxury of choice. No other offers had come his way, and he was prepared to do anything to escape the constant wails from the slave cells.

With the first rays of dawn, Captain Bass began to pace the deck. Now and then he paused to scowl at the horizon and then back toward the narrow doorway that led into the fortress—the loading gate everyone called the "door of no return." His irritation mounted, and he paced some more. As the sand in the hourglass marked the passage of time, Captain Bass's mood grew blacker and blacker.

"What's taking that devil of a priest so blasted long?" the captain demanded.

Since this question was addressed to no one in particular, no one was required to answer.

The last of the supplies had been secured on board well before sunset, including a full hold of slaves who lay chained and locked below deck. Pieter DeGroot stood by ready to cast off. He recoiled anew at the sounds of the captives' terrified screams.

"First light, says he!" continued Captain Bass, his voice rising in anger. "Well, first light's come and gone. I won't wait no longer!"

"Ye cain't leave without gittin' us blessed," a leathery sailor called Jess protested.

Captain Bass glared at him. "I never did respect them superstitions of the sea, nor the fools who persist in clingin' to them," Bass snapped. He turned his back on Jess and ordered, "Set sail!"

The Raven was the first ship to sail from Zulina in more than a fortnight, and although the hold was packed full, Lucas Bass was less than pleased with the quality of his cargo. Older men and women, children, people with deformities and wounds— that's the best he was able to purchase. He wouldn't get nearly the price he had gotten for his last shipload that was for sure. Not a strong young buck in the lot, and only a precious few supple girls of breeding age. Hardly enough to satisfy his own sailors, let alone rouse excitement at the slave markets. But what could he do? Every day that his ship sat empty in the harbor, he lost money. And with the Dutchman's offer to work for free in exchange for passage, well, Lucas Bass finally decided to take what was available to him and sail.

"'Tis a bad omen, us leavin' wi'out a blessin'," Jess grumbled.

His mates nodded their solemn agreement.

One added darkly, "Cap'n is calling a curse down on us all, 'e is. If somethin' 'appens—"

Leaving Africa in an unblessed ship didn't bother Pieter DeGroot one bit. He never did put much stock in that formality. It certainly hadn't done much to help his first voyage. And now, being most eager to put as much distance as possible between him and the African coast, he was only too happy to jump to the captain's command. Before the day was over, he proved himself an able sea hand and a willing one too. He called sheets when ordered and hopped to and handled the lines. A man who knew his business and would take orders—Captain Bass smiled and congratulated himself on getting such a crewman, and at no pay!

"That bloke'll be eatin' at the cap'n's table, 'e will," Jess muttered to his mates. "'E ain't one o' us."

On their third day at sea, Lucas Bass, his tongue loosened by ale, said to Pieter, "Too bad 'bout your lost ship. But you's a good seaman. You kin git yourself another."

"I won't sail back to Africa," Pieter replied.

The captain laughed. "Slave trade got you spooked, eh? Don't tell me you've fallen for the superstitions too."

Pieter said nothing, but his eyes fell on the hatch that led to the hold where the captives lay tight-packed and chained. Their screams and cries had died down by the second morning, but the low moans never ceased, day or night.

Captain Bass's eyes narrowed and his tone grew sharp. "Well, let me tell you somethin'," he said, his finger poked in Pieter's face. "Slave trade ain't such a bad thing. Necessary evil, that's what it is."

"Necessary? Well now, strong arguments can be made for and against that point," Pieter replied. "But of the evil, oh, yes! Of that there is no doubt. Absolutely no doubt at all!"

"Listen to you!" Captain Bass said with a snort. "Grabbing for your share of the black gold whilst at the very same minute disparaging the ship what brings it! Well, let me give you a word of advice, smart lad. There be two sides 'ere, the slave traders' side and the slaves' side. And you better choose one or t'other, Dutchman, 'cause you cain't have it both ways. Try to live in both worlds, and you jest might die tryin'."

Captain Bass was never destined to benefit from the "black gold" packed so tightly into the hold of *The Raven*. Jess would not forgive him for cheating the ship out of the protection of an official blessing, and at every turn he reminded the other men of the danger into which Bass had selfishly and foolishly thrust them all. He said it when one crate of live animals died suddenly. ("No blessin', cap'n says, so we'll all pay the price by starvin' to death!") And he said it when a slave managed to attack a crewman with a knife. ("What do we expect? Unblessed ship, it is. Like as not, we'll prob'ly all be murdered in our sleep.") And he said it again and again when the flux first showed up in the slave hold. ("Throw 'em sick 'uns over before we all git sick and die! And whilst yer at it, throw Bass over too. Pay 'im back fer runnin' out on the blessin'.") Before long, Jess had everyone frightened and on edge.

Just then an errant, rogue wave came out of nowhere, washed over the deck, and swept poor Jess overboard and out to sea. "Just as he said," the crewmen whispered one to another. "It's either Cap'n Bass or us."

The next morning, when the captain walked onto the deck and squinted into the rising sun, two crewmen grabbed him from behind. Before he could gather his wits about him, others rushed up with rope to bind him.

"'E's kickin' me!" a sailor called out to Pieter. "You . . . secure 'is feet!"

"This is mutiny!" Pieter protested. "You will all die for this!"

"Is you with us or is you not?" the sailor demanded.

"Absolutely not!" Pieter said. "Now see here—" But already, the men had Pieter down too.

Lucas Bass, they set adrift in the longboat. He was, after all, their captain. But Pieter DeGroot, who was just a sailor like them, they tossed overboard.

"You're nothing but bad luck," Bass complained to Pieter as he pulled the Dutchman into the longboat.

"I thought you weren't superstitious," Pieter replied.

"Well, I am now," said Bass.

After their second night floating aimlessly at sea, just as dawn began to break, Pieter suddenly sprang to his feet and shouted, "Look!"

Lucas Bass blinked into the rising sun and mumbled under his breath. But then he saw it too. He jumped up and stared hard, cursing the loss of his telescope. On the horizon was the unmistakable silhouette of a ship.

Pieter waved his arms in the air and screamed, "Here! Over here!"

Bass yelled, too, flapping his arms with such enthusiasm he almost tipped the longboat over.

After what seemed hours, Pieter cried, "Look, it's slowing!"

"They see us!" Bass croaked in what was left of his voice.

Before the sun reached its zenith, a slaver from the Americas, loaded with guns and rum, pulled the two desperate castaways aboard ship.

"Yer in luck," the captain told the two as he offered them hardtack and water. "We's on our way to Africa. A'fore week's end, ye'll be safely in Zulina harbor."

Four days later, Pieter DeGroot pulled his hat low to protect his face from the whipping sand and once again made his way up Zulina's loading ramp.

"Thieving bastards," Lucas Bass growled in response to Joseph Winslow's look of pity. "But at least we two is alive."

"More'n kin be said fer 'em fools wot took yer ship," Joseph replied. "Wi' no cap'n in charge, they's good as dead."

Then Joseph Winslow invited the filthy, windswept men to his cabin where he passed around the rum bottle and lifted a cup in toast. "To us wot 'ave the power!" he proclaimed.

Lucas Bass, his face hard with fury, echoed, "To us with the power!"

Pieter raised his cup and drank down his rum. He looked around him at the solemn walls of Zulina, echoing with the anguish of more Africans than Pieter could comprehend, and he held his peace.

12

The hazy African sun dipped its fire behind the fortress towers and cast a sudden pall across Grace's path. Raw anguish echoed from its bleached stone walls. *What is this place?* she wondered with a shiver of dismay. *A prison, perhaps?* A desperate scream rang out from one side, answered by yells shouted from the other. *Or a lunatic asylum?* Maybe those ships in the harbor had brought all the deranged people from Europe over to Africa. Grace remembered her father's horrible bedtime stories of his childhood journeys to Bedlam Hospital in London to watch the antics of the poor wretches locked up inside. "Cain't go see 'em no more," he lamented. "Now only folks wot 'as tickets is let in."

"This way! Move 'em on in. Bucks here, breeders over there. Not those! Bring those down this way."

Voices! And just up ahead!

Frantically, Grace searched the hillside for a place where she could hide. To the left? No, no. That wouldn't work. Maybe to the right? Nothing there. Not so much as a ditch or a gulley. Not even a thornbush where she could stomp out a hiding place.

Perhaps she could turn around and retrace her steps and escape this terrible place. Maybe go to a village up the road until she could think of another plan. She couldn't see anyone behind her. But then . . .

Slap, slap, slap.

Footsteps! The captives were not far behind her.

Grace must move forward. She had no choice.

As she crested the hill, Grace got her first full view of Zulina. Three stories of sun-bleached stone blocks, it was. Vast and menacing, it rose above two massive wooden doors. Grace could see tiny windows cut into the rock walls at intervals, but only a few. On the side away from the harbor, off to her right, a low, windowless building stretched out and around. It was almost like a second building attached to the first one.

Tight. Impenetrable. Zulina offered no respite and certainly no place to hide.

Then Grace noticed the walkway near the top of the main building.

If I could just get up there, she thought. *But how?* She could see no access whatsoever. *Perhaps around back?*

To Grace's horror, the great doors began to swing open. Frantically, she thought of excuses that could explain her presence. She might say that she was going to town and had lost her way, or that she was looking for the marketplace, then ask innocently if someone could point her in the right direction. Or maybe she could say that she was new to the area—just off a ship from London.

But when no one appeared to demand an explanation from her, Grace relaxed a bit. Alone in front of the fortress, she stared into its gaping mouth. Again she heard the familiar moans and cries, only now they sounded as if they were right beside her.

"Ye go up there, Daughter, an' ye won't never come down agin!" Grace quaked at the knees and shrank back as her father's warning echoed in her ears.

"Make room for the next ones!"

The same rough voice barked out new orders—only louder now, and from just inside the open doors. Grace dashed for the right side of the fortress. She pushed herself through a small opening where the low building met the massive one and pulled in her billows of skirt after her. A narrow staircase was cut into the wall, so she squeezed into the gap underneath.

For the first time since she climbed the ghariti tree and jumped off the compound wall, she allowed herself to breathe a sigh of relief.

With the sun now at its zenith, the shadowed gap between the stone walls offered refreshing coolness. Grace reached out and ran her hand along the rough-hewn stones of the wall. She leaned forward, closed her eyes, and allowed the dampness to soothe her stinging face and hands where sharp acacia thorns had ripped into her flesh. Of course, she couldn't stay there. And yet, as she moved deeper into the gap, she found that the space widened considerably. Maybe she could make this her hiding place for a while. Anyway, once the sun went down, it would be easier to . . .

A rock-hard hand clamped across Grace's mouth with such force it jerked her backward, knocking her off her feet.

Grace kicked and flailed her arms, trying her best to scream as she fought with everything in her. But she was no match for the muscle-bound arms that gripped her. Dragged backward through a small opening in the wall, Grace was forced into a dark, musty room and tossed to the floor. With a thud, a wooden door slammed shut.

"Don't hurt me!" Grace pleaded.

Although she could hear ragged breaths, and she could feel the steamy heat of another body uncomfortably close to hers, no one answered. Grace strained to see, but she could make out nothing in the darkness.

A sudden rush of indignation swept Grace's terror away. She jumped to her feet and demanded in English, "Just what do you think you are doing?"

No answer.

A small opening near the top of the wall let in a tiny beam of light, and as her eyes adjusted to it, Grace managed to make out the silhouette of a tall, muscular man. Definitely African. A slave, no doubt. Her captor stood directly in front of her, not three feet away.

Assuming Lingongo's famous hands-on-hips stance, and speaking with all the force and authority she could muster, Grace switched to the language of Mama Muco's people. Again she demanded, "Who are you?"

Still no answer.

Indignation thrust Grace up to a Lingongo level of courage, something she had never before achieved. "What do you think you are doing?" she demanded in Yao's language.

"I do not *think*," the man responded in a low, controlled rumble. "I *know, Lioness!*"

"What . . . ?"

"I waited for you."

"Me?" Grace huffed. "That's ridiculous! You could not possibly know I'd be coming here. I didn't even know myself. If it hadn't been—"

"Your life in exchange for my villagers," the man stated. "That is my offer."

"Really, I have no idea what you are talking about!" Grace made a grand show of annoyance. She forced her bonnet back into place and rearranged her badly disheveled clothes.

"Your husband will know what I mean," the man said. "And when he hears, he will release my people. If he does not, I will—"

"I have no husband!" Grace proclaimed. "But my father is a very important man. I just happen to be Grace Winslow, daughter of Admiral Joseph Winslow, and I demand that you let me out of here at once—or else!"

Grace lifted her head in defiance, fully intending to intimidate this impudent slave into submission. But now that her eyes had adjusted to the darkness and she could see him more clearly, her bravado faltered. She took a second look, and it dissolved completely. The man was *huge*, with a much more powerful build than she had realized. And the way he glowered at her . . . never had she seen such fierceness in any of the slaves at her parents' compound. Grace decided it would be better if she did not issue any further orders. This man was no Joseph Winslow. And she certainly was no Princess Lingongo.

"You are not the killer lioness?" the man demanded. "The one they call Lingongo?"

"I . . . I don't know about any killer lioness," Grace stammered. "But Lingongo . . . she is my mother."

"Your mother!" The controlled rumble erupted into a roar. "So she sent you!"

"Oh, no!" Grace insisted. "She doesn't even know I'm here! If she did, she would be furious with me. I just walked up here—"

"No person just walks up to this place," the man interrupted her.

"Oh, but I did!" Grace tried to explain. "Because it was the only road I could take, you see. The wide road led to town, but Jasper Hathaway is there, so I couldn't go that way, and anyway two rude seamen blocked that path. And I simply could not go back to my home. And a friend of mine named Yao, who is a slave. . . . Maybe you've seen him? He was brought here and—"

"Enough!" the African ordered. "So you are the daughter of the slave trader and the killer lioness."

"Oh, no!" Grace protested. "My father is Admiral Joseph Winslow, like I said . . . a ship captain . . . and my mother is an African princess. My father works with slave traders like Mr. Stevens, but I know nothing about a killer lioness."

Grace watched with alarm as seething rage twisted and transformed the man's demeanor. He reached out as though he would grab her. "You are here in answer to their orders!"

Shrinking back, Grace replied, "No! If they knew I was here, they would . . . they would—"

What would they do? Force her back home in chains and whip her until her back was ripped and scarred? Drag her to her own wedding with a wooden yoke around her neck? Or had they already decided to abandon her to her fate as her father had so often warned?

"I am not a slave," Grace whimpered.

"Nor am I!" the African proclaimed.

Suddenly, Grace longed to pour out her whole story to this man who hid himself in the shadows, to tell him about Yao who spoke his language and who also refused to be a slave even though his back was crisscrossed with scars, and he struggled up the road in chains and with a wooden yoke around his neck. Maybe this African would know something about that train of people she saw. Maybe he could help her find Yao—perhaps even set him free. After she told the man her story, she would beg him to let her go. But go where? To release her . . . but to what? The truth was she had no place to go.

Exhausted beyond endurance, Grace sank into a corner and wept.

The African moved away. He opened the door and quickly pushed it shut behind him. Outside, metal clanked against metal. Grace knew that sound. It was an iron bar dropping into place. She was bolted inside . . . all alone in the dark.

From all sides, and from up above and from down below, agonized moans and muffled cries wormed their way through the solid stone walls, dragging Grace further and further into the depths of despair. A panic burned in her, gathered in her throat, and grew until she thought it would strangle her.

Jumping up, Grace pushed against the bolted door. "Let me out!" she called. "Please, somebody let me out!"

Nothing.

As she pounded and kicked at the door, Grace's voice rose into a shriek.

No answering sounds. Nothing but the same cries and moans as before.

Grace threw herself against the door and screamed, "I don't belong here! Please, please . . . I am not a slave!"

No response.

For hours Grace railed and pounded until her body was bruised and her strength spent, but it was all to no avail. Finally, she crumpled to the dank floor and raised her anguished voice in a hopeless wail that blended in with all the other sounds of hopelessness.

"Don't leave me here!" she pleaded to the empty room. "Not all alone in the dark!"

The only reply was the wind that howled through the opening high above her head.

13

"Stop wasting time, Muco!" Lingongo ordered.

Mama Muco hesitated, her dusting feathers poised over the carved legs of the English dining table. "But Master Joseph said—"

"I said, stop wasting your time."

Mama shrugged and moved out to the kitchen garden to pick vegetables. Although she was in no mood to agree with Lingongo on anything, she had to admit that to constantly brush away at never-ending dust was indeed a ridiculous waste of time.

Lingongo went into the dining room and kicked savagely at the leg of the carved mahogany table. Then she grabbed up as many brocade pillows from the chairs as she could hold, and one by one she tossed them through the open window. How she hated the London house! She detested its fussy pretentiousness. *Admiral Winslow!* How could her fool of a husband not know that Africans and white men alike laughed at him behind his back? That they mimicked his strutting walk and pompous carriage? Joseph Winslow—her husband—was nothing but a silly joke.

A joke, however, that kept her people wealthy and respected, and preserved her father's position as the most powerful man on the Gold Coast.

When she heard the back door open and close, Lingongo called, "Muco! Bring a cup of comfort tea to my chambers."

"Yes, madam," Mama Muco answered.

Lingongo's locked bedchamber was at the top of the stairs, through an outer room she also kept locked to everyone but herself. The bedroom was furnished in the manner of her royal childhood. It brought her great comfort to run her hands over each of the beautiful carved wooden chests, one after the other, and to remember. No satin or brocade or embroidered fabrics could be found in Lingongo's room. Oh, no. Her furniture was overlaid with paper-thin layers of pounded gold.

In all their years together, Joseph had managed to catch only fleeting glimpses of the opulence of Lingongo's private chamber. One time, early in their marriage when he thought his wife was away, he had dared to pry the outer door open and then to force the lock on the inner door. What he saw in the instant before his wife's whip sent him sprawling came back to him again and again in his dreams. But the scar across Joseph's left cheek was reminder enough so that he never again dared attempt such a transgression.

To make the comfort tea as it should be made—the only way Lingongo would accept it—Mama Muco rushed to gather fresh bissap blossoms from the high, swaying branches that grew alongside the house. Usually, she could holler for a slave to gather the blossoms, but this day no one was in shouting distance. Just as she was about to despair, a blast of wind rattled the thick bush, and red blossoms showered down at Muco's feet. But blossoms for comfort tea were not all the wind brought to her. It also gusted in the faraway voices of the *ntumpane*—the talking drums. Mama Muco stood up, her apron filled with red blossoms, cocked her head, and listened. The drums were some distance away, but they clearly carried the beat of war.

Mama Muco was not the only one to whom the wind carried the beat of the drums.

Joseph Winslow sat at a table in his favorite corner room of Zulina fortress, where the breeze gusted through in a most pleasant way. He stopped, his hand still high in the air and the dice clutched tight, and he listened. The drums annoyed him no end. He knew they carried a message, but because he had never learned to understand the language of the talking drums, he couldn't grasp the message that whirled in the wind. For the hundredth time, he swore to ask one of his trustees to teach him the drum language—it was African, after all. How hard could it be? Then he tossed the dice across the table, rolled yet another unlucky number, and plunged further into debt.

Pieter DeGroot was on the bluffs above Zulina gazing wistfully out to the ocean toward Holland and home when the wind pushed the beat of the drums his way. For all he knew, it could have been a rhythm to accompany some tribal celebration feast, or perhaps it was a religious ritual. Still, the cadence didn't seem quite right for a celebration. And the drumbeat was so persistent, ever more intense as it went on. Perhaps that was what made Pieter shift nervously and wish with all his being that he was on a ship sailing away from Africa.

Grace was alone in her dark cell when the winds forced the drumbeats through the small opening high up in the stone wall. So constant were the muffled cries and moans that they had begun to sink into the background and she hardly noticed them anymore. But she stirred at the sound of the surf's rhythmic beat on the rocks below. Or was that the surf? It took her a few minutes to realize it was drums. Grace didn't know their language, but she figured it must have something to do with the ancestors' anger. They had every right to threaten punishment. She trembled with fear and curled herself more tightly into the corner.

Africans also heard the talking drums. Up the roads and over the paths and down the trails, across the grasslands and through the villages, into the slave shacks at Joseph Winslow's compound and through every crack in the stone walls at Zulina, the wind blew the drums' beats. Men and women stood still in the fields or gazed up from their pots of bubbling millet. They halted their business talk or ceased tracking prey. Everywhere, men and women stopped and listened to the message of the *ntumpane*:

> *War is coming . . .*
> *White men block the coast . . .*
> *War is coming . . .*
> *No guns for Africans . . .*
> *War is coming . . .*

Drums or no drums, Mama Muco had work to do. She boiled water, tossed in the blossoms, and let them steep. She strained the red bissap blossoms into a china cup. (Some things English suited Lingongo very well, including porcelain cups!) Mama then carried the comfort tea up the stairs to Lingongo's bedchamber.

"Your tea, madam," Muco called out as she rapped gently on the outer door.

Lingongo didn't answer.

The house slave rapped again, louder this time. "Madam, your tea!"

Still no answer.

For a full five minutes Muco knocked on the door and called out. When Lingongo neither responded nor cracked the door open to reach out for the tea, Muco clattered the cup down on the floor and turned to leave. She started down the stairs, but then her anger exploded, and she stomped back up.

"Your daughter is gone from you!" she stormed at the closed door. "Does nothing touch you?"

She brought her foot down on the fine English porcelain cup, again and again and again, stomping it to powder to the beat of the drums. Then Mama Muco went back down the stairs.

Lingongo would not have drunk the comfort tea anyway. In the time it had taken Muco to boil water and brew the tea on the outside kitchen stove, Lingongo had descended the stairs and left by the front door. She had marched down the cobblestone road to the gate and then down the path, her eyes fixed on Zulina. In the stifling heat of midday, drum voices whipped over Lingongo's head. She had not even arrived at the baobab tree when she saw a wagon coming toward her with Joseph perched up front next to the slave driver.

"We must talk now," Lingongo called to Joseph. Gesturing toward the slave, she added, "Without him."

Which is how it came about that Joseph took the wagon and went alone to the powerful African Gold Coast chiefdom at whose head Lingongo's father sat. Lingongo longed to go along. Actually, she longed to go in her husband's place, which she considered the only possible way to ensure that the mission would be done right. But she could not. Only Joseph, as legal owner of Zulina, was in a position to negotiate properly with the king.

Joseph drove the wagon straight into the forbidden palace enclave, past the drummers who knelt high on a ridge, positioned in such a way that the wind would be certain to catch the drumbeats and send them whirling in four directions. Warriors preparing for war, *sofos* entreating the ancestors for wisdom and guidance, *togbuis* speaking aloud the words of the ancestors, and just plain people on their way to complete everyday business—all stopped to stare at the white man, the brazen outsider, who dared drive a wagon into their sacred territory.

Without the slightest hesitation, Joseph Winslow marched up to the royal hut where the king sat on a carved wooden throne encased in gold and right to the place of the *sika'gua* without invitation. Lingongo's eldest brother tried to stop Joseph from entering, but Joseph pushed past him. "I gots business wi' the king!" he stated. "Outta me way, lad!"

The king's *okyeame* rushed forward to approach the king on Joseph's behalf. "Only talk through the speaker," Lingongo had instructed her husband. "Do not approach my father directly. The speaker knows the way to put words together so they cause no offense."

But Joseph would have none of it. If he had something to say to the king, he would just out and say it. And if the king had something to say to him, then his majesty could say his piece too.

So Joseph stood before the king with no mediator and announced, "I will be gatherin' up all the muskets and gunpowder. No one will have firepower 'ceptin' fer me."

"You must have much gold to pay for all this," the king answered.

"Gold," Joseph said. "Well, see, that's an inter'stin' thing, King. There isn't too much gold available to me jist now. But soon enough I'll have plenty, I will. The important thing fer ye to know is that ye'll git no firepower 'ceptin' through me."

"Certainly you will make the price agreeable—"

"I will make the price wot I wants it to be. An' ye has no choice but to pay the price I says ye'll pay."

"You and I have a long-standing agreement, sealed with the marriage of my daughter."

"Yes, yes," Joseph said with a dismissive wave of his hand. "We still be partners. That's why I be 'ere makin' the offer to ye and not to yer enemies. But business is business, and it's time we made us a new deal."

"Deals made and sealed are not thrown aside," the king said.

Joseph laughed. "Ye isn't left wi' much choice now, is ye?"

Because Joseph Winslow had pushed the *okyeame* aside, no one stood between him and the king to add sweetness and eloquence to his words. No one was there to carefully wipe out the insults that crept in to his talk and to replace them with words gentle and wise. No one made certain that what Joseph meant to say was what the king actually heard.

Which was most unfortunate. Because after Joseph finished speaking, after he said, "So, does we 'ave us a deal 'ere, mate?" and after the king nodded his agreement, Joseph bid farewell to his father-in-law and headed home in triumphant ignorance. He never noticed the anger that flashed across the royal face.

14

The shaft of sunlight that glinted down from the opening at the top of the wall was the only way for Grace to judge time. She had long since given up banging and kicking on the door and slumped into a corner where she lay in hopeless despair. Hours had passed . . . maybe an entire day . . . when the grate of the iron bolt jolted her to attention. The door scraped open, and the same African man stepped back through the doorway. This time, however, he was not alone. A second African followed close behind. Short and wiry, this one didn't seem much older than Grace. Ropes of muscle stood out on his arms and legs, and his wildly twisted hair gave him a fierce look.

"This is the one, Cabeto?" the second man asked in a harshly clipped voice. "This is the slave trader's girl?"

"Yes," Cabeto answered in his low rumble.

The wiry African stepped up to Grace. He grabbed a handful of her thick hair and roughly jerked her head back. "Copper," he growled. "Who is her mother?"

"The lioness," Cabeto answered.

Grace opened her mouth to protest, but thought better of it.

The wiry man barked a mirthless laugh, harsh and clipped like his speech. Grace's heart sank. This man was not like the first one, not like the one he called Cabeto. Cabeto burned with passion, yes. And he was strong and determined. Without a doubt, Cabeto was a man to fear. But if he were cruel or ruthless, something much worse would have happened to her by now.

This new one, though, he was different. Something indefinable hung over him. Something in his manner and his voice—something about his laugh—caused Grace to quake to the depths of her soul. She bitterly regretted having ever left the London house and climbing over the compound wall.

"Her father will pay for her," the wiry African stated.

"We will offer her for trade, Tungo," Cabeto said. "In exchange for our people's freedom—yours and mine."

Tungo shot a look at Cabeto. Even in the near darkness Grace could see the greedy glint in his eyes. "And for muskets and gunpowder. And for gold."

"I know nothing of muskets and gunpowder," Cabeto insisted, "and I care nothing for gold. If the white man will allow my kinsmen to return to our village and live in peace, I will not seek revenge."

Tungo glared at Cabeto. "That is not all I want. The white man and his *askari*—his soldiers—must pay for what they have done to us. We will rip this slave house out of their hands. Over their dead bodies, we will dance and beat the drums of *durbar*."

"Such wild talk!" Cabeto scolded. "Your way will kill all of us."

Tungo put his face close to Cabeto's. "Now is the time!" he hissed. "The white man's daughter walked into our lair, and he will pay richly to get her back. He will give us anything we demand. If he does not . . ." Here he gave the tangle of Grace's hair a hard yank. "If he does not, we will slit her throat!"

A scream burst from Grace's lips. With the sudden strength that comes from terror, she wrenched herself away from Tungo's grasp.

His fists clenched, Cabeto reared up to his full height. Towering over Tungo by half a head, he commanded, "No! We will not kill her!"

Immediately, Tungo's demeanor changed. "No, no," he insisted in a conciliatory tone. "You misunderstand me, my brother. I did not mean we would *really* kill her. We will only *say* we will kill her. When her father hears our words, he will give us whatever we ask. It is the way the white man does business."

For a moment Cabeto held his aggressive stance. Then with a shrug, he turned away. "Ask for guns and gold if it pleases you," he said. "I want only to see my kinsmen free."

Tungo didn't answer. He brushed Grace with a hard glance and then turned and ducked out through the still-open doorway.

Grace expected Cabeto to follow, but he did not. Awkward and silent, he stayed where he was.

"I should not have brought you here," he murmured. "This is a fight of your father and mother, not of you."

"Would . . . would he really kill me?" Grace asked.

"Certainly, he would," Cabeto answered. "Why not? After what your father does here in his prison, almost any African would kill you."

Grace stared at Cabeto in disbelief. "*His* prison? What do you mean by that? My father is the captain of a ship. He's an English admiral. Not a—" Sudden and unexpected tears flooded over Grace, and she wept. "I saw a slave mother and her baby dragged to death because she couldn't keep up with the other slaves she was tied to, so she–" Now Grace was sobbing. "My father is a proud man, and sometimes a foolish man . . . but he is not a . . . not a murderer. He does not kill mothers and their babies . . . not even if they are only slaves–"

"Your father is the captain of a ship. That much is true," Cabeto said with icy bitterness. "He is part of the *maafa*–the horrible disaster, the ships of death. He steals people from Africa and forces them across the water so he can sell them to the white cannibals. He calls them slaves, but they are my people."

Grace swiped a sleeve across her tear-streaked face. "What are you talking about?" she demanded. "My own mother is African!"

"Yes, the lioness. A traitor to her people. We all know of your mother. She is your father's partner in the work of the most wild and cruel of the bush spirits." Cabeto spat out each word as though it was poison in his mouth. "Or should I say, she is the boss of your father!"

Grace opened her mouth to protest, but the low moans echoed through the fortress walls and burrowed into her. They sent a shiver through her soul and stole every argument out of her mind. Her father's boss . . . yes, that was an apt description of Lingongo. But a lioness? And a traitor to her people?

One time, when Grace was a child and she saw her mother whipping a slave, Grace had asked, "Who are the slaves, and who are the masters?" Lingongo had answered, "The ones with the power are the masters, and the weak ones who can be beaten down are the slaves. That is why you must always have the whips and the guns on your side."

Cabeto didn't have a whip or a gun, but he did seem to have power on his side.

"Are you a slave?" Grace asked in a trembling voice.

"No," Cabeto answered, struggling to keep his voice under control. "I am not a slave. But my kinsmen are." When Grace didn't respond, he continued, "In the middle of the night, slavers attacked my village. The young men who slept at the village gate only had time to call out an alarm before they were killed. My people are strong and brave, but they could not stand against the *slattee*'s muskets. Your father—"

Grace jumped to her feet. "You accuse my father of kidnapping and killing people in your village?"

"No," Cabeto said, "it was Africans who came. Africans from tribes we did not know."

"Well, then—"

"But your father paid them for what they did. And you tell me this: if it was your father's beads and muskets and gunpowder that brought the attackers to us, then who really crushed my people?"

Grace opened her mouth to speak, but Cabeto didn't give her a chance. He wasn't finished.

"The *slattee*'s men bound our feet and hands and locked us together in chains. When my brother, the firstborn of my father, tried to protect his babies, he was struck down with a knife. He died at his wife's feet. Tungo is angry, yes, but he is not alone. I am angry as well."

"But you admitted my father wasn't even there," Grace protested. Tears welled up in her eyes again. "He isn't a bad man. My father is a respected ship's captain."

"What do you think he packs in his ship?" Cabeto countered. "Sweet potatoes and millet?"

"I . . . I don't know," Grace stammered. "I have never actually been to the harbor."

Cabeto pointed an accusing finger. "You are not an innocent

child," he insisted. "You are a woman. You live where this prison stands between you and the setting sun. You can hear, can you not? You can see, can you not? You can smell, can you not? When the very ground cries out with the misery of my people, you cannot tell me you know nothing."

"Many people are slaves," Grace sobbed. "The ones who are weak—"

With a look determined and hard, yet profoundly weary, Cabeto stared straight into Grace's eyes. "All along the horrible march, I thought about ways I could escape. When we arrived here, our captors unlocked our chains and brought us before your father. They tore the clothes off our bodies so he could look us over carefully, from our feet to our teeth to our hair. Then he paid the ones who brought us in. Your father gave beads and muskets and cloth and gunpowder to those who captured us. That's what he said my people were worth. And then your father burned his mark into each one of us."

Cabeto pulled off his shirt. He took Grace's hand, and though she tried to pull away, he forced her fingers up to his bare shoulder to the jagged scar. She jerked away as though she herself had felt the rage of her father's red hot branding iron. But there was no mistaking it. JWL. It was indeed the personal mark of the Winslow family—a mark seared into every one of the slaves who passed through their compound.

Grace sank to the floor and buried her head in her hands. What was there to say? Her head throbbed from the never-ending wails around her. It seemed that a multitude of captives together screamed out accusations against her family . . . accusations against her. She did not even look up when Cabeto left and pulled the door shut behind him. Not even when the iron bolt slid back into place.

After a painfully long time alone, the door once again scraped over the stone floor and roused Grace from her nightmarish blur of thoughts. Even though only the faintest shade of light now shone through the opening at the top of the wall, she could make out Tungo's angry face.

"We must prove to her father that we mean what we say," he was saying, evidently to Cabeto, still outside the door. "Unless the slave trader believes we will do what we say, our words will mean nothing."

Tungo pulled a knife from under his shirt and held it up before him. The dim beam of light hit its nicked blade.

15

"Oh, Lord, have mercy on my poor girl!" Mama Muco moaned. Her low, husky voice rose in anguished wails as she rocked back and forth and wrung her hands in distress. "Lord, Lord, have mercy!"

"Stop that noise!" Lingongo ordered. "I cannot think!"

Mama Muco slunk away to a far corner of the room where she slumped her sturdy body down onto the green and gold brocade settee. Never would she have dared to do such a thing in normal times, but these times were far from normal. Muco grabbed up a feather pillow and buried her face in it. She contined to beseech God on Grace's behalf, but her muffled prayers faded into a mournful background croon.

Lingongo paced back and forth, back and forth, back and forth. Each time she whipped around, her agitation increased. Suddenly, she stopped and turned on her husband. Joseph trembled at his desk and stared in horror at the bunched-up pile of bloody fabric before him. He wouldn't have recognized the blue fabric were it not for the silvery filigreed ferns. It was the self-same rich background that had first caught his eye in the London shop.

"You must be a gentleman of fine breeding," the shopkeeper

had told him. "Such a man cannot resist genuine woven silver."

Joseph had immediately bought the fabric and instructed the dressmaker to make a stylish dress for his daughter's eighteenth birthday. Or was it her nineteenth birthday? Either way, it seemed an age ago.

"We will not give those savages anything!" Lingongo exclaimed. "Not one thing—except the firing end of a musket!"

"But, me dear," Joseph ventured, his voice quivering, "Grace be our darlin' daughter! And if 'em 'eathen devils gone an' done this to 'er . . . !"

Joseph Winslow—*Admiral* Joseph Winslow—had gone positively green in the face. He cast a furtive glance at the terrible thing that lay partially exposed on his desk, and a whole new wave of horror rose up in him. It wasn't possible that one of the trustees—one of *his* trustees—could be capable of such an atrocity! Yet here the evidence lay before him, right on his desk. How could he deny what his own eyes could clearly see?

Someone to whom Joseph Winslow had generously extended extra responsibilities and privileges—someone he had *trusted*—had betrayed him! As if it wasn't enough to kidnap his daughter, that animal—that *rat*—had actually slashed off half of Grace's gentle finger and had wrapped it in a piece of cloth ripped from her dress! Then in the middle of the night, that someone had left the horrid package in his courtyard. Scaled right over his wall of protection and crept up to his very door, the rotten bugger had!

Joseph picked up the scrap of paper, and for the hundredth time he squinted at the illegible scratches the savages intended as a ransom note. He'd had to ask Mama Muco to decipher it for him:

Amatsewe family captured by Mandingo two day after last
no moon to be freed
They be named Sunba, Ayi, Okaile, Ayikaile, Ama.
5 box musket
10 barrel gunpowder
10 bar gold
today by sunset—east gate—take all guard away else daughter
die cut throat

Joseph took a deep breath and willed his hands to stop
shaking. He absolutely must keep his wits about him. He must
think clearly and act wisely and decisively.

"Grace is an idiot!" Lingongo fumed. "A disobedient
simpleton! She brought this on herself by disobeying our orders
and leaving the compound. She brought this on all of us!"

"I fault 'Athaway fer not bringin' 'er back 'ome by force,"
Joseph said. "'E 'ad the chance an' 'e didn't do it!"

Mama Muco threw her head back and once again cried out,
"Oh, if I'd only known! Lord God, have mercy on our Grace!"

Lingongo wheeled around and thrust her finger into Mama
Muco's face. "Out, slave!" she ordered. "Out of this room and
out of my house!"

Muco gave a start, and her voice froze in midcry. She looked
around, perplexed at finding herself in her master's office—and
spread out across his sofa at that! She pulled herself up and
hurried away. Once she was out the door, her agonized cries
and prayers echoed back into the room, but already her mind
was beginning to race.

Lingongo turned her outrage onto her husband. "My
father would never allow such a contemptible insult to go
unchallenged!" she declared. "He would not rest until he
regained his family's honor. He would call his warriors together,

and he would lead them right up to the traitors' refuge. He would grab up the ones who had so offended him, and he would make every one of them pay for their crimes with their lives. Then my father would personally throw their worthless remains onto the garbage heap and leave them for the hyenas to tear apart and devour."

Joseph pulled back from his wife, cringing in spite of himself.

"We'll give 'em the five slaves they asks fer," he offered. "We kin spare 'em. When the wars start, we'll git us plenty more. Ye said so yersef. An' we kin let go th' muskets an' powder they's demandin'." Then his voice hardened as he added, "But we ain't givin' 'em no gold! No, sir, that's where I draws me line. No gold!"

"You are an even greater fool than I thought you were!" Lingongo fumed. "If it gets known that slaves can set themselves up as bosses over us, that they can make threats and we will bow to their demands, where will it stop? No! We are the ones who have the power. We will give them nothing!"

"But, me dear, they'll kill Grace," Joseph protested.

"We have paid too dearly for what we have to lose it all now," Lingongo said. "Both of us." Then she turned her back. There was no more to say.

Joseph hefted himself up from his chair. As the color rose to his face, the blotches on his cheeks and nose burned a fiery red. "Aye, too dearly," he said. "But she's still yer daughter."

Lingongo swung around to face her husband. "I am the firstborn princess of an ancient and noble people," she stated, "the daughter of the great ruler who alone has the power to rest his feet on the *sika'gua*. Grace Winslow, with her English name and her washed-out skin and her rusty hair—Grace Winslow, with her fancy clothes from London and her books and her ideas to do whatever she wants and go where she does not belong—Grace Winslow is your daughter, Joseph, not mine."

"She be me daughter, then. Me English lass," Joseph answered. "An' since she's set to marry Jasper 'Athaway, soon I will 'ave me a 'igh-class English son o' me own too. One with 'oldin's and gold aplenty. Then I won't never agin 'ave to . . ."

Joseph raised his hand and rubbed it across the fiery scar on his left cheek.

"Won't have to what? Do you think Jasper Hathaway will just hand over gold for your games and your drink? He is too clever a man for that. Without my help, he will take your hand-raised English lass, and he will take your slave house too. Then he will throw you to the harmattan wind."

For some time, Lingongo and Joseph stood face-to-face—both with jaws clenched, both with eyes aflame.

"We will not give 'em gold!" Joseph repeated.

"We will not give them one single thing!" said Lingongo.

16

How Grace longed for the endless screams to stop! The noise made her head ache; it trapped her in a twilight of smothering heat and spinning blocks of stone. As consciousness slowly returned, she discovered to her astonishment that the screams came from her parched lips. Despite the agony of pain that enveloped her entire body, she tried to pull herself up, but she could not. Then she struggled to cradle her throbbing right arm, only to find that she couldn't move it more than a few inches from its uncomfortable position, which was stretched awkwardly out to one side.

Something was terribly wrong.

Where am I? Slowly, the question emerged from somewhere in Grace's muddled confusion. *What has happened to me?*

With a great force of will, she opened her eyes.

Grace was half-lying, half-sitting in what looked to be a large, steamy dungeon. Oh, how her right hand hurt! With great pain, she turned her head to the side and squinted in an effort to see. Someone had twisted a blood-soaked rag around her hand, and her wrist was shackled to an iron bolt in the wall!

With every bit of strength she could muster, Grace gave a hard yank.

"Aaaahhh," she screamed as searing pain ripped through her arm. The dungeon spun before her eyes and the room lit up like a bonfire roar. Grace fell back and collapsed into great, gasping sobs.

As the pain ebbed, an awful stench assaulted Grace. Fighting the nausea that arose in her, and taking care not to move her right arm, Grace cried out in English, "Help me!"

The strangled voice that came from her throat sounded strange and foreign in her ears. Not at all like any voice she had ever heard before.

"Mother!" Grace screamed in Lingongo's language.

No answer.

"Help me!" she called, this time in the tongue of Mama Muco's people. "Please, somebody help me!"

A rat scurried past her feet and stopped to sniff at the bloody rag twisted around her hand. With a terrified gasp, Grace tried to pull away, and then she dissolved into screams and sobs. It was all too awful! This had to be another horrible nightmare. It just had to be!

"Won't do you no good to call out," said a soft voice in Mama Muco's language. "No one will come to help you. We all called in every language we know, and no one ever comes to help."

Grace froze. She wasn't alone. She turned stiffly in the direction of the voice and squinted into the darkness. Yes, now she could make out something. There was a woman shackled next to her. Grace stared harder. A thick chain, connected to a ring embedded in the stone wall, was attached to a collar bolted around the woman's neck. Her legs . . . they, too, were chained to the floor. But unlike Grace, the woman's hands were free.

"We all hollered and screamed and cried and moaned, but we all still be here," the woman said. "All except the one where you be now. Two nights ago he went to be with the ancestors. Guard carried him away to make room for you."

"How did I get here?" Grace asked.

"Guard dragged you in," the woman said. "We thought you would die. You left so much blood on the floor. What they do to you, girl?"

Grace didn't answer. But it all began to come back to her—Cabeto and his words, and Tungo, and . . . and . . . oh! Tungo and the knife.

What would Admiral Joseph Winslow say when he was presented with the severed finger of his daughter who had dared defy him and against his orders had left the safety of his walled-in compound? And what of the proud and mighty Lingongo? Grace could still hear her mother's words: "*Why should you live like a princess when you bring absolutely nothing to my house? Even a princess must do her part.*"

Cooing, moaning sobs broke through Grace's despondency. She leaned forward as far as the chains would allow and searched along the wall. Sure enough, another woman sat just beyond the one who had spoken to her. That woman's midnight-black face was decorated in an intricate pattern of tattoos that ran down both cheeks like finely woven reeds and across her forehead in perfectly matched rows. On her chin, the tattoos formed a pattern like arrow points. Never before had Grace seen such a face. It was at the same time beautiful and terrifying. The woman's hair, wild and unkempt, was a dull, muddy red color. She, too, was shackled by a metal collar and leg chains, but her legs were so thin, they looked as if she could pull them through the rusty manacles.

"How long have you been here?" Grace asked the tattooed woman.

The woman took no notice of Grace. She continued to stare straight ahead and wail.

"She be here forever," said a man chained to the wall on Grace's left. He spoke in a rumbling dialect she recognized as the tongue of a few field hands who passed through her parents' compound on occasion. She understood it only brokenly and could not speak it well. "She not talk much," he continued.

Grace followed the voice until she spotted the speaker—a man, tall and bent, with hair heavily laced with gray. His face, like the woman's, was decorated with tiny tattoos.

"She name Udobi," he said. "Me name Ikem. She be my woman and I be her man."

In the dank dungeon, reeking with the stench of human misery and echoing with despair, Grace pulled herself as far upright as she could and strained to see around the entire room. At the top of the wall above her, three small openings let light in from the outside. Although it was extremely dim, she was able to make out still more people chained to the walls, to her right and to her left. Not to the wall across from her, however. She could just barely see, though, so she couldn't be certain. Stone steps seemed to dominate that wall, and they led up to a platform or landing of some kind. She pressed forward and stared. Behind the landing was an opening covered by what might be an iron grate.

As Grace's eyes adjusted to the dim light, she peered more closely at the people chained to the walls. Seven, she counted. On her side were the two women to whom she had already spoken. Ikem was against the wall on her left, and beyond him were two young boys. The closer one, who looked to be very small, was attached only by a single chain at his neck. He lay on the floor crumpled into a ball, moaning softly. On the wall to her right, Grace could make out a young man in a ragged *dashiki* shirt, and beyond him, a woman she could barely see. Except for Udobi and Ikem, the people looked very much like those who lived in the villages around her family's compound.

Grace suddenly became uncomfortably aware that everyone was staring at her—everyone except the curled-up boy. Embarrassed, she fixed her eyes on the floor.

"What is a fancy white lady like you doing in a slavehold?" demanded the man in the *dashiki* shirt.

"I am not a white lady!" Grace snapped more defiantly than she had intended. "My father—" She caught herself and stopped short. Perhaps it would be best to keep quiet about her father. So far, her relationship to the admiral had only gotten her into trouble.

"No mind, child. We all lost people," Ikem said in a mournful voice. "We not any of us know who we be anymore."

The pain that scorched through Grace's hand was almost unbearable. In an effort to take the pressure off it, she pulled herself first to one side and then to the other. But no matter how she readjusted, more pain pounded through her. And the rough stones of the floor and wall dug into her back and legs. Her head throbbed, and the stifling dungeon swam before her eyes. Grace leaned back and allowed her eyes to drift closed.

"Who caught you, fancy lady?" pressed the ragged man. "Mandingos?"

Grace said nothing.

"Serawoollis?"

Grace opened her eyes and stared at the floor.

"Who be fool enough to catch a white man's lady and beat her like you been beat?" he persisted.

"No one caught me," Grace answered wearily. "I just . . . I mean . . ."

Grace faltered in midsentence. Nothing made sense to her. Why should it make any sense to these people?

"Leave the lady alone," said Ikem. "She frightened and hurt. Give time to her."

"She have time enough," said the young woman next to Grace. "All she have be time and time and more time. Time until the white cannibals come for her and take her away."

"Stop that talk!" Ikem ordered. "No one never seen white cannibals. That nothing but bad talk."

"The stories say—" began the young woman.

"Stories all they be," Ikem insisted. "We hear no more stories here. They only make fear and pain grow until we not be able to bear it."

"If they don't want to eat us, why they got us all trussed up?" asked the young boy who wasn't crying.

"We slaves. That all we be," said Ikem. "We do they work and they feed us. We take care of them and they take care of us. Same as slaves we have in our *stad*—our village. Nothing more."

"No, not like that!"

This was a new voice, strong and commanding. It came from the far corner beside the stairs. Grace stretched and pulled herself further toward her painful right side and managed to make out a powerful-looking young man she had failed to notice before. Staring hard, she saw that he was shackled to the wall not only by his neck, but also by his wrists and legs. His face seemed to be battered, and his bare arms and shoulders were crisscrossed with stripes all too familiar to Grace. They could have been made only by a determined person experienced with a whip.

Although it meant tugging painfully at her injured hand, Grace strained against her bonds in order to get a better look at the man.

No, she had never seen him before. She was certain of that. And yet, there was something familiar about him. He reminded her of someone.

"In our villages, slaves are not chained to dungeon walls," the new man said with deep but quiet bitterness. "In our villages, slaves are not beaten until they die. In our villages, slaves are human beings."

The room fell silent. A smothering gloom crept into Grace and enveloped her soul.

"Mama Muco's God," Grace whispered in English. "Can you hear me through these stone walls? Can you hear my voice over all the tears? Please, please, if you can hear me, reach down and help me!"

Iron scraped against iron. At the sound, an eager hum arose throughout the dungeon. Grace watched as two African men dressed in white man's clothes pushed the door open and forced their way through. They struggled down the steps, lugging an iron pot between them.

All the while, two other Africans remained on the landing to stand guard.

The two men on the floor carried the pot over to the first boy and unlocked his manacles. The shorter African ladled a scoop from the pot and slopped it onto the boy's outstretched hand. As the boy eagerly licked it up, they moved on to Ikem.

"Give the boy a chance," Ikem said with a nod toward the curled-up boy.

The shorter African grunted.

"What is the matter with you?" the taller guard said to the shorter one. "The old man spoke. He is chained to the wall, but he is still a lord of the earth. Show him respect."

The short African stepped back and gave the boy a sharp kick. "Food!" he barked.

The boy didn't respond, and the two moved the pot on. Ikem held his peace.

As the guards unlocked Ikem's bonds and slopped food into his hand, the woman next to Grace began to weep. "Me!" she called out. "Me!"

The guards moved on to Udobi, then to the begging woman, then to Grace. As they approached her, Grace stared at the muskets the Africans carried. They were exactly like the ones her father had piled up in crates and stacked in the storeroom behind the London house. Following what the others had done, Grace held out her hand—the uninjured one. The metal spoon slopped out a scoop of pounded horse beans in slabber sauce. Grace glanced up at the African guard who served her—and she froze. It was Tungo! And the look he gave her boiled with murderous hatred.

What passed between the two did not go unnoticed.

"Who is the *señorita?*" one guard on the platform called down.

Tungo ignored him, but the other guard snickered. "Why do you ask, Antonio?" he called back up. "You want to buy her from the slave trader? You, with all your gold?"

"Not me!" Antonio answered. "She is *demasiado preciosa.*"

Even as the hungry captives continued to lick between their fingers and search the floor for one more drop of food, Tungo and his partner started around the room, jerking arms back into place and snapping on manacles. The guards gave each one an extra tug to make certain it was secure.

When Tungo came to Grace, he gave her right arm a wicked jerk. Grace screamed in pain.

"What do you want from me?" Grace demanded.

Without a word, Tungo turned and walked away.

"Don't make noise again tonight," the guard next to Antonio called down to the captives. "It will go easier with you if you are quiet."

As the four guards left, Antonio turned and waved his musket high. "*¡Adiós, amigos!*" he called. "*Sleep well!*"

17

"See what I say?" Ikem said when the guards were gone. "We be they slaves. White men not cannibals."

"I will be a slave to no man!" the beaten man in the far corner announced indignantly. "Not to a black man and certainly not to a white man!"

"And how will you stop it, Sunba?" asked the young woman next to Grace. More than a hint of sarcasm dripped from her words. "The light be bad here, but it looks to me like you be chained to a wall. And did you not lick the slop from your hands as eagerly as the rest of us? You talk big, Sunba, but just what you going to do?"

"You will see," Sunba answered. "In time, you will see."

"And what if we do not have time to wait?" asked the man who had not yet spoken. "What then?"

"The time will come, and it will come soon," Sunba replied. Then he added, "When it does come, we must all be ready."

"What . . . are you . . . saying?" a woman shackled beside Sunba asked in a soft and cautious voice.

"My brother," said Sunba. "He escaped the traders' chains. Before he disappeared in the darkness, he whispered a message to me. My brother promised he would return and make me free. When Cabeto comes back—"

"Cabeto!" Grace exclaimed. "Cabeto is your brother?"

"What do you know of Cabeto?" Sunba demanded.

From all around the room, heads turned and eyes riveted onto Grace. Only the young boy who crooned in the corner showed her no interest.

"I saw him," Grace said. "I talked to Cabeto."

"Where?" Sunba asked.

"Just outside this place."

Sunba threw back his head and roared a great, hearty laugh. His thunder of delight, a sound all but forgotten in that wretched place, rang throughout the dungeon and echoed beyond its massive walls. Then as abruptly as he had begun laughing, Sunba stopped. In a gentled voice, urgent with hope, he proclaimed, "Cabeto is here! Do not lose hope! Soon we will be free!"

Now the seven faces turned as one to stare at Sunba. Be free? What a strange proclamation to come from a beaten, whipped slave firmly shackled to a dungeon wall. As for Grace . . . well, just look at her. She was the only person to have actually met Sunba's brother, yet here she was, too, anything but free! They had all watched her dragged down the dungeon steps, bleeding and unconscious. They had witnessed her arms and legs stretched out and clamped into rusty manacles. And right here, chained to the dungeon wall, she remained. So where, in all of this, was any reason to rejoice? Where was any cause for hope?

It was Udobi, the silent woman, who finally broke the silence. "What you think?" she challenged Sunba in her reed-thin whine of a voice. "You and you brother make trouble for us? If yes, do not tell of it. If you make trouble, masters pile much more hurt and pain on us. So much it bury us."

"Udobi speak true," Ikem agreed. "You brother not get us

out from these chains. If he try and be caught, we all be the ones to suffer. Some of us suffer to our death."

"We do what they say, we have good lives as slaves," Udobi implored in a quaking voice. Tears filled her eyes and coursed down her scarred cheeks. "They take care of us. They keep us warm when it cold. They make us dry when rain pour down. We work for them and they give us food to eat." Udobi's thin body shook with sobs. "Please, please, no make them angry with us," she begged. "Please not make trouble."

Sunba's eyes flashed with disgust as he looked first at Udobi and then at Ikem. "We *will* make trouble, I promise you that," he said in a stone-hard voice. "And they *will* be angry with us—very angry. If you are happy to live as slaves, then stay in your bonds. I do not care. But as for me, I will not live if I cannot be free. Get ready, old mother and old father. Cabeto is here, and there *will* be trouble!"

Somehow, in the silence that fell over the dungeon, Grace managed to drift into a deep sleep. She dreamed of the London house, stark and tall on the African savanna. She was laughing with Yao as the two of them ran across the fields, happy and free. Overhead they heard the roar of mighty wings. When they looked up, they saw hundreds of birds soaring above them. The sun's gold caught the red and blue and green of the birds' feathers, which glistened in the sun's rays and sparkled like jewels.

"See?" Grace called out to Yao in her dream. "I'm not a slave to Lingongo! You're not a slave, Yao, and neither am I! We are free to fly with the birds!"

"Over here! This one!"

Whispered voices and the muffled cries that followed them jarred Grace out of her dream. Gone were the endless fields. Instead of Yao and the rush of brightly colored birds' wings, two men dragged the mute boy across the floor. Strangely and sadly, even as they bustled him up the stairway and out the door, the young one's pitiful croons continued.

"The old ones, too, I said!" The voice that barked this command was unmistakably Tungo's.

Udobi wailed out her distress.

"*¡Siléncio!*" This had to be Antonio. Grace wondered where the tall, lanky African slave, with his finely chiseled features, could have come from to speak a tongue so strange to her ear. "It is not for you to give orders to me, Tungo! The old *madre y padre*, we will leave them here."

"They will only bring us trouble," Tungo argued.

"We have no choice," Antonio told him. "Our time is gone. Besides, we have no place to take them. We must—"

Antonio had no chance to say what they must do because he was drowned out by the sudden sound of rock grating against rock. The second young boy screamed out in terror. Right next to where he was chained, a stone block slowly slid away to one side and exposed a black gap in the wall. Then as everyone in the dungeon gasped, an African man's head popped in through the newly opened hole. With no idea whether to be frightened or to cheer, they stared in silence as the man pulled himself up and climbed through, right next to the terrified boy.

Grace's heart raced and her breath came in quick pants.

"Cabeto!" Sunba exclaimed quietly.

Cabeto thrust his head and shoulders back down through the opening and called in a hoarse whisper, "I am up!"

"What . . . ? What . . . ?" stammered one of the women.

"That tunnel," gasped Cabeto. "It is steep!"

"On purpose, *señor*. Because it leads to the door of no return." Antonio pronounced the words solemnly. "It is meant only to go *abajo*—just down to the slave ships. No one is meant to come *arriba*."

The three men struggled together to heft a wooden crate through the opening, then to drag it out onto the floor. Immediately, Tungo clawed at the slats that sealed the top. Antonio rushed to assist him, and then Cabeto joined in. The three men forced their fingers into the spaces between the boards and pulled together at the wooden slats.

"Kwate!" Tungo called to a fourth man who was just emerging from the tunnel. "Help us!"

With two more strong hands, they managed to tear away the slats. Eagerly, they peered inside. But the excited anticipation quickly froze into stunned silence.

"This is all you got?" Tungo demanded. "Eight muskets and one bag of gunpowder?"

"No more was in the arms storeroom," Kwate protested. "The crate was supposed to be full." Then he added, "It does not matter, Tungo. When we get your ransom for the girl, we will need nothing more."

"No," Tungo said. A twist of disgust crossed his face. "The white slave trader and his killer lioness will part with nothing. Not one thing will they give in exchange for the life of their daughter."

After a moment of confused silence, Kwate asked, "What do you mean?"

"I mean they will not meet my demands. Not even to save her life."

Cabeto stared at Tungo. "They will not let my family go?"

"No," Tungo said. "Not even that."

Cabeto staggered as though he had received a physical blow. He shook his head and looked again at Tungo. "They would let their daughter die?"

"That is their answer. They will do nothing to redeem her life."

Tungo glanced over at Grace, and for the first time, a flash of pity glistened in his eyes.

Grace could not stop the wild howl that exploded inside her and poured out, long and loud and awful. It made no difference to her who heard her grief. At that moment it didn't even matter to her whether she lived or died.

When her horrible lament had run its course, Grace, emotionally numb, slumped exhausted to the floor. The room was silent. Even Tungo seemed unable to speak.

The first words uttered were both strong and strangely gentle. They came from Sunba's mouth. "Free me, Brother," he entreated Cabeto. "I must be ready for the coming fight."

Silently, Antonio removed a key from the chain around his waist and handed it to Cabeto. Cabeto moved swiftly to his brother and unlocked the manacles from his wrists, legs, and neck. Sunba unfolded himself and painfully moved one cramped limb after another. Slowly, he got to his feet and stretched himself to his full height. Grace could see that he was almost as tall and powerful as his brother.

"We fight tonight!" Cabeto said, his black eyes flashing. "We fight tomorrow! And the next day, we continue to fight!"

Antonio looked down at the half-filled crate. "I fear we will die fighting," he said.

Tungo spun around and pointed his finger at Grace. Once again fire flared in his eyes. "Then she will die first!"

18

"The very idea of an engagement party in this . . . this filthy desert of a place! Why, it would be laughable were it not so ridiculous!" Charlotte Stevens stormed to her mother. "At home in London, yes, but here I cannot think of one person I should care to invite!"

"This is certainly not a desert, my dear," Henrietta Stevens said as calmly as she could. "It is a jungle. You certainly shall have a party in London when we return home, but right now, this is where we happen to be. Furthermore, since it will likely be your last trip to Africa—"

"One can only hope!"

"Try to be patient, my dear," her mother answered, a note of exasperation in her voice. "You know perfectly well it is your father's slave house here that keeps us in genteel comfort in London. Do remember that. I dread our visits here as much as you do, but it is a small price to pay for our comfortable years at home. You may start your list with the Winslow girl. What is her name?"

"Grace." Charlotte pouted. "But she is an African. If I invite her, I might as well invite all the slaves too."

"Very well! Have it your own way," Henrietta said. She lifted her billowing skirts and swept toward the door. "Forget about the gifts your guests would bring. Forget the gold jewelry for which the African people of this coast are so well known."

After her mother's footsteps had faded into the distance, Charlotte sat down at the desk, took the pen from its holder, and dipped it into the inkwell. Then in a flowing hand, she wrote:

1. *Grace Winslow*

Yes, Charlotte complained mightily about the voyage from London to Africa—and for good reason. The trip truly was horrendous. But truth be told, she would miss her time here. Her father did spoil her terribly. Every time she came to Africa, he indulged her in every way imaginable. Was there any possibility that Reginald Witherham would treat her even half as well? She had no idea, for she hardly knew the man. Only that he was rich and that he came from a well-connected family. Only that her mother could not stop bragging about the superb marriage deal she had made—single-handedly, too, as she was always quick to point out. Only that he still called her Miss Stevens, and that she had spoken to him so seldom that she had not yet had to decide what she would call him . . . if she called him at all.

Grace dipped her pen and added to her list:

1. *Grace Winslow*
2. *Lingongo Winslow*

Well, if she invited Grace, she would certainly have to invite Grace's mother. That didn't mean she would have to actually talk to Lingongo, of course. But her mother was quite right. An African princess just might bring a gift of gold—perhaps even handcrafted royal jewelry, which was always wrought in solid gold. Since Reginald Witherham had refused to accompany her to Africa—"Oh my, no! Never, ever!" were his exact words—he would know nothing about such a gift, and so it would be hers alone to do with as she pleased. A delightful thought indeed.

Charlotte placed the pen back into its holder and sighed. Her last trip to Africa! No more horrendous months on the ocean. No more endlessly boring days in a cramped cabin interrupted only by storms and seasickness. And no more of those Quakers with whom anyone even remotely connected to the slave trade was forced to contend these days. Really, those people insisted on causing such a commotion on the London docks, singing and chanting about the fate of the poor heathen Africans. As though they knew anything about it! Grace Winslow was an African, and she seemed just fine. And certainly no one oppressed Lingongo. No one would dare try!

Reginald Witherham was no Quaker. And certainly no one ever accused him of possessing a social conscience. The plight of the Africans was not at all the reason he complained so about travel to Africa. With him it was a question of class.

"I shall allow you to go this one last time," he had stated in his stuffy way, "but only because your father is there, and I believe a woman is obligated to honor her father. I shan't allow it ever again, however, even should your father choose to remain. Nor must you ever reveal to any of my friends, relatives, or even casual acquaintances that you have ties to . . . *that place.*"

Yes! He had actually said *that place!*

Charlotte had sputtered out some response—though, as usual, Reginald Witherham paid her no mind. But to her mother she had raged that she would not be ordered around by a stuffy, pretentious man.

"Charlotte, my dear," her mother had soothed, "this is a *marriage.* Once the wedding has taken place, Mr. Witherham will go on with his business life, and you will go on with your social life—only you will do it on the beautiful Witherham estate with servants at your side ready to do your every bidding. You will never want for anything again as long as you live. Soon you will have children to fill your life. And, my dear, you will never again have to leave England."

"And you, Mother?" Charlotte had said. "It will greatly enhance your social standing, too, will it not?"

That question did not sit well with Henrietta. "Are you being impertinent, Charlotte?" she challenged. "It is a mother's duty to see that her daughter marries well. You should be thanking me, not making criticisms." She had sniffed, turned away, and swept out of the room.

Charlotte picked up the pen and dipped it in the inkwell. Then she wrote:

1. *Grace Winslow*
2. *Lingongo Winslow*
3. *Joseph Winslow*

Entire families must be invited together. For the one evening, she would have to force herself to abide the men who worked with her father, however objectionable they might be.

They would dance at the party—though where the music would come from, Charlotte had no idea. And plenty of food—only English food, of course, not the awful native stuff. Her mother had been wise enough to bring some specialties along with them from London. Perhaps her father could send out a hunting party. Surely, there was something decent to be found in the jungle. Oh, and the gifts, of course. That would be the most important part of the party.

Charlotte put the pen back in its holder, and then she leaned back and allowed herself to daydream. Gold. Yes, that would be the perfect gift for a young English bride preparing to wed a gentleman of the highest class. Gold jewelry. Or gold coins, if they had such things in Africa. Maybe someone such as the Winslows, who owned Zulina, would even bring a block of gold.

Perhaps she should write a notation at the bottom of the invitations stating that she would be receiving gifts on behalf of her upcoming wedding, just in case someone might not understand. Just to make certain the event was worth her trouble.

I suppose it would be a bit too much to suggest gold, though, she thought. Too bad.

19

When Joseph Winslow strode into the entry hall of the London house, he was walking proud. In his boisterous search for Lingongo, he swaggered through the inside kitchen and on to the dining room. She wasn't there, so he marched up the stairs to her bedchamber, and when she didn't answer his knock and calls, he made his way back down again. He found his wife pacing in the parlor. She did not immediately acknowledge him, but when it finally pleased her to look his way, Joseph grinned, puffed out his chest, and strutted back and forth. He took great pains to jangle the bag of gold coins he held out in front of him.

"Fool, is I?" he crowed. "Simpleton, is I? Ain't wot 'em blokes at the docks is sayin' 'bout now!"

Lingongo glared suspiciously. "Where did you get those coins?" she demanded.

"Lucky streak wi' me dice," Joseph bragged. "Won me the 'ole pot, I did! Wot ye be sayin' to me now, Woman?"

Lingongo's eyes narrowed as her gaze moved from her gloating husband's rum-flushed face to the bag of coins he clutched in his pudgy fist.

"What I say is, *what of Zulina?*"

"Wha' of it?" Joseph answered with a hiccup and a shrug. "We's made no concessions to 'at ruffian up there wot 'acked off our Grace's finger. An' the bugger's crawled off like the coward 'e be. Soon Grace'll be draggin' 'ome like a whipped dog, beggin' an' pleadin' fer our fergiv'ness."

"The painful end of the whip is what she will get from me," Lingongo interjected.

Joseph took no notice. "After 'er weddin', Jasper 'Athaway's money'll be ours. 'Tis good as done. Our troubles'll be no more, me luv."

Joseph crossed the room unsteadily and sank his besotted body down into the feather-stuffed cushions of the brocade settee. Just the previous month this wonderful piece had arrived from London by ship. He had intended it for his office, but Lingongo insisted on the parlor. *Jist wait*, he thought as he settled in. *Soon this'll be in me office where it rightfully belongs, fer me an' me alone!* A satisfied smile spread across his bloated face. Joseph unbuttoned the top button on his cotton shirt, folded his hands over his extended belly, and heaved a contented sigh.

"Zulina—" Lingongo persisted impatiently.

"Our storeroom 'ere is piled 'igh wi' muskets an' gunpowder jist so's to satisfy ye," Joseph retorted with more than a note of impatience. "'Ad ever'thin' toted down yeste'day. Cain't say as I's pleased 'bout it, but it's done. An' I won't 'ear another word."

"Did you—"

"Not another word!" Joseph's smile had faded, and a flush of temper quickly replaced his look of contentment.

For a moment, Lingongo considered her husband. Then she rose in silence, carried herself with regal grace to where he slumped, and stood over him. Without a word, she reached down and grasped hold of the bag of coins clutched in his hand. Joseph opened his mouth to protest, but the threat of Lingongo's face caused him to reconsider. In that one instant of indecision, he loosened his grip just enough for Lingongo to jerk the bag from his fingers.

"'Ere now!" he protested, but Lingongo had already turned her back on him and was on her way out of the room.

"An' one more thing, Woman," Joseph called after her lamely. "Don't ye be makin' mock o' me no more! I ain't standin' fer it, I ain't!"

Lingongo swept through the house along a swift, circuitous path and headed for a place in the game room known only to her. It was a foolish room, really, used by no one at all—a section cut out of the dining room because Joseph Winslow insisted every proper English home must have a game room. Bending low over the fireplace hearth, Lingongo pried a loose stone out of its position in the lower back corner of the cold fireplace. She glanced quickly over her shoulder to make certain her unsteady husband hadn't followed her, and then she stuffed the bag of coins into the hole. Lingongo replaced the stone and used her foot to force it securely back into place. The gold would be safe there alongside the other coins she had been able to secret away. Not the royal jewelry her father had given her at her wedding, of course. That she kept in an even more secure place under the floorboards of her bedchamber along with the gold bars she had saved in the hope of someday buying her freedom from Joseph.

"Lingongo! *Lingongo!*" Joseph stumbled from room to room in search of his gold coins. The fool didn't even have enough sense to sneak around quietly. Lingongo was in no mood to listen to him whine and wheedle. And she certainly had no intention of allowing him to gamble the coins away. Oh, no. She had plans of her own for that gold.

She hurried back through the house, taking care to avoid her husband, and headed for the storeroom on the other side of the courtyard. The storeroom was a substantial building constructed of stone and mortar, with a heavy wood-plank roof. At one time, Joseph had six field hands living there. In Lingongo's opinion, it was the perfect place for storing guns and gunpowder, and she was determined to make certain Joseph had kept his word.

Before she even reached the storehouse, Lingongo spied the gleam of new metal against the door. Padlocked! Yes, of course, it would be. And Joseph would have the only key. Irritated, she walked around the building, looking for some way to see inside. But it was impossible. The walls and door were solid and sound, and the small windows were boarded up at Lingongo's insistence.

As she rounded the back corner, Lingongo almost ran into Joseph coming the other way, red in the face and out of breath.

"Lingongo, me darlin'," Joseph wheezed. Even though he clutched his chest, he did his best to smile. "I tol' ye, the store'ouse be full!"

"I want to see for myself," Lingongo stated. "Where is the key?"

"Right 'ere, me tur'ledove," he said. He held up a ring of keys and swung them triumphantly in the air.

"Open the door!"

Joseph fumbled with the ring. His hands shook as he tried one key after another, all to no avail. When he managed to locate the right one, he jammed it into the lock, turned the latch, and shoved the door open.

Except for a narrow path down the middle, the room was filled with stack after stack of boxes and kegs.

"These be muskets," Joseph announced as he slapped the boxes next to him. "Twenty-five to a crate, they be." Then he gestured to the wooden barrels and said, "Gunpowder." His face clouded momentarily. "Sure do 'ate 'avin' it 'ere, though." He forced his way down the narrow path between the stacked crates and then called over his shoulder. "All the balls and sech fer the guns be back 'ere."

Flashing a smile of triumph, Joseph returned to where Lingongo waited.

"Done an' done!" he said.

"What about the slaves who carried it all down?" Lingongo asked. "Are they dead?"

Joseph hesitated. Then he said, "I done as ye wished me to, me dear." Then he reached out and caressed her arm. "Come now, me luv," he wheedled. "Where's me gold, 'ey? Give a bit to yer man."

Lingongo locked her husband in a steady gaze that belied the mockery of her words. "Since you are a master with the dice, *Admiral* Joseph Winslow, why don't you demonstrate what a truly great man you are by bringing home a bag of gold with the help of no one and nothing but yourself?"

Color rose up in Joseph and set his face aglow. The smile vanished from his thin lips and no more sweetness dripped from his tongue.

"Damnation, Woman, them gold coins be mine!" he growled. "An' I demand ye gi' me wot belongs to me!"

"What belongs to you?" Lingongo shot back. "The fury of cheated *slattees*—that belongs to you! Debts to more traders than you can recall—that belongs to you! A daughter who would rather be a slave than have you as a father—that belongs to you! The most profitable slave fortress anywhere around, boiling with rebellion and slipping out of your grip—that, Joseph Winslow, belongs to you!"

"Aye, Woman, Zulina *is* mine!" Joseph shouted back. "An' I will run it me own way, I will! An' I'll do it wi' no 'elp from the likes o' ye!"

For the first time in their life together, Joseph turned his back on his wife. Then as steadily as he could manage in his condition, he strode across the compound, across the fields, and out through the front gate. His head much cleared—more by the confrontation than by the outside air—he marched down the road toward the baobab tree and then headed toward the narrow road that led up to the fortress. He did not slow his pace, and never once did he look back.

20

L ow moans of hopeless despair echoed through the grate in the wall above the dungeon door to drift into the night shadows and mix with Grace's uneasy dreams. Then the hiss of Tungo's angry voice seared her sleep. "They will feel my wrath! I will slash her throat and throw her body at their door!"

Grace jolted awake. Was the voice real? Or was it just another attack of the night terrors? She couldn't be certain. But through the rest of the night, she lay perfectly still, her eyes and ears on guard. Something was happening, of that she was certain. And because so much danger prowled the air, she must keep a watchful vigil.

Snatches of urgently whispered arguments reached her: ". . . risking our lives to be in here so long!" Hushed, angry voices: ". . . must kill or be killed! It is not us who are at fault, but we will pay the price."

Although Grace heard these snippets, try as she might, she could not follow the disjointed conversation. Nor could she identify who said what, so swift and urgent did the whispers fly through the air. Several times she heard a key turn in the lock, and each time it was followed by the cautious scrape of the door opening, then closing. And throughout the night, shadowy figures crept past her.

To the best of Grace's reckoning, four nights had passed since she left home. Just four nights since she climbed onto the compound wall and jumped over into another world. Just four nights since she made her way to the baobab tree. Four nights since she turned left at the tree and ran up the narrow road to Zulina. Only four nights! Was it possible?

When she tried to picture the London house, it seemed so distant and long ago, almost too far away to remember. How could she have lived there all her life?

Concentrating on one room at a time, Grace mentally walked through the only home she had ever known: the dining room, with its ornate mahogany tables and fancy chairs with legs that ended in carved goat's feet . . . the parlor, with its brocade settees that her father forbade her to sit on because they must be preserved for the most important people, which obviously did not include her . . . her father's office, which she was allowed to enter only when bidden . . . the library—the most comfortable room in the house, as far as she was concerned. It contained the books her father had brought back from Europe and pretended he could read when anyone he wanted to impress was in the house. In truth, she was the only one who could read them because her father said all proper English ladies knew how to read and write and it wouldn't be fitting for an admiral like him to have a daughter who was not a proper English lady.

Grace sighed. Her poor father just could not accept the fact that half the blood in his daughter's veins was African. Of course, her mother couldn't accept that the other half was English. And since she could not change her blood, Grace could do nothing but forever disappoint both of them.

Grace concentrated on each piece of furniture in her bed-chamber, which wasn't difficult since she knew it so well—the quilted coverlet on her feather bed, the silver brush and comb side by side on her dressing table, each handkerchief neatly stacked in her dressing table drawer. Then she pictured her father's bedchamber. Actually, all she could remember were the shelves he built to hold the many things he collected during his sailing days. Then on to Lingongo's bedchamber—first the small entry room and then her sleeping room, both of which her mother kept locked with a key she fiercely guarded. Since Grace had never seen inside her mother's rooms, she had little to picture. Once Lingongo had carelessly left the outer door ajar, and being a curious child, Grace had peeked in just as her mother opened the inner door. In the second before it slammed shut, Grace caught sight of a glorious flash of sun shining on gold. At least she thought she did. But it could have been her imagination.

Next Grace pictured the inside kitchen, which Joseph wanted because it was English, and the outside kitchen, which Lingongo wanted because it was African. Early every morning while everyone slept, Mama Muco built cooking fires in two very different ovens so that the family could awaken to a break-fast of fried plantains and porridge (outside oven) and hot bis-cuits for Joseph Winslow (inside oven).

Oh, Mama Muco! Grace's eyes flooded at the thought of Mama's love and gentle touch. How she longed for the one person who ever truly cared about her. When Grace had first whispered her escape plan to Mama—sprinkled with assur-ances that Yao planned to meet her and embellished with allu-sions to a ship waiting at the harbor—Mama had grabbed her and held her close. "No, no! Oh, no!" she had cried. But then she pushed Grace out at arm's length and declared, "Slave life is no life at all," and she set to work.

Carefully, Grace cradled her injured hand in her lap. The pain had subsided some, but now she tucked her hand in out of habit. Grace took a deep breath and purposely relaxed her clenched jaw and stretched the edges of her mouth just the tiniest bit until anyone looking at her would insist she had just the shade of a smile on her face. Yao was wrong, she thought with a strange sense of satisfaction. *I did* leave the London house. *So I'm not Lingongo's slave. Not any longer!*

What was it Yao had said? *"I need nothing but my wits, and so I will not stay."*

Well, I have my wits too! Grace determined. *And I am out of there. But I will not stay here, either. I will also find a way out of this dungeon.*

As the first glimmer of morning light worked its way through the dungeon grate, Cabeto stood up from his place in the huddle of men. He positioned himself so that the faint shaft of light shone on his face and everyone could see him, and then he spoke in a strong, clear voice:

"The wise men say no matter how long the night, the day is sure to come. Though the night seems too long to bear, we are a patient people. Two more days we will wait while Tungo and Antonio and Kwate play the part of trustees in the white trader's service. They will gather my family and bring them to this room. On the third night, when the moon is gone from the sky and the night too black for white men to see, we will leave here and we will return home. Then we will be slaves no more. You can go back to your villages, or you can come with us. It is for each of you to decide."

Grace called out, "Oh, please! My friend Yao—he was brought to this place in chains, in a yoke like an ox. But he says he won't live like a slave. He must get out too! Please, can't you find him?"

"I know this Yao," said Antonio. "He came here with the brand of your padre burned into his shoulder."

A menacing growl rolled up from Tungo. "Branded like an animal!"

Grace looked away, her face burning with shame.

But Cabeto stepped forward and stood in front of Grace. Despite her shame, she looked up at him and dared to fix him in her gaze. So much had happened since the day he clapped his hand over her mouth, dragged her inside the fortress, and locked her inside, yet Cabeto had barely acknowledged her existence. Not until this day. This day he looked straight at her and slowly shook his head back and forth.

"I am sorry I brought you here," he said softly. "This is not your fight. None of this is of your making. It never was."

Grace didn't know how to answer, and so she remained silent.

Freed from their shackles, Grace and the other two younger women settled together on one side of the room. The woman who had been chained next to her—Safya was her name—was older than Grace by a good ten years. Now she turned her golden brown eyes on Grace. Her low-hung eyelids made it look as though she was half-asleep, but Grace was not fooled. She knew Safya watched her closely. Not like Oyo, the shorter, rounder woman—the lovely one who was locked to the wall next to Sunba. Oyo watched no one. She kept her face turned away and her eyes on the floor.

The trustees, along with Cabeto and Sunba, had spent the night huddled together on the side of the room opposite the women. At some point, the man in the ragged *dashiki* shirt joined them. All night long the men argued among themselves, their voices rising in anger and passion and then falling off into urgent whispers.

In another corner, Udobi and Ikem huddled together. Udobi crooned and moaned as her husband petted her and whispered words of comfort.

Only the boy remained alone.

Abruptly, Ikem rose to his feet and strode over to Cabeto. "My woman and I leave now," he announced. "We not be part of this trouble. We not wish you ill, but we go now. Take us to different room and leave us in peace."

"We cannot do that," Cabeto said. "When we leave, you can come with us, or you can stay here. But now you cannot go."

"Ikem will not fight your fight," he said firmly.

Tungo shoved Ikem aside. "You have no choice, old man! And if we refuse to crawl away like frightened children in the night—" Here he made a point of casting a disdainful look in Cabeto's direction. "—If we stand and fight like the warriors we are meant to be, either you will fight beside us or you will die at our feet!"

The man in the ragged *dashiki* jumped up. "I am a warrior!" he proclaimed with pride. "It is my name—Gamka. In the tongue of my people it means 'one who is a warrior.' I will fight alongside you!"

This Gamka looked nothing at all like the tall, muscular Cabeto and his leopard-like brother. Gamka was much shorter. His skin was not black like theirs, but a dusky brown, more like Mama Muco's. His face was round like Mama's too. Yet Grace knew from watching the workers at the compound that a person could not tell the value of a man by the way he looked. Nor was it possible for someone to gaze upon a man and accurately predict what danger he posed.

"Warriors do not slink off like hyenas in the night!" Gamka scowled.

"Many white men are in this place, and they have many Africans working for them. We cannot fight them all," Cabeto argued. "Is it not enough to free our people and return to our homes in peace?"

"No!" shouted Tungo. "It is *not* enough! Gamka and I say we fight!"

Now Sunba was on his feet. "The white men have many guns and much gunpowder. All of them carry muskets. We have only a few muskets. No matter how strong and brave we are, we cannot stand up against the white man's guns."

"Put a spear in my hands and I will be worth twenty white men with guns!" boasted Gamka.

"You talk of peace," exclaimed Tungo with scorn. "Do you know what will happen when you get back to your village? The slave trader and his lioness will send slavers to hunt you down with whips and muskets—to punish you and prove they are your masters. They will rape your women and murder your children in front of your eyes. Then they will beat you and drag you back up here in chains."

Tungo paused, and for many minutes the dungeon was silent. When he spoke again, the scorn in his voice was replaced by weariness. "Perhaps you believe if that happens, you will be as you are now. But you will not. No, it will be much worse for you . . . and much worse for your people."

He gazed hard around the dungeon and fixed his eyes on Cabeto. "You talk of peace? There will be no peace! If you believe differently, you are a fool. All of you—you are all nothing but fools!"

Grace squeezed her eyes shut and grasped her throbbing head, and then she rocked back and forth, back and forth. Think! Think! She must think! But how could she think among so many voices of misery?

People were locked up in all the other dungeons and cells. What about them? All the men and women and children would not be able to escape with Cabeto and Sunba in the dark of the night. What would happen to those who were left behind? What would the slave trader and the killer lioness do to them? Her father and mother . . . what would they do to the ones who were left?

21

"**D**on't ye be goin' down into the dungeons wi' them Negroes no more! It jist ain't civilized! They's savages! Wot ye think ye doin' anyway, mixin' wi' the likes o' them?"

It wasn't unusual for Pieter DeGroot to be rebuked for what he had come to think of as his daily rounds. Since he was forced back to Zulina a second time, every seaman at the fortress had taken a turn at upbraiding him at least once, and that included the captain of the filthiest ship in the harbor who was himself on the receiving end of most tongue-lashings.

At first, after he returned to Zulina, Pieter had answered each challenge by patiently explaining his position. "I have no other use for my time," he would say. "And if I can bring the poor wretches even a small measure of comfort and relief from their sufferings, well, where is the harm?"

The retort he received was always the same, and it never failed to bristle with what one English captain labeled "righteous and just anger."

"It jist ain't befittin' a white man," the captain said, "an' right there is where the 'arm is! We gots to 'old up our standards as civilized Christian men, is wot!"

So Pieter DeGroot gave up any attempt to answer the

critical voices. As for the belligerent ones, he never tried. He shut his mouth and let those around him rage. But this time was different. This time it was an ultimatum, and it came from Joseph Winslow himself. With the owner of Zulina—his host, upon whose kindness and favor he depended—Pieter tried a different tack.

"I was concerned for the condition of your . . . your valuable merchandise . . . Admiral," Pieter said with careful and measured respect. "Since your reputation as a shrewd businessman and a respected English gentleman is known far and wide, I was certain you would be equally concerned. I am correct, am I not?"

Joseph Winslow's bluster failed him completely. He wasn't at all prepared for such a response.

"Well, yes," he sputtered. "But ye doesn't wants to . . . that is, ye cain't be going to . . . see 'ere, me lad, the problem is . . . well, wot I means to say is that when ye . . ."

Pieter's silent gaze remained steady.

"Jist stay away from me slaves!"

Pieter didn't respond.

Slapping the Dutchman on the back, Joseph suggested in his most conciliatory tone, "Now then, me good fellow, won't ye come along an' toss the dice with me an' the lads? 'Tis a right proper way fer the likes o' us to while away the time. Got me a lucky *juju*, me does, an' I's of a mind to show 'im off. Come along now and we'll 'ave us some fun."

To watch this man quiver with anticipation—to *actually* salivate at the idea of gambling his money away—well, it intrigued Pieter immensely. Which, in addition to pure boredom, was why he finally consented to allow Joseph to pull him along one corridor after another, with Joseph stopping to look in cell after cell in search of his mysterious *juju*—his magic amulet. Turning a corner, they ran up against three African trustees toting a large pot of boiled beans between cells.

"'Tonio!" Joseph exclaimed with glee. "Ye be the very one I's needin'! Drop that pot and come along wi' me. Now, me lad!"

"*Sí, señor*," mumbled Antonio. He set his end of the pot down on the stone walkway and followed the white men.

"'Tonio talks *juju* to the gods," Joseph informed Pieter. "If'n 'e prays over 'em dice, I cain't lose. Jist last night I got me more gold pieces than I could 'old in me two 'ands put together. Jist ye watch an' see."

High up in the corner room of Zulina, where the sun shone in through three windows and the breeze blew comfortable and cool off the water, half a dozen boisterous men were throwing ivory dice. Each had a tankard of rum beside him at the large table. Off to one side sat a basket containing a handful of gold coins. When Joseph and his companions entered, the dice stopped rolling and the room fell silent.

"'Ere I is wi' me *juju*!" Joseph announced. He turned to Pieter and said, "While 'Tonio is prayin' over the dice, me lad, you toss some gold into the basket fer the both o' us."

"I'm not a gambling man," Pieter protested.

"Suit yersef," Joseph said with a shrug. "Jist toss in me share then." When Pieter didn't promptly reach for his purse, Joseph said impatiently, "'Ere now, lad. Ye's livin' in me quarters and eatin' me food, ain't ye? It's time ye done right by me. Throw somethin' in the basket. 'Urry now!"

It was not a request; it was a command. Reluctantly, Pieter opened his purse. He had only one gold coin left. Sadly, he tossed it into the basket.

As Joseph took his chair, he grabbed up the dice and handed them to Antonio. "Pray the juju!" he ordered. His eyes shone with greedy anticipation.

Antonio lifted his head and intoned: "*¡Escuche, Dios! ¡Escuche!* May the gods pour out their blessing upon us. *Tsua Tsua Tsua manye aba . . .*"

Even before Antonio finished, Joseph whipped the dice around in his two hands and tossed them onto the table. A double six. Joseph laughed out loud and snatched up the basket of coins, and then he emptied the pile of gold in front of him.

"Git me some rum, 'Tonio," Joseph told him. "A 'ole tankard. Then start another *juju* prayer! We's on a roll agin today, we is!"

They had been playing long enough for Joseph to lose all his gold and win some of it back again when the door flew open. Lingongo stood in the doorway, hands on her hips and fire in her eyes.

"Here you are, you worthless fool of a no-good husband!" Lingongo exploded. "You gamble away our gold while some wretched savage cowers within these very walls and plots evil against us. You allow him to snatch up your daughter and then to hide out under your own roof! Can you not understand? He makes you look like a feeble buffoon in front of everyone, and you do absolutely nothing to stop him!"

Joseph struggled to his feet, his face crimson. "'Ere now, Woman . . . don't ye be carryin' on so, or I'll 'ave to raise me 'and to ye, I will!" But the tankards of rum made him unsteady, and the humiliation muddled his brain. So, buffoonlike, he stumbled and staggered and slurred his words.

With lightning speed, Lingongo's hand shot out. Her whip slashed across the table and sent tankards, dice, and gold pieces flying in all directions. As the men ducked and scattered, desperate to escape this wild woman, they knocked chairs over and pushed into each other. Only Pieter, beside Antonio and well behind the others, did not make a move.

"Go!" Lingongo shrieked at Joseph. "Find the troublemakers and hang them by their necks over the front gate. Let everyone see what happens to those who dare challenge the owner of Zulina!"

22

It was Antonio who carried the warning to the dungeon. When Tungo heard it, his face contorted in fury. He thrust his finger in Grace's face and demanded, "Her! Rip off her fancy white man's clothes! Then chain her to the wall where she cannot betray us!"

"I'm not a part of them!" Grace protested in frustration. "Look at me! If I was, would my father and mother have deserted me like this? Would they have left me in your hands even after you chopped off my finger?"

"He who sleeps in the jungle must be aware of the leopard," Tungo stated coldly. "When the fight starts, black will stand with black, and white will stand with white. What color will you be then?"

"I'm just as black as I am white!" Grace implored.

"How will we know for certain before it is too late?" Gamka challenged.

Cabeto raised his voice and pleaded for calm. "We do not have to fight the lioness and the white traders!" he insisted. "We can go to our villages and live honest lives in our own homes. If we must come against the white man, we can do it another day. A day when we are united and well armed—"

But Gamka had heard enough. "I am a warrior, and I for one will never dare turn my back on you!" Gamka yelled at Grace.

"If the slave trader searches the cells as Antonio said, he will also come here," said Kwate. "When he does, he will find his daughter. And he will see that all of you walk free with chains unlocked—"

"Grace and I can hide in the tunnel," Cabeto said. "Then you and Tungo can put the rest back in chains. Let the white trader and his woman come and look, if that is what they want to do. They will find everyone just as they left them. Then they will be satisfied and they will go."

"No one will put chains on me again!" Gamka shot back. "I am a warrior, and I will fight!"

With a sudden wail of despair, the boy rose up from his place all alone on the floor. Safya rushed to him and pulled him to herself. She hugged and caressed him and gently crooned, "There, there, young one. All we have done is to frighten you. No one even stopped to ask your name."

"I have no name," the boy sobbed. "They call me Guedado because I am wanted by nobody."

"We will not call you by that name," Safya said firmly. "No, here you will be called Hola—one who saves. You will bring us good fortune and hope for a future. Come, Hola, you will sit with me."

But the boy wouldn't move. So Safya sat down beside him, and there she remained.

"The muskets!" Tungo ordered impatiently. "Come, we must make ourselves ready."

He and Gamka hurried to the chest Cabeto had dragged up from the tunnel. Tungo lifted out a musket and waved it high in the air as he shouted, "I will take one! Who else will do the same?"

"I will!" said Gamka, and he, too, grabbed a musket. "But I will toss it to the ground the moment I find a proper spear."

"Who else will take one?" Tungo called. "Come, arm yourselves! Kwate! Antonio! Sunba! Will you fight like warriors? Or will you cower like frightened slaves?"

No one moved.

"Cabeto speaks right," Kwate said. "We do not need to fight. It is better to be a calm and silent water than a raging flood."

Tungo sneered. "It is true that the wise men have much to tell us. But they also say it is the calm and silent water that drowns a man."

The talk came to an abrupt end at the sound of Lingongo's voice. She was in the corridor just outside. "Throw this door open," she commanded. "I will inspect the dungeon myself!"

Tungo sprang to his feet and raised his musket high. Bellowing, he charged wildly toward the still-closed door. With the speed of a panther, Cabeto pounced on him and slammed him to the floor.

Outside, the voices stopped short.

"Get her into the tunnel!" Cabeto commanded in a ragged whisper as he nodded in Grace's direction.

Antonio grabbed Grace's arm and pulled her across the room. But before they reached the tunnel, Gamka leaped over the gun chest and positioned himself squarely between them and the grate. He raised his musket and pointed it directly at Grace's face.

"No!" he said with a menacing growl. "We will not run. And none of us—not even the white one—will hide."

Like a leopard stalking his prey, Sunba sank down into a silent crouch. His muscles tensed as he faded into the shadow of the wall. Ever so slowly he inched his way toward Gamka.

A key rattled in the lock outside the dungeon door. After some effort, it slipped into place and turned.

"Let me up!" Tungo raged as he struggled against Cabeto. "A warrior fights, and I am a warrior!" But he could not break Cabeto's iron hold.

As the heavy wooden door scraped over the stone floor, a baleful wail arose from Hola. Safya enfolded the terrified boy in her arms and hugged his trembling body tight as she gently rocked him.

In one confusing instant, Sunba sprang toward Gamka just as Antonio shoved Grace away from him. Gamka whirled around toward the opening door and fired the musket.

A high-pitched shriek pierced the air and echoed off the stone walls. In a terrified panic, Udobi, the quiet one, tore free from her husband's grip and dashed toward the dungeon stairs, screeching like a wounded animal in mortal pain.

"No!" Ikem cried out in alarm.

But he was no match for his woman's blind hysteria.

In the confusion, Grace and Antonio made a dash for the tunnel and tugged on the door.

"¡Ojalá! ¡Qué lástima!" Antonio exclaimed. "The door to the tunnel . . . it has been bolted from the outside! We are locked in. All of us!"

Udobi, still hysterical, was now at the foot of the stairs. Kwate jumped forward and grabbed her arm, but she wrested herself from his grasp. He grabbed again at her withered, fleshless body, and then he picked her up in his arms.

Just at that moment the door flew open. A deafening explosion shook the dungeon and filled it with blinding smoke.

Then silence. Terrible silence.

On the wooden landing by the open door, Lingongo stood with a smoking musket clutched in her hands. At the bottom of the stairs, crumpled together on the floor, lay Kwate and

Udobi. A bright red pool oozed from under them and slowly spread out across the rough stones.

A universal gasp enveloped the dungeon. Everyone stood still and gaped, too horrified to move. Everyone except Tungo. He sprang to his feet, musket in hand, and returned the gunfire. Although his musket ball missed Lingongo completely, it knocked a large chunk out of the stone wall next to her head, which was far too close for her comfort.

"Lock them in!" Lingongo bellowed in fury as she ducked out through the open door.

The door banged shut behind her, and the iron bolt clanged into place.

A shocked silence fell over the dungeon.

But Lingongo was not through yet.

"Grace!" she called from the other side of the grate. "We saw you in there. We saw that you were walking free."

The room swam in front of Grace's eyes, and she reached out to steady herself on the slippery stones of the wall.

"Do you hear me?" Lingongo demanded. "You are not bound and you are not chained. You could get out of there if you wanted to. So I ask you, Grace, which side are you on?"

Grace stepped away from the wall and forced her feet to move forward, one step after the other, until she stood directly under the wooden doorway landing. Her heart pounded so fast and so hard, she had to gasp for breath. Her hand throbbed with more pain than she had suffered since that first horrible day.

"Ye ain't one o' 'em, Grace."

It was Joseph's voice now.

"Ye's a lady, ye is. Them's nothin' but worthless savages in there. Jist slaves. We's goin' to kill the lot o' 'em, jist as they deserves. String 'em up by they necks, we will. So ye come on out o' there right now, girl! Ye 'ear me, Grace?"

Grace would not look at the others. She didn't dare meet anyone else's eyes. Not just then.

"Your time has come to an end!" Lingongo called. "What will it be—them or us? Slaves who kidnapped you, or your mother and father?"

Grace was well acquainted with the sound of rage in her mother's voice, but for the first time in her life, it failed to strike a panicked frenzy in her heart. Every part of Grace's existence had already been devoured by fear. Fear lurked in the carved mahogany furniture and the brocade settees of the London house. It hid behind the baobab tree where the chiefs are buried and the road divides and goes in two directions. It masqueraded as a smile on Jasper Hathaway's jowly face just as terrifyingly as it prowled the shadows and dungeons of Zulina. Yes, Grace was well acquainted with fear. So she took a deep breath and let her mother rage and threaten. For once in her life, Grace—and not her fears—would do the deciding.

"Speak!" Lingongo demanded. "I will wait no longer!"

Grace looked around her—at Oyo, her beautiful face streaked with tears. At Safya, who still clutched the terrified boy forced into this horrible place, nameless and unwanted. And at the men, clustered together as one, their eyes fixed on her, waiting for her answer. Then she looked down at Udobi and Kwate at her feet, the withered old woman almost hidden in the embrace of the powerful young man. She looked up at Ikem who stood over the two of them, paralyzed in grief, his feet soaked in their blood.

Grace lifted her face, and her eyes flashed defiantly. "I am not a proper English lady, Father! And I am not an African princess, Mother!" she said. Then in a voice clear and strong, a voice that did not belie the tears in her eyes, she proclaimed, "But neither am I a slave!"

"Do not waste any more of my time with your idle prattle!" Lingongo commanded. "Make your choice! Will you come home and face your punishment, or will you stay here with these worthless slaves?"

"I will stay!" Grace answered. "And I, too, will be free!"

Lingongo's rage roiled within her. "You will not be free!" she exploded. "I will crush you under my foot like a troublesome insect. You will hang by your neck from the gates of Zulina. And when you do, there will not be one person, African or white, who will mourn you!"

Outside the door, Joseph, his face deathly pale, whispered to no one in particular, "I brung me daughter up to be a fine English lady, I did! I brung 'er up to marry me a gentl'man o' class."

Through clenched teeth, Lingongo hissed, "That daughter of yours, Admiral Joseph Winslow, with her haughty ways and fancy clothes, is no fine lady. And she certainly is no African princess. I will whip the faded flesh from her scrawny back. Then I will heat your branding iron to white hot. Since Grace has chosen to be a slave, a slave is how she will die."

23

The dungeon reeked of gunpowder and of death. Grace had grown accustomed to the foul stink of human misery, but this new stench was far worse. It was the smell of finality—the smell of hopelessness.

Grace slumped back against the wall and slowly sank to the floor. The finely woven silvery filigreed ferns that had made her blue day dress a matter of such pride to Joseph Winslow snagged and ripped as the silver threads scraped against the rough stones, but Grace could have cared less. She hated this dress. She hated every piece of fancy European clothes she had ever worn. Not only were they tight and uncomfortable, but it humiliated her to wear them. No wonder people stared at her with such contempt! No wonder they assumed she was just another one of their detested oppressors!

In the aftermath of Lingongo's murderous attack, the dungeon echoed in a cacophony of despair. The boy Hola's howls could not be quieted despite Safya's attempts to cajole him and soothe his fears. Ikem's wails and chants rose and fell as he rocked his dead wife in his arms. Beneath those howls and wails hummed Oyo's soft sobs—the beautiful one, whose soul was broken in two.

And without letup, from the men's corner, increasingly bitter arguments jarred through the cries of sadness and loss.

"We need time to gather our people!" Cabeto insisted. "Then we will break through the tunnel and swim to shore. Make a way where there is no path, then go on to our homes in the village to gather strength and numbers. White men cannot follow us if we leave here on the blackest night with no moon to give light to them."

"No!" Tungo argued. "We do not have time to wait! I say we use the guns we have—kill them all before they kill us! First the lioness and then the white trader. Then all the other white men we can find—kill them one by one—and then the *slattees* who do their bidding as dogs serve their masters. Their bodies will warn other white men who think they can make us their slaves!"

"You speak, but you do not think," Cabeto argued. "Few cannot stand against many. Before we could kill them, we would all be dead."

"Then we will die heroes!" Tungo shot back.

Other voices rushed in . . . angry voices. Argue, argue, and argue some more, until Grace could stand it no longer.

Grace stifled her desire to scream. She cradled her aching head between her good hand and her throbbing, injured hand, and clamped her mouth tight. Oh, how tired she was of all the arguments! What good did it accomplish, anyway? Not one single bit! They were all still locked in the dungeon. Only there were fewer of them now because two were dead.

Why did it have to be Kwate? Of all the men in the dungeon, he was the kindest, the most gentle. He spoke with a voice of reason the way Cabeto did. If Kwate had not been killed, he and Cabeto could have stood together against Tungo.

And why Udobi? All she wanted was peace—even if it meant

a lifetime as a slave. Right now she should be sitting in front of her mud hut, stirring a pot of millet porridge as she watched her grandchildren at play. It made no sense! But then, nothing made sense anymore.

Grace wondered whether the harmattan winds had stopped blowing yet. She couldn't tell through the stone walls, of course. But maybe when the winds finally stilled, maybe when the sand settled and no longer darkened the sun, maybe then her world would regain its reason. Maybe, if any reason continued to exist.

The huddled men were too busy trying to outyell each other, to see who could shake his fist highest and hardest, to notice when Ikem stopped his chant and gently laid his woman on the floor. But Grace noticed.

Slowly, deliberately, Ikem pulled himself up to his full height. Then he turned to the huddled men and spoke in his rumble of a voice.

"No more!" Ikem ordered with such authority that everyone immediately fell silent. "Look what your guns do to my woman! The white man and the lioness now see what strength we have. Now they know for certain what we can do. Everything, they already know it all. They be no surprise arrows left in our quivers."

Ikem strode over to Antonio. "You, please," he implored. "You say to the white man no more have to die. Say we be good slaves to them. Then they be good masters to us. You say that to them. Make them understand."

With an outburst of fury, angry voices broke out again. But this time they were aimed at Ikem.

"Sit down, Old Grandfather!" Gamka ordered with a sneer. "Stay with your grief, but do not give us advice. Your words are foolishness!"

Cabeto turned on Gamka and demanded, "What is happening to us? Are we becoming like them? We have among us a lord of the earth, an old man. And you will show him respect!" Yet when he spoke to Ikem, Cabeto's voice remained respectfully firm. "Good or bad, we will not be slaves, my father. Good or bad, we will allow no one to be master over us!"

"Five men alone, they cannot fight the—" Ikem began.

"Five *warriors!*" Gamka bellowed as he lunged forward.

Tungo, right beside him, exclaimed, "Five *angry* warriors who refuse to live as slaves!"

Antonio joined in, and Sunba, and Cabeto, too, until Ikem's single voice was drowned out by a whole new torrent of angry words. In the midst of the wave of passion, Grace stood up. At first she swayed unsteadily, but she planted her feet and willed herself to stand firm. "You do not have just five men," she announced.

The arguments faded as all eyes turned to Grace.

"You have five men and *one woman.*"

Fading sunlight fell through the grate and cast a slanted beam down the wall, directly across Grace's face. She stood proud with her head held high and looked for all the world like a royal princess of a noble people. The sun lit up the natural golden fire sprinkled through her hair. Surely her grandfather, king of the most powerful nation on the African coast, would have been proud.

"Five men and *two* women!" said another voice, this time from behind Grace. It was Safya. She, too, rose to her feet and held herself tall and proud and confident.

"Three women." Oyo turned her tear-stained face to Grace. Had the room not fallen so silent, her soft voice might never have been heard. But in the hush of amazement, it rang sweet and clear.

Next to Safya, the boy slowly rose to his feet. In a voice still a bit shaky, he said, "And me, the one you call Hola—*the boy who can save*. You have me too."

"Nine of us! One for each gun, and one more to hand around the gunpowder!" Tungo roared as he leaped jubilantly into the air. "Now we *will* fight! And we will keep up the fight until every last bit of our gunpowder is gone!"

"Even then we will not stop!" exclaimed Gamka. "Not as long as one of us still has breath!"

Ikem's shoulders sagged as though a heavy sack had been thrown onto his aged back, and he stumbled back to where Udobi lay. "I not mourn for my woman only," he said with a sigh. "My chants be for us all. For now we be all dead." Once again he sank to his knees at his wife's side. Once again he raised his head. A long, mournful cry poured forth from deep within him. Then his cry formed into words, and the words became chants that he repeated again and again and again. No one raised a voice of protest, and no one moved away.

At long last Ikem lifted his face and slowly gazed around him. First at Oyo and Safya and Hola, but all three quickly averted their eyes. Next he focused on Antonio, then on Cabeto, then on Sunba. He stared at each in turn, but not one could hold his piercing gaze for long. Next, Ikem locked Tungo in his stare, and for a long while, Tungo glared right back. But in the end, even Tungo's defiance wavered, and he, too, lowered his eyes. As for Gamka, he didn't even try to meet the old man's challenge.

When he looks my way, I'll stare down at the floor, Grace determined. *I won't look into his eyes.*

But that's not how it happened. Ikem's eyes grabbed Grace in spite of her resolve and forced her into his resolute gaze. Try as she might, she could not pull her eyes away from his.

When Ikem finally released her, his head dropped to his chest. He placed one hand on Udobi and the other on Kwate and continued to grieve in silence.

Thinking it an intrusion for anyone to watch Ikem in his deep grief, Grace got up and positioned herself directly in front of him so that her flowing skirt blocked him from view. Then she said to the others, "Tungo told us that if we left quietly in the night, there would be no peace for us. He is right. I know Lingongo, and she will never allow us to leave here and live in peace. But Cabeto is also right. We are too few to fight against the armed slavers."

The strength and authority in Grace's voice hushed even Ikem's lament.

But she was not yet finished. Her eyes flashed and her voice roiled with passion as she exclaimed, "If we ever again hope to walk free, we must have more people willing to fight beside us. That leaves us with only one choice . . ."

Thrusting her wounded fist high into the air, Grace proclaimed, "We must take Zulina!"

24

Braced against the billowing wind, Pieter DeGroot stood alone on the hillside behind Zulina fortress and gazed down at the dozen ships anchored in the harbor below. Azure sea stretched out so far before him that it seemed to become one with the heavens. With rhythmic predictability, foamy whitecaps whipped up far out in the distance and swept onto the deep-red sands of the shore below before they washed back out again. Along the shoreline, coconut palm trees bent and stooped in wild dances. Only back here, shaded by the high fortress walls, where his face caught a fresh wind, could Pieter find a bit of relief from the oppressive African heat. How he longed for the foggy coasts of Europe where a sailor actually needed to pull a knit cap down over his ears and tug his coat collar up around his neck to keep out the chill of the sea air.

Even more, he longed for the lush green veldts of his boyhood. Pieter closed his eyes and conjured up a picture of those fields that had seemed to stretch out so endlessly when he was a boy—fields framed by the high dikes he used to know so well. Oh, to see them again in the winter, frozen over into solid ice! How many happy hours he and his brothers and sisters had spent skating across those frozen ponds!

Pieter opened his eyes to the reality of ships anchored at Zulina. He kicked at the loose rocks strewn around his feet until he cleared away a spot of dirt, and then he sank down and settled himself on the hillside. He found it more and more difficult to remember those long-ago days—more and more painful. So much had happened since he was a boy in the Dutch countryside. It was not just that things had changed; he himself had changed.

A piercing wail echoed from inside the fortress and jerked Pieter out of his reverie. He turned around to face the stone wall, grimaced, and looked away. All he could think about was that other horrible shriek. It, too, had come from inside. It had assaulted him as he hung back behind the others in the passageway. Lingongo was just outside the dungeon door, ready to push it open, but when that unearthly scream pierced through the walls, it paralyzed all of them with horror and dread.

"'Tis the cry o' the devil 'imsef, it is!" Joseph had gasped, and not one person doubted that he was right.

Pieter ran the back of his hand over his sunburned face. The memories tumbled over and over and chafed his mind until it was worn raw. With the tail of his shirt, he wiped the dust from his weary eyes.

Suddenly, something caught Pieter's eye. He jerked upright and leaned forward for a better view. Down below, a lone figure moved toward the notorious door of no return. Over the years, more African captives than anyone could tally had been driven in shackles and chains from the main floor of the fortress, through a dank and narrow passageway, and out through that very door to longboats waiting to take them over to the slave ships anchored in the harbor. Once captives passed through that door, they were gone forever. Some were resigned to their fate, crying perhaps, maybe even moaning. Many fought and struggled, but they were quickly whipped into submission. A few resisted so ferociously that they were finally beaten unconscious and dragged to the longboats.

But now, no longboats waited, and the slave ships at anchor stood empty and unmanned. The steady gale seemed to push that lone figure forward. Palm trees whipped wildly on both sides as blue ocean lapped white and foamy in front. What could it mean?

Pieter shaded his eyes and squinted hard at the unknown person. African? Yes, almost certainly. Surely a man. But who? What was he doing out there all alone and unguarded?

The man disappeared into the passageway, and then he quickly reappeared at the small window on one side of the door.

Pieter cringed. At that very spot he had loaded his slaves onboard *Dem Tulp*. On that day an African trustee stood guard in that self-same window. The longboat was almost full when the guards forced one last slave through the door—a huge young man—a Mandingo in extra shackles. Pieter had sighed with relief when he saw him prodded toward the longboat. That Mandingo was his prize purchase. Just the sight of him filled Pieter with pride and caused his imagination to swim with visions of riches. Then, suddenly, the Mandingo hurled himself over the side.

"Man overboard!" Pieter had yelled. "Haul him out!"

Instead, to Pieter's shock and horror, the trustee took careful aim and fired. The musket ball struck the Mandingo in the shoulder. He reeled and splashed about, bellowing like a wounded water buffalo. Before Pieter could gather his wits, a second trustee in the opposite window also fired. His shot blew a gaping hole in the Mandingo's chest. The Mandingo pitched forward and sank into the sea like an iron bar.

Without so much as a backward glance, the sailors pushed the rest of the terrified captives into the longboat. When it was full, the sailors climbed in, dipped the oars into the bloody water, and rowed out to *Dem Tulp* as if nothing had happened. It was at that moment that Pieter vowed he would never again sail a slave ship. No profit, however fabulous, was worth it.

"Now, then, Dutchman! Ye be keepin' yersef outta the admiral's way too?"

Pieter forced his attention away from the shadowy figure at the window and shaded his eyes. Captain Cummings puffed down the stone steps toward him.

"Blamin' me, 'e is," Cummings complained. "Now, 'ow's it me fault when 'e's the one wot grabbed the musket, I asks ye? Ye knows wot 'appened. Ye saw it all wi' yer own eyes!"

The whole awful scene flashed back: Lingongo unbolted the dungeon door, and Joseph and Cummings pressed right up behind her, panting like a couple of yard dogs. Then they heard that unearthly shriek that turned their blood to ice. Yes, Joseph had grabbed Cummings's gun, but immediately, Lingongo snatched it from her husband. Not one other person had moved. Joseph's hands shook and sweat dripped down his face, soaking the collar of his shirt. He didn't want to let go of that gun. But then, he never could hold his own against Lingongo.

"So wot if we witnessed 'er makin' a fool of 'im?" Cummings said. "Ain't the first time we seen it, an' won't be the last time, neither. Standin' up to her weren't goin' to change that none."

At first, Joseph had refused to back down. But so had Lingongo. Pieter thought she would blow a hole clear through him; she was that furious. Old Joseph must have been thinking the same thing because—although under his breath he bid all powers in heaven and earth to plunge her straight below—he finally gave in and let her have her way.

The roar of the musket blast ricocheting in that narrow stone passageway had knocked Pieter to his knees. Cummings and the others scattered like rats on a blazing ship. They let go with more cursing than Pieter had heard in any tavern in any port city of the world. Even Joseph rushed to put as much distance as he could between himself and his wife. Only Pieter hadn't moved. It wasn't that he didn't want to. It was that he couldn't. His legs had gone completely numb and useless.

Cummings shook his head in puzzlement and lamented, "I ain't like ye, DeGroot. Me, I don't mind killin' slaves. I figures they's lots more where we got those ones from. But turnin' guns on our own kind? On the admiral's own daughter? Now that, I says, is a sin. Yes, sir, fer sure it is a sin!"

Pieter shot Cummings a look of undisguised disgust.

"I will stay, and I will be free!" Grace had yelled back in answer to her mother's ultimatum. How that had caused Lingongo's face to twist in murderous rage. Although it took every bit of effort she could muster, she had composed herself enough to call back to her daughter, "Then you will hang from the gates of Zulina!"

But that wasn't all. As Lingongo pushed her way down the corridor, only Pieter, still hunched back in the shadows, heard her final vow: "No food and no water will go into that dungeon! We will wait until they are close to death from hunger and thirst. Then we will go in with guns and knives and slaughter every one of them!"

"An' the tustees . . . ," Cummings continued. "Where is they now, I asks ye? Where is they?"

"I don't know."

Pieter got up and picked his way across the rocks, back

toward the fortress. But when he glanced back over his shoulder, he again caught sight of the figure at the window below. He stepped as far to the edge of the embankment as he possibly could. Yes, now he could see. It was an African dressed as a white man. A trustee, then. But which one? He stretched forward to get an even better view.

Badu! It was Badu, one of the trustees with whom he had shared a pot of porridge the day before that poor, desperate mother and daughter had tried to escape. One of the two trustees who had shot them dead.

Badu climbed onto the window ledge and stood in the exact spot where the trustee with the gun had waited as Pieter loaded *Dem Tulp*. And then, as Pieter watched in horror, Badu let go and dropped into the sea.

With the tide rolling in, strong waves smashed against the foot of the door of no return. But Badu did not reappear. There was nowhere to swim, nowhere to go. Badu had joined the ancestors.

"It's not right!" Pieter exclaimed out loud. "It just is not right! The Africans should have a fighting chance. We even give an animal in the jungle that much!"

25

The rhythm of African working songs that sailed on the wind and drifted through the windows of the London house washed a flood of melancholy over Mama Muco. Joseph Winslow's slaves were busy in the nearby cassava fields. Muco stretched herself out the window to watch them beat the rhythm with their hoes and digging sticks as they chopped at the hard ground.

In a strange way, it comforted her to hear those old chants. She still remembered them from her childhood, even after so many years. Despite the ache in her heart, Muco lost herself in the beat and picked up the music:

"*Yama o yama do deo, Yama o yama do deo . . . dede dshamalomba,*" Muco intoned in her husky voice as she rubbed oil deep into the carved crevices of the mahogany chairs that were pushed up around the dining table. "*Yama o yama do–*"

Without warning, Muco abruptly hushed and cocked her head. The workers had stopped singing. She hefted herself up from the floor and hurried to the window to gaze out at the fields. The workers were still there, all right, but they no longer chopped and dug. Now they were staring in the direction of the stone wall, over toward the accursed fortress, whose name Muco had vowed never to utter again.

With a gasp, Muco dropped her polishing rag and ran for the door. "Oh, Lord, Lord," she prayed, "let it be my Grace come home!"

But it wasn't Grace. Muco was halfway across the dusty courtyard when she met Joseph Winslow rushing toward her. The moment she saw his flushed face and heard his ragged breathing she knew something was terribly wrong.

"Master Joseph," Muco called out. "What is it?"

"Leave me be!" Joseph scowled. He didn't slow his steps, and he took pains to avoid her face.

"Master . . . is Grace . . . ?" Mama Muco began anxiously.

"Don't ye never say that name in me 'ouse again!" Joseph barked. He pushed past Mama Muco and hurried on.

Terror gripped Mama Muco's throat. She looked back toward the compound wall and, to her astonishment, saw that the gate, which was always kept tightly bolted, stood wide open. Whatever did it mean?

For many hours, Muco paced back and forth through the courtyard, waiting and watching and wondering. All the while she beseeched God on Grace's behalf. Joseph Winslow had long since retreated to his study. As for Lingongo, no one seemed to have any idea where she might be.

Long after the sun had set and blackness enveloped the night, Muco continued to stand watch in the courtyard. A sprinkling of pale stars came out and a tiny sliver of moon rose in the sky, yet still she lingered. When the moon was almost overhead, Muco finally heard the rustle of someone at the gate.

I must not be caught where I do not belong! Muco worried.

In a panic, she hurried to secret herself in the closet off her kitchen pantry sleeping quarters. Quickly, she pushed aside the buckets of sweet potatoes and squash, and she squeezed in between the sacks of flour and the store of dried beans and millet. Then she pulled the door almost closed behind her. It was a perfect place to keep her eye on things without being seen.

"Joseph!" Lingongo's voice rang through the kitchen, and it blazed with fury. "You had better be here!"

Muco poked her head out in time to see her mistress storm into Joseph's study.

Slaves were not allowed to enter the private living quarters unannounced, especially not at night. But Mama Muco was more worried about Grace's well-being than about a beating from her master. So she followed Lingongo, taking care to stay hidden in the shadows.

". . . with no food and no water," Lingongo was stating with a gratified grin, "because I had the tunnel door bolted shut!"

"Tomorrow mornin' I'll send me trustees in wi' muskets blazin'," Joseph said. "Blow the 'ole lot o' 'em to bloody 'ell, I will!"

"Have you ever stopped to consider that those jailers of yours are nothing but slaves themselves?" Lingongo challenged. "Did it ever enter your mind that they just might turn their muskets on you?"

"Naw, they won't, neither. They's faithful to me, they is. More faithful than me own flesh an' blood!"

"How can you be so certain?"

"I ain't no dolt, Woman!" Joseph retorted. "That Spanish 'un—'Tonio. The one wi' the *juju* powers. I'd trust 'im wi' me own life, I would!"

"You cannot trust anyone, Joseph!" Lingongo cried in exasperation. "Those white sea captains you call friends may all be far away from here by tomorrow. If the trustees think they have a chance to go free, they will turn on you before you have time to fit a musket. Even the *slattees'* fighting men will turn against you if they see it to be for their good!"

"Wot o' the *slattees*? They ain't even involved in this, Woman!"

"Everyone is involved in this! After all your years in this land, you do not even hear the *ntumpane*, much less understand the language of the talking drums. You have no idea that even now they pound out your name and mine too. Now everyone in every village up and down the coast knows slaves at Zulina fortress drove us away from our own slave house!"

Joseph hoisted himself out of his chair and glared at his wife. "White men sticks together wi' white!" he said. "And them Africans wot fight again' us, they'll pay a sore price fer their trechery! Ye jist mark me words on that."

"You fight in your way, Husband," Lingongo said. "Then I will fight in my way. Your way will injure, but my way will kill."

"Now, see 'ere!" Joseph protested.

"No, you see here," Lingongo shot back. "You do what you do. Then I will finish what you start."

Mama Muco barely had time to jump back into the corner and press herself against the wall before Lingongo swept past her and out of the room and then on down the hall. For a long time Muco hung back in her hiding place, hardly daring to breathe. The door to the office still stood open, and she could see Joseph Winslow hunch-shouldered beside his desk. Finally, he sank back into the chair and dropped his head into his hands. This was her chance. Swift and silent, Muco eased out the door and slipped back into the safety of the pantry room.

At the foot of Muco's bed stood a small, unpainted wooden chest, its top fastened with worn leather hinges. It was where she kept her few possessions. Muco opened the lid and carefully lifted out the Book of God that a long-ago missionary had brought to her village when she was just a child. Never would she forget the day he opened that book and showed her people the marks that talk. How amazed she had been at the stories they told!

"Yes," the villagers told the missionary. "We understand. You adore Jesus because he speaks to the Creator. He is your mediator with the spirit world."

But then one day the missionary fell ill with jungle fever, and the next day he died. *"Obeah!"* the villagers had whispered to each other. Witchcraft. And so the book was snatched away and tossed outside the bamboo gates of the village.

Young Muco didn't believe that *obeah* killed the missionary. And she didn't want the God stories to be gone from her life. So while the village was sleeping, she left her mat and crept outside her family's hut, and then ever so silently, she went outside the bamboo gates. She retrieved the missionary's book, and she brought it back with her. Oh, so careful, so quiet, she had been as she pushed aside the banana leaves that covered the roof of her sleeping family's mud hut and tucked the book deep into the thatched roof. Later, when the slavers came to her village with their flaming firesticks, she had just enough time to pull the book down and hide it in her clothes before she was shackled and dragged away.

One day, when Grace was young and the two were alone, Mama Muco took out the God book, opened it up before the girl, and pointed inside.

"These marks can talk and tell wonderful stories," she told Grace.

"Oh, Mama Muco, you are so funny!" little Grace had said. "Those aren't talking marks. They are words written in English! I can read them. Do you want me to teach you to read them too?"

The reading lessons started that very day. Letter by letter, word by word, little Grace Winslow taught Mama Muco how to read the white man's marks.

Tenderly, Mama laid the book on her cot, and then she went back to rummaging through her chest. Tonight she needed something else. She pulled out one thing and then another—her other dress, her two aprons, her headcloths. A ragged green, yellow, and red checkered headcloth caught her eye. Yes, that would do nicely!

Carefully, Muco folded the colorful cloth in half and folded it in half again. She continued to fold it until the cloth formed a small triangle with two extra points, one hanging down on either side—one shorter and one longer. Then Muco tucked the folded headcloth into her clothes and silently stole out of the room. Watching to make certain she wasn't seen, she crept through the inside kitchen and out the back door to the walkway to the outside kitchen and on to the courtyard.

"Please, God," Muco prayed, "make a way for this slave through the stone wall, just like you made a way for the old-time slaves through the Red Sea."

Despite the near black of the night, Muco's steps were quick and sure. Rapidly, she crossed the courtyard and walked through the kitchen garden without the slightest concern for what carefully tended plants her feet might crush. Then she struck out over the fields in the direction of the stone wall.

When Muco was first brought to this compound and set to work as a house slave, she had barely begun to bud into a young woman. Actually, she was relatively fortunate. Joseph Winslow directed her straight to his house—no imprisonment, no beating, no horrific sea voyage. She had always been able to gather news of the surviving members of her family from other slaves who passed through her master's compound.

And Grace . . . well, Grace had grown up in her care. Muco had learned to speak English from Grace's tutors.

Mama Muco loved Grace.

Muco knew by the rise in the ground that the wall must be near. When her outstretched hands touched stone, she turned and followed it until she reached the gate.

"Please, oh, please!" She breathed her prayer out loud. "I can't open the lock and I can't climb the wall. Please, Lord God, make a way through!"

Mama Muco threw her full weight against the gate, and to her amazement, it creaked open. In her anger, Lingongo must have forgotten to lock it behind her.

"O God, whose hand divided the Red Sea," Muco breathed into the night air. "Thank you! Thank you!"

Mama passed through the gate and hurried down the road toward the baobab tree where the road divides and goes in two directions.

"Now, O God, open the best eyes to see and know," Mama breathed. "Open the best eyes."

26

Silently, Oyo moved over next to Grace and positioned herself in such a way that the stream of sunlight fell directly across her shoulders. Then she stretched her arms upward toward the beam of light.

"Outside the sun is hot," Grace said softly.

"I like it hot," Oyo replied.

Grace moved over a bit so that Oyo could fully enjoy the warmth of the slender ray.

"Do you think we will ever see the sun again, Grace?" Oyo asked. "I mean, really see it—up in the sky? Do you think we will ever see the moon and the stars, or hear the birds call in the trees, or see a fish pulled from the river? Do you think we will ever again walk free?"

Grace reached over and put her arms around Oyo's shoulders. "Oh, yes!" she said. "I do! I truly—"

That's when they heard the scratches.

"Ugh!" Oyo winced. "Rats!"

But Grace jumped up. "No! No, it isn't rats. It's something behind that door!" she said, gesturing to the tunnel entrance behind them.

Antonio jumped up. *"No es posible,"* he said. *"¡Somos todos aquí!* All of us are here."

Tungo leaped into position and took aim with his loaded musket. But then the locked tunnel door swung open, and a tall white man with a bush of yellow hair climbed up and into the dungeon. He carried no gun or knife in his outstretched hands, and when he spoke, his voice was gentle and calm.

"I've come to offer you help," Pieter DeGroot said.

Because Tungo didn't understand the English words, he responded to the intrusion by waving his musket in as threatening a manner as possible.

"Grab him!" he shouted. "Chain him to the wall!"

Pieter raised his hands in a gesture of surrender and answered in English, "I can't understand your talk. You can't understand me, either, can you?"

Grace stepped forward. "I understand you," she said. "I can tell him whatever you want him to know."

Pieter stared at the beautiful bronze-skinned young woman before him. Her clothes, although filthy and tattered, were obviously European made of quality material. And her right hand—it was wrapped in a blood-soaked cloth. Pieter knew immediately who she was. Still, he found it almost impossible to connect this graceful young woman to the crude Englishman who had so rudely jolted him from his bed only a few hours earlier.

"Is ye gone like all 'em other buggers?" Joseph Winslow had demanded as he pounded on Pieter's cabin door. "Did ye lift yer anchor in the black o' the night and sail wi' the tides wi' the rest o' 'em? Bloody cowards, ever' one! Ain't too proud to eat me food an' down me rum, or take me shelter ever' night, but come a bit o' trouble and they's up and gone!"

So this was the daughter whom Joseph Winslow had deserted and left to her fate.

Tungo glared at Pieter. "What can you do for us?" he demanded. He raised the musket and aimed it directly at Pieter's face.

"I can make certain you have food and water. And I'll provide you with any other supplies I can secure," Pieter answered evenly. "Oh, and this door that prevents you from entering the tunnel will no longer be locked. That I can also do."

Grace repeated his words to the others.

Safya and Oyo laughed for joy, and Hola clapped his hands. Tungo, however, was not impressed. "You are a white man!" he insisted. "Why should I believe that you would help us? It may be that you set a trap."

"Not all white men are like Joseph Winslow," Pieter answered, "just like not all Africans are like Lingongo."

Pieter DeGroot was a man of honor. That, as a matter of fact, lay at the heart of his quandary. Without a doubt, he had an obligation to his host. Joseph Winslow, though a man with many faults, had been generous to him. Now the man was under double attack—these armed rebels in the dungeon of his slave fortress on one side, and the blind fury of his wife on the other. Yet Pieter could not abide the thought of him attacking—and killing (for the eventual outcome would certainly be killing)—a defenseless group of people who had been forced into a corner and trapped there. What choice did they have but to fight back with everything at their disposal? So it was that on that very morning, after Joseph Winslow had awakened him and then had walked away and left him standing alone and half-naked in the corridor of Zulina, Pieter DeGroot had come up with his plan.

In just two swift strides, Cabeto was upon Tungo. The two struggled, and Cabeto knocked the musket from Tungo's hands. As soon as the gun clattered to the floor, Grace snatched it up.

"You best not close your eyes tonight," Tungo hissed at Cabeto.

"We must not fight each other, Tungo," Cabeto stated evenly. "If we are to survive at all, it will only be together as brothers."

Cabeto looked at Grace and said, "Ask this white man why he comes to us."

Grace repeated the question, but Pieter didn't answer her. Instead he stepped up to Cabeto and spoke directly to him. "I come to help you . . . because I don't want to see the white men die."

Behind him, Grace repeated the words in Cabeto's tongue.

"But even more, I don't want them to kill you," Pieter continued. "It seems that the scales always tip in the white man's favor. I cannot prevent that. But I want to do what I can to make the scales weigh a bit more equally."

Antonio chose that moment to step out of the shadows. *"Buenos días, señor,"* he said to Pieter.

At the sound of Antonio's voice, Pieter looked around in confusion. Quickly, though, a grin of recognition spread across his face.

"Ah, Winslow's good luck man!" Pieter said. "What's that he calls you?"

"Juju. His magic charm."

"But you were not in here before, were you?" Pieter asked, bewildered.

"Sí," Antonio answered. *"Lo vi todo.* I was right here, and I saw everything that happened."

Pieter DeGroot laughed out loud. "You must have hidden yourself well because Joseph Winslow certainly doesn't know that! He is searching everywhere for you. He considers you the most loyal of all his trustees. In fact, at this very moment he is telling everyone who will listen that he can always count on you and your magic to fight at his side." Pieter shook his head at the irony. "If he only knew!"

"Oh, but he must not know!" Grace exclaimed. "Don't you see? This way, Antonio has a safe way in and out of the dungeon. He has access to my father too." Turning to Antonio, she said, "And he trusts you!"

Grace translated everything for the others. Before she had even finished, excited voices rang out from every direction. Everyone seemed to have a question, an answer, or just an exclamation.

"*¡Siléncio, por favor!*" Antonio pleaded. Then to Pieter, "*Señor, estos dos son muertos.*" He gestured to the place where Udobi and Kwate lay. "You and I must carry out the dead and lay them to their rest."

The blood drained from Pieter's face as he stared at the two bodies.

"Then we will return with water and food," Antonio added. "All of us here—we must drink and we must eat. *Es muy importante.*"

Grace laid her hand on Pieter's arm. "I don't even know your name, sir," she said.

"DeGroot. Pieter DeGroot, miss."

"How did you get in here, Mr. DeGroot?"

"Not really such a clever plan," Pieter said. "I offered to buy your father his fill of rum, and when he fell asleep, I lifted the keys from his waistcoat."

"Yes, that would work," Grace said. "Well, I do thank you. You brought us hope just when we needed it the most."

"He is a *thila*," breathed Ikem. "The ancestors sent a guardian to us to stand by our side and protect us."

Pieter, who could not understand the old man's language, only considered Grace's words. He looked around at the faces fixed on him. "Please," he said to Grace, while looking at the others, "tell them I am so sorry for my part in all this." Then he gently took Grace's injured hand in his large calloused ones. "Perhaps, in some small way, I can do something here to help atone for my own mountain of sins."

"A *thila* from the gods!" Ikem repeated.

"A man sent from Mama's God," Grace declared.

27

"Tonio, me *juju!*" Joseph cried in joy when he caught sight of Antonio standing at the doorway of the corner room. He forced himself up from the cot and made a feeble attempt to smooth the rumples from his clothes. Then his face darkened. "We gots us trouble 'ere, 'Tonio. Bad trouble! I needs yer *obeah* mumbo jumbo. Ye must 'elp me wi' yer witchcraft."

"*Sí, señor,*" Antonio responded with a slight bow.

"Call down some *obeah* that'll make 'em rebels all sick an' die!" Joseph ordered. "Ye kin do that, cain't ye?"

Hesitating, Antonio reluctantly agreed, "*Sí, señor.* I can do it."

Joseph, who finally gave in to his hangover, sank back down onto the cot and moaned, "Owww! Me poor achin' 'ead! Give me a bit of restin' time, 'Tonio, then ye kin work yer *juju* fer me. Once I is feelin' some better . . . then ye'll set things right fer me."

Bowing slightly, Antonio gratefully backed out of the room. Pieter would need time.

Finally, everything was assembled, ready and waiting for Antonio and Pieter to move up the tunnel and into the dungeon. This was their chance. A barrel of water. Two loaves of bread that Pieter had managed to sneak out of the kitchen. Dried fish from the storeroom. A sack of raw vegetables he had pulled from the garden. Alcohol for treating wounds. A keg of gunpowder. And a yarrow poultice for Grace's wounded hand.

But where was DeGroot?

After his hangover abated, Joseph insisted Antonio hear his plans to storm the dungeon. He boasted about his cleverness and led his trustee all the way around the fortress, but now that Joseph had finally made his way back to his cot, the Dutchman was nowhere to be found.

Then Antonio remembered DeGroot's comment about the solace and comfort he found on the back side of the fortress, so he made his way around to where the road led up from town. As he walked past the road, something caught his eye. It was a brightly colored piece of cloth—green and yellow and red. It seemed to be snagged on a thornbush, and yet . . . Antonio drew closer. It was only a ragged piece of worn cloth, the kind many African women wore wrapped around their heads. Still, something struck him as unusual about this cloth. It wasn't just caught on the bush. No, it looked as if it had been deliberately folded into an unusual shape. And to Antonio's eye, it looked almost as if it had been hung on that thornbush on purpose. Carefully, Antonio pulled the cloth free from the briars and tucked it into his shirt.

Sure enough, he found Pieter behind Zulina, gazing wistfully out to sea. When Antonio asked for his help, DeGroot quickly headed for the tunnel opening, with Antonio a respectful distance behind.

"What took so long?" Tungo hissed as he eased up behind Antonio. "We came to find you."

They opened the door to the tunnel, where Gamka waited

just inside. "I thought you went white with the Dutchman," he said to Antonio.

Getting the pile of supplies up the tunnel and into the dungeon was difficult work—hot and sweaty. It took much more time than they expected.

"Master is going to be looking for me," Antonio said anxiously. "I must get back to him."

"Don't call him 'Master'!" Gamka snapped.

Antonio said nothing. Gamka was young. There was much he did not understand. He had not lived long enough. But the time would come when he would know and grasp it all— perhaps—if he were fortunate enough to live that long.

Antonio had been born a slave in Spain. When he was little more than a boy, he was taken aboard a Spanish ship to help with the new African slaves on a Spanish-run plantation far up the river—to *domesticado* them. He was at Zulina assisting his Spanish *jefe*, Señor Miguel De La Vega, in selecting new slaves when Joseph Winslow lured Antonio's master into a game of lanterloo. De La Vega had never played the game before, a fact that caused Winslow's eyes to glisten with eager anticipation, and the ivory fish flew faster than either the Spaniard or Antonio could follow. De La Vega's gambling blood was flowing hot, and although he was on a losing streak, he could not stop. Before he knew what happened, Antonio belonged to Winslow.

In shock and desperation, Antonio had fallen to his knees and made the sign of the cross the way he had so often seen his master do. At the same time, he had tried to repeat his master's Latin prayer—although he couldn't remember the right words, since they had no meaning to him. As his hands fumbled and his tongue twisted, Antonio cried out in exasperation, first in the language of his master, then in the language of his African father. And Joseph Winslow, who had been losing badly for many days, won that game and every other game until not a single man had anything left to wager.

Joseph Winslow, his eyes glistening with greed, looked at his new slave and exclaimed, "*Juju!* Magic!"

Antonio gazed at Hola, so eager to help, and his eyes filled with unexpected tears. This boy, so young! When Antonio looked at him, he saw himself not so many years ago.

"Oooh!" Grace cried out as Pieter unwound the filthy cloth from around her hand. It was the piece of fabric Tungo had ripped from her skirt, now stiff with dried blood. Grace's wound had not been tended since her finger was hacked off almost a week before.

For the first time, Grace saw what Tungo had done to her—a jagged, crosswise cut between the first and second knuckles of her first finger. Already the flap of skin that crookedly covered the exposed end had started to grow into place. But her finger was fiery red, and when Pieter touched it, Grace screamed and jerked her hand away.

"Hand me the alcohol," Peter instructed.

Oyo stepped up. "I will help my sister," she stated.

Kneeling beside Grace, Oyo gently took hold of the injured hand and held it in her lap. With a steady hand she poured out a small stream of alcohol, and when Grace cried out, she murmured words of comfort. Then, with Pieter's help, Oyo tied the yarrow poultice firmly in place.

"The *samanka*, it pains now," Oyo said tenderly. "But it holds a powerful death spirit that will suck the poison out and ward off harmful powers. Tomorrow your hand will be on the way to healing."

Antonio started to squeeze back through the tunnel opening, but halfway through, he stopped. "*¡Mire!*" he called back to the dungeon. "Look at this!" Pulling the green, yellow, and red-checked cloth out of his shirt, he said, "I found this on a bush at the head of the road." He tossed the cloth to the floor and then squeezed on through and slid the door closed behind him.

"Mama!" Grace exclaimed as she sprang to her feet. "That's Mama Muco's headcloth!"

But before Grace could reach the folded cloth, Gamka rushed over and grabbed it up. He carried it under the grate so that the shaft of light shone on it, and there he stood for some time carefully studying it. He turned the folded cloth over and over in his hands, inspecting it from all sides. Cabeto, Sunba, and Tungo hurried over to gaze at the cloth with him.

"It is folded into a message," Cabeto stated. "But it is not of our people. I cannot read it."

"The triangle speaks of danger," Tungo said.

"It is the folding of my people," Gamka said. "But . . . it isn't right. It must have been done by someone who is forgetting our ways."

Grace pushed her way through the men. "The cloth belongs to our house slave!" she exclaimed. "It must be a message from her! Read it, Gamka. Please! What does Mama Muco say?"

Gamka held the cloth up. "Tungo is right. This shape gives a warning of danger. But whether the danger is here now or is to come, I cannot tell, because it is not the right size for either. These . . ." Here he indicated the two extra points that hung down on either side. "These are warnings that danger will come from two sides."

"The danger comes only from the white man!" Tungo stated.

"Two sides," Gamka repeated. "That is the message of the cloth."

"Maybe the danger comes from two directions," Cabeto suggested. "Maybe from the door and from the tunnel."

"No," said Grace. "It comes from Joseph Winslow and from Lingongo. From the slave trader and from the lioness."

"The second is far more dangerous than the first," Gamka said. "But that is all I can read."

"The slave trader first," Grace said. "Then the lioness."

28

"'Ear, 'ear!" Joseph called out from his perch atop Zulina's rough-hewn community dining table. "We don't need 'em cowardly buggers wot crawled off in th' night an' sailed wi' th' tide! Ye is th' real men, ye is. An' ye is 'ere an' ready fer a bloody good fight! 'Ooray fer the fightin' men!"

Just a fortnight before, an assortment of captains and whatever was left of their sailing crews crammed around this same table—more than three dozen hungry men all told—more than willing to stuff their bellies with the cook's stewed meat and gravy-soaked biscuits. Now only seven white men could be found in all of Zulina fortress, and that counted the cook, who flatly refused to pick up either a sword or a firearm. Cummings was still there, and Thomas Pitts and Henry Taylor. And the Spanish Capitán Carrillo and his first mate, Gonzales.

Joseph had given up on Pieter DeGroot and counted him among the deserters. Yet at the last minute DeGroot slipped in and took a spot at the far end of the table with the trustees.

"This be yer fight, Joseph," Henry Taylor called out. "What're you offerin' to do to make it worth our while?"

"If'n these savages gits away wi' this rebellion, none o' us is safe, 'Ank!" Joseph bellowed back. "Ain't that reward enough fer the likes o' ye?"

Joseph Winslow's face wore the increasingly common ruddy-red mask of too much drink, yet he managed to stand fairly steady and hold his sword high. Over his shirt he had donned a heavy leather vest, though it didn't have quite the warrior-like effect it could have had if it had not been hanging on him at such a comically lopsided angle.

Before anyone else had a chance to speak against him, Joseph waved his sword high and wide and called out almost jovially, "'Ear, 'ear, me brave lads! This right 'ere today is what we was made fer!"

The men around the table raised their weapons and responded, "'Ear! 'Ear!" But it was nowhere near a resounding answer to Joseph's call to arms. The conviction and commitment simply were not there.

"But why is ye makin' us go in there?" Cummings said with the tinge of a whine in his voice. "They gots guns! Cain't ye jist starve 'em out?"

"No!" Joseph responded. "This thing 'as gone on too long already! It gots to be finished 'ere an' now. An' we is finishin' it up today!"

"His woman won't put up with it no more!" Tom Pitts told Hank in a loud snicker of a whisper. Hank guffawed, and all around the table, Tom was rewarded with hoots and smirks.

"We 'as to show 'em we is in control 'ere, we does!" Joseph insisted. An edge of desperation crept into his voice and the blush deepened on his cheeks and nose. "Else there's to be more an' more trouble. I says it stops right 'ere an' now. I says it stops today!"

"And *su hija*, Señor Winslow?" asked Capitán Carrillo. "What about your daughter?"

Joseph's face darkened. "I ain't got no daughter!" he shot back.

At the end of the table, the trustees sat apart from the white men, except for DeGroot, who purposely squeezed in next to Adisa. The trustees' impassive faces gave no clue about where their sympathies lay. Joseph turned to them, and the light suddenly beamed back in his face. Gesturing with his sword, he commanded, "You, 'Tonio! Say a *juju* over us!"

Antonio slowly stood to his feet. Raising his face toward the ceiling, he intoned,

"Akui nah itung taksi ka',

o tuhan, tenangan kui, ika' aleng uh nyelung akui nai jadi'

jam ika' dahin nyepida ika'

Bah.'u'll.h"

Then he folded his hands and bowed low at the waist.

"'Aa, 'aa!" Joseph responded, clapping his hands together and laughing with glee. With help from Cummings, he managed to stagger down off the table without falling. He grabbed up his sword in one hand, and with the other he hoisted a pistol high in the air. Then he yelled, "Charge!"

Joseph forged ahead, down the main corridor and through the winding passageways. Not until he approached the dungeon grate did he halt and look behind him. The Dutchman and the two Spaniards were there, but the Englishmen had fallen behind. As for the unenthusiastic trustees, they were dragging as far back as they possibly could.

"'Ere now, we's in this together!" Joseph hissed back in an angry whisper. "Quit yer laggin', ye beastly cowards!" Then an idea came to him and he quickly added, "'Tonio! To the front wi' ye!"

As Antonio made his way up to Joseph, the reluctant Englishmen grabbed the other trustees and eagerly forced them forward as well.

"Them Africans in that room . . . they ain't had neither water or food fer nigh on to three days now," Joseph whispered back down the corridor. "They be too weak to fight back. Jist go on in there shootin'. I'll be right behind ye."

With an unsteady wave of bravado, Joseph did his best to make a grand show of unlocking the dungeon door. The entire effect was ruined, however, when he could not get the key into the lock. He struggled and struggled, spitting curses as he did his best to force it in. The key finally found the hole, and then the bolt slipped free. Just before he pushed the door open, Joseph grabbed hold of Antonio and held him back. Then he pushed the other trustees forward and one by one shoved them through the door.

Immediately, the dungeon exploded in gunfire. In the chaos that followed, Antonio wrenched himself free from Joseph's grasp. He dashed through the door and plunged headlong into the billowing smoke and shrieking chaos.

29

Cummings folded almost double as he gasped and choked in the smoke. The others, stupid and stunned, stood and gawked. Not Joseph Winslow, though. He was far too pleased with himself to pay Cummings any mind . . . or the rest of them, for that matter.

"'Elpless as toothless ol' women, they be!" Joseph chortled.

Perhaps he was right. Inside the dungeon, after the initial shrieks, everything had fallen breathlessly still.

Joseph hesitated only a moment before he tentatively called through the doorway, "'Tonio?"

"¡Entre, Master!" rang out the confident reply of his trusted slave. "Come on in!"

Joseph laughed out loud. "Jist ol' women, that's all they be!" he chortled to the others. "Didn't I tell ye as much? Didn't I, now?"

Joseph flapped his hands in front of his face to clear a path through the smoke and marched triumphantly though the doorway and made for the stairs. Cummings recovered himself in time to jump to and follow at his heels, and both Spaniards stepped up to march behind them. The very picture of victory, they were! But then, swift as a cheetah on the attack,

Antonio sprang out in front of them, leaped over the side of the stairs and down to the dungeon floor. The other trustees immediately dropped to their bellies, rolled aside, and pressed themselves tightly against the walls. As one, eight armed men and women rose up out of the smoky shadows.

As musket fire roared, Tom Pitts and Henry Taylor, who had not yet crawled in through the grate, threw down their arms and ran back through the corridor. As for Pieter DeGroot, he dropped to his knees and hunkered down, clasping his hands over his ears. It was a futile effort, of course. Nothing could block out the screams and shouts that poured from the smoke-filled dungeon.

In the tangled confusion, Capitán Carrillo managed to crawl back out the door, but when the smoke dissipated, his man Gonzales lay dead. Cummings, blubbering and wailing like an injured water buffalo, lay on his back, his shoulder a bloody mess. As for Joseph Winslow, he stood stock-still at the foot of the stairs, wild-eyed and face-to-face with Grace. In her hands was a musket—*his* musket—loaded and ready to fire!

"Well now, me darlin' daughter," Joseph sputtered in a voice so shaky he could hardly spit out the words. "I been 'opin' an' prayin' I'd see yer lovely face 'ere. That is, to see ye agin before—" But his voice failed him before he could finish the sentence. He couldn't even make *himself* believe his lame words. How could he expect anyone else to believe them?

As his desperation mounted, Joseph's eyes darted from one face to another. When they landed on Antonio, he brightened. "'Tonio!" he exclaimed. "Is this all part o' yer *juju*?" He took a step toward the African. "'Tis magic that's workin' 'ere, ain't that right?"

Tungo sprang forward and grabbed Joseph by his fleshy jowl. Then he jerked a knife against the pale throat and pressed it so hard that a thin stream of blood trickled over Joseph's sweat-drenched collar and down onto his lopsided leather vest.

"Grace!" Joseph whimpered. "Grace, me darlin' daughter. Is ye goin' to let this madman harm yer lovin' father?"

"Tungo, stop!" Grace ordered.

What Grace had in mind, no one would ever know, because she was interrupted by the sudden snap of a whip that ripped across Tungo's hand and sent his knife flying. Unfortunately for Joseph, he was between the whip and the knife. The whip caught him in the face and slashed him from his forehead all the way down to his throat.

"Come!" Lingongo called to her husband.

But bleeding and in shock, Joseph seemed to have taken root.

In the silence that followed, all eyes locked onto Lingongo. She didn't hesitate. Lashing her whip, she cleared a path.

"Now, Husband!" she ordered. "Come!"

Cabeto and Sunba scrambled for the muskets Lingongo had whipped from their hands.

With blood streaming from his face, Joseph shook loose from his stunned paralysis and scrambled up the stairs. But then he stopped abruptly and pulled back. Cummings splayed awkwardly between him and the grate door.

"'Elp me!" Cummings cried out. "Joseph, fer the love of God, don't leave me 'ere to die."

Joseph paused, but for only a moment. Then he stepped awkwardly over Cummings, who writhed on the stairs and reached out to him. Without a backward glance, Joseph forced himself through the grate.

Never had Grace seen her father move so quickly. By the time Cabeto could grab up his musket and ready it, Joseph was out the door and had slammed the bolt into place. Cabeto waved his loaded musket in the air and bellowed in fury.

But then he stopped. He strode up to the locked door and ran his hand across one hinge and then the other. He closely examined each one. The two were not the same. One had been damaged. Cabeto stepped back and took careful aim with his musket. Then he pulled the trigger.

The shot was dead-on. When the smoke cleared, a large crack ran down the entire length of the door. The damaged hinge was now destroyed.

As one, Sunba and Tungo ran forward, throwing their full weight against the door. Wood cracked, yet the door stood. Gamka and Cabeto joined, and together they hit it again and again and again. Finally, with a great splintering crash, half the grate door ripped away.

The dungeon thundered with shouts of victory.

Grace caught her breath. "Are we free?" she asked. "Can we just walk out?"

"Out of the dungeon, yes, but not out of the fortress," Tungo said.

"*Es verdad,*" Antonio agreed. "The doors at the ends of the passageways—surely they are bolted tight. Probably nailed shut, *también*. To make certain that we cannot leave."

The dungeon filled with excited chatter as everyone talked at once.

Everything had changed. No longer could Antonio come and go openly. No more did he have Joseph's ear, and he certainly could not rely on the slave trader's trust. And what of Pieter DeGroot? Where did he stand? No one knew for sure. Only one thing was certain: this day—this one day—they had been victorious! Now the precarious tunnel was no longer their only way in and out of the dungeon. Although Antonio no longer had Joseph Winslow's ear, he still had his keys. All of Zulina was potentially theirs.

In the midst of the euphoric chatter, Cabeto looked at Grace. "No, we are not free," he told her softly. "But we will be!"

Ikem, who had remained aloof from the others throughout the entire confrontation, suddenly stood up. He raised his hands high in the air and commanded, "Listen!"

Immediately, everyone stopped talking. In the silence, the others could now hear what only Ikem had heard through the noise. The ever present moans and cries of the fortress had ceased. In their place was the undulating sound of voices calling out to them from hidden places beyond the dungeon's walls.

In mixed languages and many tongues the voices pleaded, "Me, too . . . oh, please, me too! Do not forget about me, my brothers and sisters! Come and free me too!"

30

"Benjamin! Benjamin, where are you off to?" Henrietta Stevens, still in her nightdress, called out from her bedchamber. "You promised you would spend this time with Charlotte and me, yet here you are, off once again!"

Henrietta didn't like to show her irritation because it was not the way civilized ladies behaved. Nor did she appreciate being forced to step out of her room still in her nightclothes. But how, pray tell, was one to behave in a civilized way when forced to exist for two entire months on the edge of a heathen jungle with a husband who appeared to have deserted even the vaguest pretense of living as an Englishman? Every other year she dutifully sailed across the ocean—at great personal inconvenience and peril, she was always careful to point out— and forced herself to stay for two long months at her husband's side on the African slave coast. And being an exemplary wife and mother, she not only saw to their daughter's proper upbringing in London, but she also insisted that the girl accompany her on her trips to Africa.

Fortunately, Henrietta had the good sense to make her position quite clear the moment Benjamin first told her he was giving up his slave ship in order to manage a slave house on Africa's coast. Otherwise, she would most assuredly be expected to spend even more time out here. Yes, her husband earned good money. For that she was most grateful. And as he told it, he was much safer here than he had ever been on the slave ships. But Henrietta had her own health and well-being to consider. And there was, of course, Charlotte.

"Go back to your room, my dear," Benjamin Stevens urged. "You and Charlotte stay inside today and busy yourselves with your lace."

At the first light of dawn, before his wife and daughter had even begun to stir, before the infernal wind had a chance to get the better of them all, Benjamin Stevens had eased out of his house and headed down the sandy shore.

Despite Henrietta's opinion of his living conditions, he found his house here most comfortable. Simple and utilitarian, that's what it was, exactly what a white man's abode on the coast of Africa should be. He had not the slightest use for the foolish extravagances of Joseph Winslow, who forever crowed about his ridiculous London house. Why should Stevens build anything for Henrietta and Charlotte anyway? They were in Africa so seldom. And now with Charlotte being married off to a man he had never even met, he knew full well that he was not likely to see her again. Not unless he left the slave house without an overseer for a minimum of three months. How could he possibly do that?

So long as the sun was not yet high in the sky—or if he waited until after it had begun to set—Stevens enjoyed the comfortable walk to the slave house he managed for a group of British investors. It was just a complex of shelters on the sandy coastline actually, but a most effective operation. African traders marched captives in coffles into the factory where he checked them over and had them manacled. Then they were securely chained to the walls and floors inside various rooms according to their age, sex, and value. When Stevens had a good supply of slaves ready for sale, he hoisted a signal flag to alert nearby ships that he was open for business. His was not a huge fortress like Zulina, but Benjamin Stevens worked hard, and his profits were enviable.

It was just as the ship carrying Henrietta and Charlotte and their trunks from London arrived in the harbor that the drums had started. In the days since, drumbeats whirled through the air ever more urgently. Stevens couldn't understand what they said, but the slaves chained up in his holding cells clearly did. Something was happening, and it made him most nervous.

"Benjamin!"

"Go inside, I told you!" Stevens ordered. He was a patient man, but there was a limit to his endurance.

This morning, as he had headed toward the slave houses, Benjamin Stevens had shaded his eyes and gazed out to sea, the same as he did every morning. But to his amazement, he saw that three ships had anchored during the night and that at least two more were sailing his way. What did it mean? Slave pickings were slim right now. Almost a month had passed since he had flown the signal flag. Why, then, the sudden rush of ships?

It was Charlotte Stevens, as she stared out the window because she had nothing else to do—"Not even glass to keep the wretched bugs and mosquitoes out!" Henrietta had groused when she saw her daughter resting her chin on the window ledge—who first saw Benjamin approach with the strangers.

"Look, Mother," Charlotte called. "Father has one . . . two . . . three . . . four . . . five . . . six—he has *nine* white men with him!"

Henrietta had already composed the speech she would pour

out on her husband when he finally returned home. She had given up so much and suffered so desperately just to spend some time with him, she had planned to say, and look how thoughtlessly and rudely he treated her. And Charlotte—on the very eve of her marriage! Why, it was little wonder his daughter did not plan to come back to Africa. As a matter of fact, in consideration of his present behavior, she herself might be forced to come to the very same decision! (Here, Henrietta had planned to pause long enough for the effects of her threatened punishment to soak in.)

Righteous indignation. That was the tone she would assume. And she would sprinkle it with a generous helping of personal pain.

Henrietta waited at the door, the words of her recriminating speech already filling her mouth. But when she saw the set of her husband's face, she forgot all about the speech. Instead, she asked, "What is it, Husband? What has happened?"

Stevens motioned the men toward the parlor. Then he took his wife's arm and led her to the back of the house.

"Joseph Winslow!" he said. "That arrogant old windbag has really done it this time!"

31

Grace sank wearily back against the coolness of the stone wall. She brushed unruly wisps of hair away from her eyes and mopped the dripping perspiration from her face. She was exhausted—utterly and thoroughly exhausted. Forty-seven people, she had counted. Forty-seven men, women, and children chained in the dank stone holes and locked rooms. It had taken hours to unshackle all of them. But now one entire wing of Zulina was free.

"*Can ton!*" a gap-toothed man behind her proclaimed in a loud, gravelly voice.

Grace looked over at him and then at the small clutch of people gathered around him. In spite of her weariness, she couldn't help smiling. In the Dogon language, *can ton* meant "a village of their own." At first, with so many desperate souls from such a variety of tribes and tongues, confusion reigned. People scurried from room to room in search of family, or even desperate to catch sight of a villager they recognized. Something familiar, that's what they longed to find. But now everyone was beginning to settle into small groups with others who spoke the same language or in some other way reminded him or her of home.

"Muskets . . . pistols . . . gunpowder . . . lead balls—" From the far side where they hunkered together, Grace could hear Cabeto's voice as he ticked off his list to Antonio. Then Cabeto stopped abruptly and demanded, "The Dutchman. Can he really get all these for us, Antonio?"

"He will try," Antonio answered. "He can promise no more than that."

"Knives too. And spears," Gamka interjected impatiently. "Tell the Dutchman Africans do not fight like white men. Firearms are not enough for us. We need knives and spears. Tell him bows and arrows too."

"Knives, maybe," Antonio answered with a wave of his hand. "But not spears or bows and arrows. He will not find those in the white man's storehouse."

"You tell him—" Gamka began, but Cabeto interrupted in a rock-solid voice.

"You tell him, 'Thank you,'" Cabeto said. "The Dutchman can only get us white man's arms, and he risks his life to do that. We understand, and we are thankful. We ask nothing more."

Grace turned slightly away from Oyo and readjusted herself. She slumped down until her left shoulder rested firmly against the hard stones, then she propped her hand under her head. From this position, she could see Cabeto framed between Antonio and Sunba, with Gamka on his other side.

What a strange man he is, this Cabeto! Grace thought, and a strange flutter moved through her. *I do not understand him in the least.*

Cabeto raised his hand as he talked and gestured toward the door. It was that same rock-hard hand he had clamped down on her mouth just before he dragged her out of her old life and into this violent new world. His voice rang with enough authority to still Gamka and save her life from Tungo's murderous scheme, yet it had filled with tears when he told of the slavers' assault on his village. Cabeto, who kidnapped her, was the same man who humbly asked her forgiveness. Cabeto, who consistently argued for peace, was the same man who commanded this desperate band of men and women preparing to fight a battle they could not possibly win. Who was this Cabeto—a man of peace or a man of war? A man she could learn to trust, or a man in whose presence she must forever be on her guard?

"*Ah keen!*" Tungo cried from atop the water barrel where he had positioned himself. "*Ah keen!*"

Grace sighed. One thing was certain—Cabeto was nothing like Tungo. Tungo, who bellowed out his battle plans for all to hear, then boastfully pronounced himself *ah keen!* A strong warrior doesn't need to announce himself. Soon enough, what he is will be obvious to everyone simply by his actions.

Yet the more Tungo called out his self-proclaimed "strong warrior" title, the more his confidence grew. He jumped down from the barrel and strutted about waving his arms and his gun in the air, and then he proudly proclaimed himself the honorable leader of the victorious rebels.

"*Ohla!*" he yelled as he leaped into the air and thrust his musket high. "*Ohla Tungo!*"

Men and women stopped what they were doing to stare up at him. They silenced their talk in order to listen. And yet, it was not to Tungo that they turned for guidance. No, it was to Cabeto. Cabeto, who didn't announce himself or proclaim a proud title. Cabeto, who got busy and did what needed to be done. When Cabeto gave instructions, people not only listened but also rushed to obey.

Grace watched Cabeto, and she smiled.

"Tungo, we must have a strong leader who will make certain the doors are at all times secure from the inside," Cabeto said in a voice that did not allow for discussion. "You will be that man. Take whoever you need to help you."

Then Cabeto turned to his brother: "Sunba, you will guard the passageway. You, also, take who you need."

He put Gamka in charge of the door from the dungeon to the tunnel.

Antonio would be responsible for getting messages down the tunnel to Pieter DeGroot and also for bringing supplies back up through the tunnel.

"Food!" Safya called out to Cabeto. "With so many hungry ones, we need more food." She shook her head in exasperation. "And we have no cooking fire! What are we to do about that?"

"Ask the Dutchman what he can do," Cabeto instructed Antonio. "What he brings us, we will eat. Cooked or not, we will be grateful for it."

It was now midday. Grace noticed that Cabeto periodically shifted a few inches to the left—just enough so that the shaft of light from the grate fell directly across him. How his face glistened in the sunlight! Such a strong profile he had! Such piercing eyes! In spite of herself, Grace pushed away from the stone wall and inched forward. Never before had she seen so powerful a man as this Cabeto, not even among the well-muscled slaves who toiled in her father's fields. Perhaps—though she could not say for certain—not even Yao.

"*Ohla,*" Grace breathed. "*Ohla Cabeto!*"

Cabeto turned and looked into Grace's face. "You call me honorable leader?" he asked her in disbelieving puzzlement.

Grace looked away as humiliation flamed in her cheeks.

"An honorable leader would not drag a lady into a dungeon. An honorable leader would not allow an innocent lady's hand to be mutilated. No, Grace. Do not call me *ohla*. I do not deserve it. Most of all, not from you."

Grace reached out and touched Cabeto's arm. "If not leader, may I call you 'friend'?" she asked.

Cabeto didn't get a chance to answer because at that moment the boy Hola ran up to him and demanded, "I want a musket too!"

"A musket is not easy to shoot," Cabeto told the boy.

"But—"

Ikem called out to Hola, "You and me, we not shoot white man's firesticks. You stay by me, boy. I teach you to fight brave like a son of Africa. You be African man, not white man."

No longer did Ikem speak of being a good slave and cooperating peacefully with his master. To Cabeto, Ikem said, "I be old and full of experience. The time has come that we must fight. I not fight like white man, but I have understanding of many years. I ask you, Cabeto, give me men to be my own—old men like me. We fight, too, but in ways of Africa. Boys too young to fight with you, like Hola here, we bring them with us and we teach them to fight in the old ways."

Cabeto considered Ikem's words.

"You the leader, my brother," Ikem pressed. "No other has the power of your hand. The ancestors be with you alone."

"Are you asking my permission to lead a group of African fighters?" Cabeto asked.

"No, my brother, not permission," Ikem said. "Lead them I will. I ask your blessing."

"Then you have it, my friend," Cabeto told him.

As Grace watched from the shadows, two men who had pleaded separately for peace—a ritually scarred old man and a powerful young *ohla*—clenched hands in a united alliance for battle.

32

The ruler of the most powerful chiefdom in the Kingdom of Gold, the king, the Great and Powerful One, had permitted his daughter to stand before him and freely voice her complaints. He had even tolerated the abominable behavior of her boorish husband who pushed his way in, unannounced and on his own. Perhaps that is why his son dared approach him with neither invitation nor permission and presumed to speak on behalf of the ancestors.

"A new swarm of locusts blew in on the wind," Obei declared in a most inappropriate voice of insolence accompanied by a careless wave of his hands.

Did the prince think him both blind and deaf? Even as they spoke, men and women spread out across the millet fields to slap and stomp at the swarming insects. Witch doctors and diviners were also at work, their *ase* increasing with each potion they concocted and with each animal they sacrificed.

"It is as the wise men say," Obei continued, a tone of accusation coating his voice in bitterness. "The land mutters and complains."

Because Obei was his firstborn son, the king listened to him, but with every word his displeasure grew. Such arrogance! Such insulting audacity! Prince or not, how could he dare speak in such a way to the only great ruler, the one who dressed in the black kente cloth woven with broad gold strokes, the one who had the right to richly bedeck himself with the heaviest royal gold jewelry, who alone could put the porcupine ring of military prowess on his finger? Why, his feet rested on the Golden Stool! Did his son have no respect for the spirit of the nation?

What Obei was careful not to mention was that purpose and intention stood behind both his visit and his words. Whether the king agreed or disagreed with his statements mattered not in the least. The point was to hold his father's attention while the elders gathered with other dignitaries of the chiefdom in a secret meeting to discuss whether the king was still capable of carrying out his responsibilities, or whether it was time to pass the power of the *sika'gua* to Prince Obei.

The locust invasion was but the latest disturbance of the natural order that the wise men took to be signs that it just might be time to dispose of the ruler. They had already endured long, dry months when the rain that should have come stayed away. That was also a sign. Still, it was true that such things did occur in the natural order of life. Of more concern than these was the king's decision to melt down some of the royal gold to buy weapons from the white man. No! A successful king should be adding gold to the treasury, not taking it away. But the gravest alarm arose from the matter of the alliance the king had forged with the Englishman—the alliance he paid for with his favorite daughter.

"This nation was created by the ancestors," an elder stated at the beginning of the secret meeting.

"Yet it must be maintained by war," responded a respected warrior.

"White men look at Joseph Winslow and they laugh," a second elder said. "Because he is the husband of the daughter of our king, when they ridicule him, they also ridicule us. Joseph Winslow is an offense to the pride of our nation."

"A wise king would not give his daughter to an outsider in marriage," the oldest and wisest of the elders said. "Certainly not his favorite daughter. Not even in exchange for many, many ships filled with guns and enough kegs of gunpowder to fill an entire village." Everyone nodded his agreement. And the oldest and wisest added, "He certainly would not give her to a white slave trader. And most certainly not to such a one as Joseph Winslow."

This talk had been said before. But now word had come to them of the rebellion at Zulina slave fortress. "Lingongo herself appealed to her father for help," yet another elder exclaimed. "It is one thing to make war on an enemy people and take captives for sale. Even our ancestors made slaves of war captives. But to fight alongside the white man against Africans in chains?"

"No!" shouted the warrior. "I will not!"

The nation teetered on the brink of disaster. On this point, all the elders agreed. It was punishment from the ancestors, they insisted. Well-deserved punishment.

"But he is king," the oldest elder pointed out. "And as such he has magical powers we do not possess. We must be careful. We must be very wise and very careful."

At that same moment, the king—who had heard enough of his son's endless babble—gestured toward his golden snake sword, then to his shield emblazoned with the likeness of defeated enemies, and then around the throne room to the horns of buffalo and the teeth of lions.

"My magical powers raised me high to this throne," he informed his son, "and they will keep me seated here. Do you doubt that? If so, then challenge me, O great prince, and see what happens."

At the mention of a personal challenge, Obei drew back and blanched.

"Does it surprise you to know that your plot does not take me by surprise?" the king asked. "By challenging me, my son, you have angered the spirits. For the past several nights they have given me warnings in my dreams. Oh, yes, this is why I listened to your sister, and it is also why I endured her fool of a husband. It was because of what I already knew."

Obei, whose mouth had been running over with so many words, suddenly found himself stricken silent.

"You say we are in a time of crisis. In that you are correct," the king said. "As are the elders who plot alongside you. But what you and they have neglected to see is that crisis makes people careless and desperate. And so it is precisely such times that give others the opportunity to bring new life to our nation. But only if we act carefully and wisely."

For a long time, the king did not dismiss his son. Instead, he sat on his throne, cool and comfortable in his royal *kente* cloth and gold adornments, and watched the prince sweat and worry.

No wonder the king's people respected him so deeply. No surprise that their fear of him was so intense.

33

√   Gunpowder barrels—3
√   Crate of muskets, pistols stacked on top—1
√   Lead balls in leather sacks—4
√   Knives—5
√   Barrels of fresh water—4
√   Bread loaves—4
√   Buckets of dried fish—3
√   Pot of boiled meat—1
√   Sacks of fresh vegetables—2
√   Pot of boiled beans—1

Pieter DeGroot shoved the checked-off list into his pocket and pushed the last of the supplies up the tunnel to Antonio. Only then did he rock back on his heels and heave a sigh of relief. Had the fortress not been in a state of absolute pandemonium, it would have been impossible for him to gather such a great store of supplies without raising suspicion. But as it was, no one paid any attention to the kitchen, nor was a guard posted at the storage room where the munitions were kept.

The last time Pieter saw Joseph Winslow, he was heading for

his bed, bellowing in pain and anger. Lingongo raged in fury on the grounds outside. She had slipped her passageway bolts free only to discover that the doors had been secured from the inside, locking her out of an entire wing of her own slave fortress! What enraged her even more was the knowledge that slaves walked around inside, unshackled and armed.

Where the English sailors were, Pieter could not begin to guess. But he did know he could not keep up his thievery for long. The kitchen pantry was growing sparse and so was the arms storehouse. Besides, Joseph Winslow had already sent out a desperate call for help to all the slave-holding establishments up and down the African coast. It was only a matter of time before reinforcements and armaments of every kind would flood in and crush the rebellion. The poor wretches in the dungeon would all be slaughtered; he had no doubt of that. But at least they would go down fighting and with their bellies full. He would see to it.

Pieter waited until Antonio, still inside the dungeon, pushed the cover back over the upper opening, and then he made his way down the tunnel. At the bottom, he leaned back in the inky darkness and listened. Silence. He eased the lower door open just wide enough to squeeze through and dropped down to the stone landing.

Immediately, a tongue of fire ripped across his back and sent him reeling to the floor. Stunned and confused, Pieter struggled to his feet. But before he could clear his head, another blow ripped around his legs and he crumbled to his knees. The next lash knocked him flat. This time Pieter didn't try to get up. He lay still, screaming in agony.

"Put him in irons!"

There was no mistaking the voice. It was Lingongo.

Pieter strained to turn his head in her direction. Lingongo

had her eyes fixed squarely on him. They never wavered, not even as she carefully rolled up her whip and tucked it under her arm. Across her face spread a stone-cold smile that offered not one bit of mirth.

Tom Pitts and Henry Taylor rushed toward Pieter and grabbed hold of his arms, but Pieter managed to shove them away. He forced himself upright.

"Stop yer fightin', you rotter of a traitor!" Tom sneered as he kicked Pieter in the stomach.

Pieter reached out to grab Tom's booted foot, but it spun before his eyes and his arms flailed helplessly in the air. More blows, then everything went dark, and Pieter dropped to the floor.

When Pieter regained his senses, Henry Taylor was lashing him to a hook in the wall.

"Henry—" Pieter gasped.

"You gone and done it to yersef," Henry whispered. "Don't think I's enjoyin' this, bindin' you down like any old slave."

Henry jerked Pieter's arms back over open wounds, cut clean through to the muscle by Lingongo's whip. Pieter yelped in pain.

"I's bindin' you, but I won't chain you, mate," Henry whispered with a strange gentleness. "That I will not do."

Between cries and groans of agony, Pieter did his best to mumble his gratitude.

When Henry offered him a drink of water from the jug, Pieter gulped ravenously.

As Henry stepped up to leave, Pieter said, "She was right there waiting for me, Henry."

"Aye, that she was," Henry agreed. "Knowed you was in the tunnel, she did."

"How did she know?" Pieter asked. "Who told her?"

Without a word, Henry picked up the jug and walked to the cell door. But just before he stepped out, he paused and turned back to Pieter. "I'll tell you this much, mate," he said with a sad shake of his head. "I'd rather 'ave a anchor tied 'round me neck and be tossed clear to the depths of the deep blue sea than be in yer 'ide, Pieter DeGroot. I sure 'nough would."

"Who told her?" Pieter asked again.

The door shut. Outside, a key turned in the lock.

Pieter's blood trailed all the way from his prison cell, down the stone hallway, through to the landing, to the tunnel opening where Lingongo had lain in wait. At that very moment, under Lingongo's watchful eye, two slaves worked with hammers and spikes and freshly cut planks, erecting a wall to seal the tunnel opening.

"Make it solid!" Lingongo ordered. "No one or no thing must ever pass through there again."

But Pieter knew nothing of this. Pain settled over him like a heavy cloud, and he drifted in and out of hazy consciousness. Once again he saw himself aboard *Dem Tulp*. He heard his crewmen's dying gasps and watched helplessly as Africans threw themselves overboard, then bobbed in the sea and reached out to him before they sank forever. He listened again to the cries of horror and despair that poured from the mouths of every person—black and white—on that doomed ship. And, oh, the unbearable agony of his mangled back. Surely that, too, was just a part of the terrible nightmare. With great effort, Pieter struggled to awaken from the awful dream that reverberated and echoed with howling screams. As he dragged himself back to consciousness, he discovered the cries were his own.

Pieter squinted through swollen eyes and peered into the dusky gloom. He was alone in a rank, rat-infested cell. At the sight of the sodden mess of a floor, befouled with his blood, he groaned and squeezed his eyes shut again. Then he faded back into a hazy twilight of agony.

Sometime later—minutes? hours? days?—racked with pain and groaning for water, Pieter once again forced his eyes open. Before him stood the despicable Lingongo. Pieter jerked awake, but the apparition did not disappear.

"I watched you from afar because I thought you might be an exception for a white man," Lingongo said, her voice even and controlled. "One who could reason and make rational decisions. Not a fool like the others. Not like Joseph Winslow."

Pieter said nothing. Though it took every bit of self-control he could muster, he refused to give Lingongo the satisfaction of hearing him groan.

"When I heard whispers of a traitorous white man, I thought it could be any one of that pitiful lot of sailors. I even suspected my own husband. But I never thought it would be you. I am disappointed by your betayal, yes, but even more, I am disappointed in myself because I did not suspect you."

Pieter struggled to his feet so he could look Lingongo in the eye.

"And you, Lingongo, royal princess of a proud and ancient people," Pieter said, his voice thick and his words slurred. "Who are you to speak to me of traitors? Are you not the worst of traitors to your people?"

Lingongo's eyes flashed. "Do not dare speak to me of such things!" she snapped. "Long ago a choice not of my making was forced upon me. I could be a slave trader, or I could be a slave. I made my decision, and I made it well. I will be a slave to no man. I will not!"

"I, too, made a choice," Pieter said. "I am pleased to inform you that those poor wretches now have a fighting chance to also be slaves to no man—and to no woman."

"You made a foolish choice," Lingongo replied flatly. "One of those poor wretches betrayed you. All I had to do was promise free passage out when the rest are killed."

"You are wrong. I made a wise choice," Pieter replied. "Eight of them did not betray me. And those eight will fight all the more bravely because I gave them what they needed most. I gave them hope."

34

Just after Antonio closed the opening, while Gamka and Cabeto heaved the heavy pot of beans over to the corner and Ikem complained that no one got him a lion's tail to use as a proper good-luck war charm, the first sounds of trouble echoed up from below. Antonio had started to explain that white men had no lions' tails because they didn't use them, but his words were cut short by sudden scuffles pierced with cries. Antonio sprang into action.

"Water barrels . . . ammunition crates . . . push them in front of the door!" he commanded.

Stacked together, those barrels and crates formed a sturdy blockade. Tungo and Gamka took up defensive positions, muskets tamped and ready to fire, just in case anyone should climb up the tunnel and attempt to force through.

Horrible screams had followed—something beyond the usual fortress distress—something less distinguishable, but equally unsettling and ominous.

"Lingongo!" Grace cried in alarm. "It's her! I know it is! Oh, she must have caught the Dutchman!"

While Lingongo stood over Pieter DeGroote down below and lashed him with her whip, up in the dungeon the captives caught their collective breath in a gasp of pure horror.

Antonio lurched backward as though he had been punched in the stomach. "*¿Como puede saber?*" he demanded. "How could she know? The Dutchman was always *muy* careful when he came in and out of the tunnel. How could the lioness know?"

"You underestimate my mother," Grace said in a voice hushed with grudging respect. "She is not easy to fool. The admiral talks and yells and boasts and threatens, but Lingongo, she is the one to fear."

Not an hour later, the pounding began.

The boy Hola looked up at Safya. "Maybe it's the Dutchman coming back?" he asked, his small voice quivering with hope.

"Hush," Safya told him a bit too roughly. "It is not the Dutchman. It is her. The lioness is sealing us in." Instinctively, Safya reached for Hola and pulled him close. The boy didn't resist.

Since Safya and Oyo were in charge of provisions, Cabeto said to them, "We must watch our rations, both of food and of water." There was no need to say more.

"Come," Ikem called to the group of older men he had assembled. In his pile of armaments were the five knives Pieter DeGroot had delivered through the tunnel. Then Ikem went over to Hola and grasped the boy by the shoulders. "You also," he said. "Come now. It is time you learn the way men of Africa make war. Come and see boys become men. We teach you the way our fathers taught us, the way our grandfathers taught our fathers."

Safya gasped and clutched the boy more tightly. But when she looked up at Ikem, respect flooded her eyes, and she slowly released her grip. Without a word Hola got to his feet and followed Ikem and his men. Single file, they climbed to the open grate and out through the broken door.

There was no time to spare.

"Sunba! Tungo!" Cabeto called. "Have you set men to guard the doors to the outside?"

"Yes, Brother," Sunba answered. "Men armed with muskets and plenty of gunpowder."

An unexpected rush of tears flooded Grace's eyes. In Cabeto's powerful black face, in his gentle voice that knew how to be strong and challenge others to strength, she saw a reflection of Yao's determination. Oh, how long ago and far away Yao's words seemed! Where was he now? If only he could be here to see the birth of a new hope. If only he could join the fight for freedom!

". . . three cells and one dungeon," Cabeto was saying. "Tungo, Gamka, Antonio—each of you will oversee one cell. Choose between you who will take which one. Sunba, you will oversee the dungeon. Ikem, it will be for you and your men to guard the corridor."

Tungo swaggered forward. "And you, Cabeto?" he called out with a touch of sarcasm. "What is it that you will be doing?"

Cabeto stepped forward to meet the challenge. "I will oversee the fight, my friend," he said in an even voice. "I will make certain we all work together. As the wise ones say: when spider webs unite, they can tie up a lion. Those are good words for us, for alone we are but single strands, and we have a lioness to defeat."

Although Cabeto's words were controlled, an unmistakable blade of authority cut through his voice and gave his words a razor edge.

Tungo frowned and swaggered, but he said no more.

"Tungo," Cabeto called out, "you assign each person to one of the four rooms, and give each a job to attend to when the fight starts. Sunba, it is up to you to guard the guns. You decide who will use them and when. Antonio, you take charge of the gunpowder, balls, and wadding. All the munitions are your responsibility."

"The lioness is nothing to us!" Tungo yelled, waving his musket wildly.

"You are wrong," Grace said gravely. "To underestimate her is a great mistake. Lingongo is always something. Cabeto does well to plan and prepare."

Tungo glowered at her, turned his back, and stalked away.

Bent over the case of guns, Sunba pulled one out and held it up, and then carefully laid it aside. One by one, he unpacked the others and also stacked them along the wall. Antonio and Gamka moved off to begin their preparations too.

Grace turned to Cabeto and pressed, "What of me? What is my job?"

"I will not ask you to fight your own mother," Cabeto said.

Grace turned away and fixed her attention on the activity that buzzed all around her. But she didn't move away, and neither did he. After a few minutes, she turned back and searched Cabeto's face.

"When I was very young, herds of elephants occasionally trampled the grasslands outside our compound," she said softly. "They stripped so many young saplings that nothing remained but bare limbs. Those elephants uprooted entire trees. Everything in their path, they destroyed. But the elephants never grazed near villages. My mother would tell me, 'I am stronger than those elephants, Grace, because I would not spare the villages. I would trample them first because that is where the grass is the most tender, and because no one would expect to find me there.'"

Cabeto watched Grace, his expression unchanged. When she paused, he waited in silence for her to continue.

"It is a great mistake to think my mother will show mercy because I am here," she said.

"But your father—"

"No," Grace said. "I am a disappointment to the slave trader. He could not make me white, and I failed to make him rich and respected."

Tungo's men reluctantly gave up their guard positions at the opening that now led nowhere. Impatiently, Tungo paced back and forth, back and forth. The endless hammering jangled his nerves. Suddenly, he sprang to the door and slid it open.

"*Alto!*" Antonio called out in warning. "Stop!"

Tungo never glanced in Antonio's direction. He forced his way past the others, thrust his head into the tunnel, and bellowed, "Thank you, Lioness! You do our work for us! You keep your murderers out of our fortress!"

Cabeto grabbed Tungo, and with one blow of his fist he knocked him flat. Sunba dropped the musket he had just lifted out of the crate and dove into the fray. With one quick move, he pinned Tungo to the floor.

"You will die, Killer Lioness!" Tungo screamed as he struggled and kicked. "My hands will squeeze the last breath from your throat! With your own blood, you will pay for the blood of my people!"

The hammering stopped. And from the far end of the tunnel, Lingongo's answer echoed back.

"You want a contest between you and me, little man? Then you will have your contest."

With a leap, Grace raced past Tungo, whom Sunba still held pinned to the floor. Without the least hesitation, she rushed through the open doorway and plunged into the dark tunnel. Half running and half sliding, she charged blindly downward until she ran up against the planks nailed across the opening. Her face flooded with tears, Grace slammed against the barrier and screamed, "Mother! It doesn't have to be like this! You don't have to kill everyone!"

"Never again call me 'Mother,'" Lingongo declared in an icy voice that chilled Grace's soul. "If it will ease your mind, not *everyone* will die—but you will. And now that you finally have friends, so will they." She paused a moment. "You have squeezed from me the last drops of pride and honor. On my word, Grace Winslow, not one person who is important to you will leave Zulina alive."

35

G race stirred from a restless sleep and opened her eyes to
the first beam of dawn. Instantly, she was alert and on
guard. Something was wrong.

Long ago—back in another life, it seemed—Grace had learned
to be wary of fears that crept up and attacked in the dark of
night. Back then, she blamed it on the cries that wafted in on
the howling wind to stalk the darkness and haunt her dreams.
But now the harmattan winds couldn't be to blame. Now the
sounds of anguish and terror came from inside the stone walls,
and they never stopped. It was the cries of men and women
on her left and on her right, in front of her and behind, all
of them forced to endure yet another sweaty night crowded
together on the stone floor.

As Grace lay still, Safya shifted uneasily next to her and
cried out in her sleep for Hola. But Hola wasn't there. He had
taken to sleeping with Ikem and the old men.

Oyo felt Safya push against her, too, then groan and pull
away.

As Grace's apprehension grew, her body tensed. Menace
floated heavy in the air. She forced herself not to tremble.
Slowly, she sat upright. A few people had begun to stir, but

most were still asleep, bunched together in small groups. Grace slipped her hand along the floor until she felt the musket she had tucked up close. She clutched it and moved into a crouched position. Grace crawled on her hands and knees along the crowded floor, picking her way over to where Cabeto lay with the other men.

Cabeto's eyes were wide open, watching Grace.

"You feel it too?" Cabeto's mouth hardly moved as he spoke, and his voice was barely perceptible. He more breathed the words than spoke them.

Grace nodded.

Smoothly and silently, Cabeto eased onto his haunches and slipped his hand over his own musket. Just at that moment an explosion ripped through the walls, rocking the dungeon. Chunks of stone broke loose and rained down on the sleeping people. Men, women, and children jumped up and screamed in terror. In their panic, they ran into each other.

"Stay low!" Cabeto ordered in a hoarse whisper.

A blast of musket fire roared through the sagging grate, and the dungeon immediately flooded with smoke. A new wave of terror swept over the already panic-stricken Africans. Their dreadful shrieks ripped the darkness. People clawed over each other in a desperate attempt to get to the stairs.

As the smoke cleared, Grace saw two newly freed captives dead on the floor. Several other captives cried out that they were injured. When a panicked woman next to Grace started to shriek, a wild-eyed man behind her covered his ears and begged her to stop. But her cries only grew louder and more shrill. So the frantic man grabbed a chunk of rock and hit her over the head. The woman sank to her knees and fell to the floor, silent.

The first guard of attackers—a strange assortment of white

men—immediately prepared their muskets to fire again, but Cabeto and Grace were ready. Their shots rang out—Cabeto first, then Grace—and two white men Grace had never seen before fell to the floor. The attackers stopped short. In blind puzzlement, they stared into the smoke-filled dungeon.

"Who be shootin' back at us?" one mumbled. "No resistance is wot Winslow told us. No weapons in 'ere, he said."

Hurriedly, Antonio and Sunba rammed charges into their muskets. Tungo and Gamka scrambled for their weapons.

"Each of you look to your leader!" Cabeto commanded. "Then do exactly what he tells you! Ask no questions. Just obey!"

Two shots rang out and then another and then one more as the four Africans fired into startled attackers. Three white men fell. All the while, Cabeto and Grace worked their ramrods and prepared their muskets for the next round.

Lingongo pushed the immobilized men aside and shoved her way into the dungeon. "Attack them, you cowards!" she bellowed. "Attack them!" Her whip whistled through the air and ripped Antonio's gun from his hands, slashing his wrists and arms.

Grace aimed and fired. A trustee next to Lingongo grabbed his shoulder and fell to the floor. Then Cabeto aimed and pulled the trigger. Screaming in fury, Lingongo ducked down just in time to avoid becoming the next casualty.

"Retreat!" one of the white men cried. "Retreat!"

"No!" Lingongo shrieked. "Fight on! Fight on!"

Leaping to her feet, Lingongo turned her whip on the white fighters as they tried to turn back. She drove them forward, down onto the dungeon floor and directly into the line of fire.

Then seemingly out of nowhere, Ikem rose up before them.

"This be our time, African warriors!" he cried. "Follow me to war!"

Before the wide-eyed white men, Ikem's tattooed face transformed from a frightening shadow into a war mask of pure terror—alive and in person! Fearlessly, Ikem dashed toward the attackers, his long-bladed knife high in the air. The attackers dissolved in howls of panic.

"'Tis a demon come to drag us all to 'ell!" Henry Taylor gasped before he fell down in a dead faint.

More than one man chose Lingongo's whip rather than face the black tattooed specter who charged toward them with his killer knife.

Whether or not the captives were actually moving toward their assigned rooms as the leaders directed, Grace could not tell. *If I could just get these people out of the middle of the fight!* she thought. She dropped to her hands and knees and crawled through the confusion and blinding smoke. She reached her hands out to hysterical men and women, one by one, and she held on to them with a reassuring, gentle firmness.

"We'll be all right," she whispered into the ears of each one. "Do not be afraid. Cabeto is in control."

Despite the ferocious din around her, Grace continued to crawl from one person to the next. "The attackers are moving down onto the floor. Go up the steps just as soon as you can get through," she softly instructed each person. "Here, let me help you. Let me show you the way. As soon as you get out of the dungeon, go to your leader's room and wait for instructions. Don't be afraid."

Again and again, Grace whispered words of hope. "Today is the beginning of our victory! Tomorrow is freedom day!"

So, one person at a time, panic began to die down. But even as the screams and shrieks of terror faded, they were replaced by cries and moans of the injured and dying.

"Grace!" It was Oyo's voice, and she sounded urgent. "Over here!"

Grace followed the call. When she reached the far wall, she anxiously asked Oyo, "Are you all right?"

"Yes," Oyo said. "But I have three people here who are bleeding badly, and I don't have anything to stop the blood from flowing."

Without hesitation, Grace stood up and ripped the skirt off her blue day dress and tore the material into two flat pieces. "Here," she said as she handed one piece to Oyo. "We can tear this into strips to make bandages." Together they set to work.

Only then did Grace look down at the wounded one whom Oyo had carefully and tenderly tucked back against the wall. What she saw caused Grace to fall to her knees.

"Hola!" she gasped. "Oh, poor Hola!"

The boy looked up at her. "Ikem said I fought . . . like an African warrior."

"And you will fight again!" Oyo promised him. Then she quickly turned away so the boy wouldn't see her tears.

Together, Oyo and Grace wrapped the boy's bloody arm in strips of cloth woven with ferns of silver.

"Are we winning?" Hola asked.

Musket fire echoed from the corridor outside. But when Grace looked around the dungeon, she was amazed to see that not nearly so many white men remained in the fight.

"Why, yes, I do believe we *are* winning!" Grace answered.

Just at that moment another round of gunfire erupted. Sunba and his group burst through the door. It didn't take them long to roust the last of the attackers and push them back outside the dungeon into the narrow passageway. Lingongo and Joseph's forces seemed to grow sparser by the minute. They had the weapons, it was true, but now that the rebels had shown their strength and were actually fighting back, the intruders lost their desire to attack. They were definitely on the defensive.

More musket fire rang out, though less and less by the minute. Outside the dungeon, angry voices burst through and then died away. Grace didn't recognize any of them—other than her father's, on occasion.

"I'll let you know everything that happens just as soon as I know," Grace promised Hola. "You won't miss a thing."

Grace made her way up to the broken door and ducked through. For the first time since she was dragged unconscious into the dungeon, she stepped back outside its walls. But when she gazed around her, she caught her breath. The stone passageway was a mass of rubble. At each end the blue sky showed through gaping holes knocked into the fortress wall. What could have caused such damage? Did these men actually bring cannons off their ships?

"We cannot be that important to your parents," Cabeto said, shaking his head in perplexed disbelief. He had come up behind Grace, and now he stood alongside her to stare at the destruction. "Why would the lioness and the slave trader destroy their own fortress just to get back at a few captives? What sense does it make?"

Grace sighed. In a voice weary from far too much experience, she said, "You don't know Lingongo. She will not rest until her pride is avenged, no matter what the cost."

36

Charlotte Stevens sat in the straight-backed chair she had pushed up against the front window of her father's house. She leaned forward and thrust her head as far out as she could manage, paying not the least attention to the wind that raged and whipped at her white-blonde hair. Half-written invitations stood in a neat stack on the table behind her, but Charlotte was too intrigued by the activity outside to pay them any mind. Along the beach, half a dozen men scurried this way and that with a flash of swords and pistols. Some rushed boxes and barrels into longboats and then rowed them out to load onto waiting ships.

What was happening?

"Charlotte and I will leave Africa immediately!" Henrietta proclaimed in a voice shrill with fear. "This very day! Arrange a ship to London for us now, Benjamin."

"Have you not listened to a thing I've said?" her husband exclaimed. "You cannot leave. That would be the most foolhardy action of all."

Charlotte turned to face her parents. "Personally, I think this is all quite wonderful," she announced.

Both Henrietta and Benjamin stopped short, their mouths

hanging open and the next arguments poised on their tongues, as they stared at their daughter.

"I truly do!" Charlotte insisted. "Chain up Africans and push them here. Whip them and push them there. You always talk about Mr. Winslow and Lingongo, Father, and of the horrible way they treat their slaves. Well, if they truly are as bad as you say, I think it time the Africans made a stand on their own behalf."

"You do not know what you are talking about," Benjamin Stevens snapped.

"If Mr. Winslow and Lingongo are so horrid, then Grace must be a true heroine for risking her life to—"

"Charlotte!" Henrietta exclaimed. "I must say your attitude shocks and distresses me! Your own father could fall victim to a rebellion provoked by those soulless heathens. How can you possibly defend them?"

"Mother, the Quakers at the docks say—"

"Never you mind what Quakers say," Henrietta shot back. "Low-class emotionalism is all one can expect from the likes of them. Religious drivel and nothing more! Not one of them has ever had to cross the ocean in a ship loaded with Africans, who would like nothing better than to see all white people dead. Your father knows what these . . . these *beasts* . . . are really like. And as for Grace, well, one can hardly expect more from her, can one?"

Benjamin sighed and ran his hand through his thinning hair. Yes, he did know. He knew far more than he wanted to acknowledge, especially right now. The horrors of the Middle Passage—every day, lugging the bodies of those who had not survived the night up from the hold and dumping them overboard. When rations ran short, he cut them so close he had to choose which captives were to eat and which were to starve . . . packing them together in such misery that men and women chose to plunge overboard and drown in the icy sea rather than continue to sail on his ship. Oh, yes, he knew. He knew.

"I did my part," Benjamin said. "When Joseph called, I sent men to fight alongside him. That they did not stay and fight to the death is neither my fault nor my business."

"What about those men out there?" Charlotte asked, gesturing to the ones at work on the beach.

"What they do is no concern of mine," Benjamin answered. "Or yours."

"Will they fight the slave rebels?" she asked.

"They may wait a bit, my dear, but in time they will surely fight because it is the right thing to do," Henrietta said. "Things will go much differently when those horrible rebels are well starved for food and water. I actually think it a very clever idea to cut off their supplies."

Now she had Charlotte's attention. "Admiral Winslow and Lingongo are going to starve them? Grace too? Her own parents?"

"Never you mind," Henrietta said. "Grace made her decision and her parents made theirs."

"Well, I wash my hands of the entire affair," Benjamin declared. "We will carry on with our lives, and we will pray to God above that the troubles stay up at Zulina and do not affect us here."

"And you will search for a ship to take us back home to England," Henrietta reminded him.

"Not right now," Benjamin answered.

"The soonest possible then."

"The soonest possible," he said.

Charlotte said nothing. She leaned her head back and shut

her eyes tight. Grace Winslow. She was more African than English—that was certain. Mother always said there was more of their kind in her blood than ours.

Suddenly, Charlotte had an overwhelming desire to talk to Grace—to ask her what she thought about the Quakers, and about men like Charlotte's father who ran slave houses, and to tell her about Reginald Witherham's unpleasant way of knowing everything about everything. Oh, and to tell Grace she thought it was absolutely wonderful to do something in one's life that really mattered.

A great gust of wind roared through the window and whipped the neatly folded party invitations off the table and down to the gritty floor. Charlotte did not even bother to pick them up. She had more important things on her mind.

37

"**D**urbar!"
Throughout the dungeon, voices rose up and joined together to shout out the joyful cheer. Soon it rang from one liberated cell to the next.

"*Durbar!* This day we celebrate!"

But in the midst of all the laughter and singing and shouting and dancing, Grace sat apart from the others and wept. Too many men and women had died. Too many lay injured. Although others made light of Lingongo's threats, Grace knew full well that the worst was yet to come.

"To our chief!" a wide-faced man called out in an enthusiastic salute to Cabeto. With a rousing cheer, the others shouted as one, "To our chief!"

Grace watched Cabeto's face. She could tell by the way he avoided looking the others in the eye that he was uncomfortable with his new position. Nor could she miss the jealousy in Tungo's gaze.

Although Tungo joined the others, his voice was neither pleasant nor cheerful. Grace looked at the laughing, cheering people, and wondered, *Am I the only one to hear the harsh, brittle edge to Tungo's voice? Can no one else detect the cutting bite of his comments?*

It wasn't only that Tungo seethed every time the others called Cabeto "chief." The real problem was that he knew the same thing Grace knew—that the day to celebrate was not yet here. Danger had hit from one side—the smaller point on the folded cloth message from Mama Muco. But what about the longer point? What about the greater danger?

Oh, Mama, if only you could tell us more!

With all the dancing and singing, no one noticed Grace stand up and ease along the wall. No one saw her slip out through the broken dungeon door and into the rubble-strewn passageway. According to Oyo, who kept careful count, twenty-three of their number had perished. Hola was not among them.

Grace stumbled through the broken stones and entered the next cell. Blessedly, it was empty. The noise of the celebration made her head throb, and she longed to be alone for a while. She cleared a space for herself in a far corner, sat down, and leaned back against a sagging wooden crossbeam. The walls were blessedly cool, and when she rested with her head back and allowed her eyes to drift closed, she dreamed of mango groves . . . of a small black and brown gazelle with a white flick of a tail . . . of sweet potato fields seared black by a roaring fire . . . of a new silk taffeta dress stained with innocent blood.

"Sunba!"

Grace started at the sound of so urgent a whisper just outside the door.

"I come to make a deal with you."

Shaking the dreams from her head, Grace looked around in confusion. Where exactly was she?

"It is you who are the strong one. We can all see that."

Tungo! It was his voice she heard. She was certain of it.

"You are the wise one, Sunba. Why is it, then, that your brother takes the place that should rightfully belong to you?"

The deadly attack . . . the celebration . . . her throbbing head . . . her desperation to get away. Yes, it was all coming back. Grace could still hear the shouts and the songs—even the sound of the makeshift drums—as they drifted from the next cell. Perhaps it was time for her to go back and join the others.

"Do not accuse me of wanting to be chief," Tungo was saying. "No, I want only what will set us free and what will keep us alive. But here is what I think, Sunba. The two of us together will be best for everyone. You are the strongest and the bravest man here. You proved that many times over. And I have the experience. Together you and me, Sunba—together we can defeat the white oppressors!"

Grace was already halfway to her feet, but at the sound of Tungo's urgent voice so close by, she thought better of it and sank back to the floor. What choice did she have? She pulled herself as far into the corner as possible and listened.

"Cabeto is my brother," Sunba answered.

"We are all brothers," Tungo responded. "Is that not true?"

"Cabeto is the son of my father," Sunba persisted.

Evidently, Sunba walked away because Tungo called out, "We will talk again, Sunba!"

But he was met by silence.

Grace waited until she was certain Tungo had left and then returned to the dungeon. No one seemed to have missed her. Antonio, who was taking stock of their dwindling supplies, announced that the bean pot was already empty. Two men hefted it through the open door to the tunnel, and it clattered all the way down until it crashed into the wooden barrier at the bottom. The boiled meat was also gone.

There has been way too much celebratory eating! Grace thought with rising frustration.

"Many vegetables . . . plenty of dried fish . . . some bread," Antonio reported. "And that cheese the Dutchman brought."

"Huh," Safya scoffed. "Africans do not eat white man's cheese!"

Someone from the other side of the room shot back, "Depends on how hungry we get."

Antonio said no more, but it wasn't difficult to read the look on his face. With so many hungry people, the meager stores would not last long.

Questions whirled through Grace's head. There were so many things she wanted explained. But in the end, she asked only the one question that troubled her most: "Antonio, why was Lingongo waiting for the Dutchman at the end of the tunnel?"

Antonio laid down the muskets he was counting and looked up at her. "*Es una buena pregunta, señorita*," Antonio said. "A very good question. I, too, have asked it—*muchas veces*."

Tungo and Sunba walked in just in time to hear Grace's question.

"The lioness is cunning," Tungo said. "Surely she followed him and then lay in wait for his return."

"Seems to me the Dutchman was cunning too," Grace said. "Too cunning to fall into such a simple trap."

"*Sí*," Antonio agreed. "And he was careful, *también*. I do not believe she could have followed him."

"What then?" Cabeto asked.

"The lioness must have known the Dutchman would be there," Antonio said solemnly. "If that is true, there is only one way she could have known—only from one of us."

The room fell silent.

Grace's face burned hot as all eyes turned in her direction. How Grace wanted to stand up and scream out her innocence!

She would pour out the sad tale of her poor Bondo, served up on a porcelain platter because Lingongo thought him useless and because it was to her parents' advantage that she marry the snake Jasper Hathaway, even though it meant she would have to spend the rest of her life beating him off with a stick. How she longed to shout that Yao was wrong, that she was no longer a slave in the London house because she dared to climb over Joseph Winslow's stone wall, because she followed the narrow road away from the baobab tree up to Zulina. She wanted to scream out that she could be safely in the library of her parents' house right now, surrounded by her books, instead of here in this dreary dungeon waiting to die. That she could have been an English lass and not an African slave. She wanted to scream that she had chosen to be one of them!

Grace's mouth was open to say all this. But as she looked around her, from one person to another, all her fair-minded arguments died within her. Who was she to lecture these people—these men and women and little ones who had been ripped away from their burning villages, who had been forced to watch in helpless horror as their families were torn away from them and killed or shipped to faraway countries? These people who had been shackled and bound in chains, and whose backs bore the scars of her own parents' cruel whips? What did Grace possibly have to say to these people about suffering?

So she closed her mouth and kept her peace.

"One of us is the betrayer," Tungo stated. "I will make it my job to find out which one. And when I do—"

Tungo unsheathed his knife and flashed it in the waning beam of sunlight. Then with one vicious movement, he plunged it deep into the corner wooden beam.

38

"Evenin', Mr. Hathaway," Tom Pitts said. "You kin go on down t' the house. Jist follow the cobblestone path."

"I know the way!" Hathaway snapped.

Tom Pitts and Henry Taylor stood guard at the front gate in the wall around the Winslow compound. Each man held a musket, loaded, tamped, and ready to shoot. And just for good measure, each man also had a razor-sharp knife tucked into a sheath at his waist. Tom and Henry knew exactly who was to be allowed inside, and they knew what they were to do if anyone else tried to get past them.

When Jasper Hathaway arrived at the house, Muco opened the front door, admitted him, and then showed him to the library, which was set up to accommodate twenty-two men. Never before had so many people been inside the London house at one time.

"'Ere now, Jasper, set yersef down," Joseph said with exaggerated hospitality. The wound Lingongo's whip had slashed across his face was red and swollen and still looked quite nasty. When he tried to smile, his eye watered and his lip drooped.

Most of the chairs were already occupied by grim-faced white men who grumbled impatiently to each other. All except for Benjamin Stevens, who sat stiffly in a seat in back, as far away from the others as he possibly could.

"Let's get this meeting started!" boomed a man with a shaved head and a bushy mustache. Turning to Joseph, he accused, "We shouldn't even be here, Winslow. This ain't our fight."

"Oh, but 'tis, Nate," Joseph argued. "Them 'eathens is always tryin' to take over wot by rights is ours. If'n they gits by wi' it 'ere, then the slaves at yer place'll git wind of it and next thing ye knows, they'll be fightin' ye too."

"He's right," Benjamin Stevens agreed with a sigh. "Like it or not, the trouble has already been stirred up, and tomorrow it could be us."

"I already lost two good men in your battle," Nate said. "What more do you want from me?"

What Joseph wanted was encouragement . . . and men he could depend on to stand up and fight alongside him no matter what . . . and money (preferably gold) to finance the battle . . . and respect. Respect most of all. It was indescribably painful for him to stand by and watch as slaves grabbed away so much of his property. But what he absolutely could not abide was all the talk he overheard about his personal failures and his weaknesses and a whole array of other purported inadequacies. He would do anything to get this mess behind him—absolutely anything. Which was why he had told—no, *ordered*—Lingongo to stay away from this assemblage. It was his meeting, he said. He had called the men together to get their help. Starting today, he, Joseph Winslow—Admiral Joseph Winslow—would be the one in control of Zulina.

"Such a trouncing at the hands of slaves is *un insulto* to every one of us and also to God on high!" Capitán Carrillo pronounced.

Joseph opened his mouth to answer, but Jasper Hathaway stood up and demanded his attention.

"Where is Grace, Joseph?" he insisted. "You promised me I would have her hand in marriage, yet when I last saw her, she was walking the streets by herself! Now I ask you, *where . . . is . . . your . . . daughter?*"

"This ain't 'bout Grace!" Joseph snapped testily. "'Tis 'bout us. Is we to keep control o' our rightful pro'pity, or ain't we?" He had tried to keep Grace's presence at Zulina a secret from his future son-in-law.

"Grace is as good as my rightful property, Winslow! If she is a captive up in that fortress, as some say she is—" Hathaway began.

He didn't get the chance to drive his point home, however, because at that moment the library door flew open and Lingongo swept in. She strode straight to a dais, which was fortuitously positioned directly in the path of rainbow hues cast across the room by the library's diamond-cut window panes. Regally and with measured purpose, Lingongo mounted the dais and stood, haughty and disdainful, before the gaping men. She had wrapped herself in a *kente* robe of gold, woven through with a pattern of black and red and green. But her stunning clothing did not cause the men's mouths to drop in unison.

No, it was the astounding collection of heavy, gorgeously tooled solid gold jewelry that transformed Lingongo into such a dazzling sight. Thick chains festooned with enormous solid gold pendants hung from her neck. Heavy bracelets decorated both arms, and rings glinted on her fingers and toes. On Lingongo's head rested a golden crown with row after row of birds and animals and flowers, all tooled in gold by the most expert African craftsmen. Even Lingongo's beautiful chocolate face was flecked with fine gold dust.

A unified gasp arose in the room. Jasper Hathaway plopped back down into his chair, his mouth frozen in an open position. As for Joseph Winslow, he reeled backward and fell directly onto Capitán Carrillo's lap, although the Spaniard was so transfixed he hardly seemed to notice.

It was some moments before Joseph was able to regain either his footing or his voice. But he finally managed to croak out a strangled, "Lingongo, I tol' ye to stay away t'day. I tol' ye—"

Lingongo turned on him. "No, I told *you!*" she said. "I told you I would not be humiliated without demanding vengeance! I told you I would not compromise with ruffians and thieves and *slaves!* I told you I was born a princess and no one could take my royalty away from me!"

Lingongo looked out over the clutch of white men still gaping in wide-eyed, open-mouthed amazement. "You disgust me!" she spat at them. "Every one of you!" She turned to Joseph and said, "You! You are the worst of a bad lot!"

"Lingongo, me dear—" Joseph whimpered.

"Go ahead and make your plans," Lingongo said. "Talk all night if you like. But remember this, white men are not in control here. You never were and you never will be. Africa is not your land. Africa's men and women do not belong to you."

With an air of regal superiority, Lingongo swung around until her back was to the men, and then she swept out of the room.

For many moments, the men remained transfixed. It was Joseph Winslow who finally rallied himself and made his way back up to the front of the room. He attempted to carry on the meeting as planned, but no one could get the sight of Lingongo out of his mind. One by one, each man suddenly remembered a compelling reason why he must be off.

"Good-bye, Admiral Winslow. So sorry I have to leave," each said with an exaggerated pretense of respect before he made his hasty retreat. "You do have my support, of course, but . . . uh . . . well, right at the moment . . ."

There was no doubt in anyone's mind that come the dawn, something would happen at Zulina, and when it did, Lingongo would be leading it. And everyone in the room was certain that Lingongo would get no argument from her husband.

Mama Muco opened the door for each man as he left. She prayed the right person had found her folded headcloth—someone who knew where Grace was, someone who could read the long point to her. Grace would understand. Grace would be ready.

39

"No, no, no! Don't put your hand in the *foufou*, you stupid fool!"

Grace looked over the crowded knots of people, searching for the source of this latest angry commotion.

"You be filthy!" a woman scolded as she shoved another woman away from the common pot of food. When the rejected woman hungrily grabbed at the pot, a man jumped in and sent her reeling with the back of his hand.

Grace ran to the woman and helped her to her feet. "Never mind, Moussa," she murmured. The group, talking together angrily, closed their circle against both Grace and the rejected woman. Grace took Moussa's arm and led her to another pot of food in a different part of the room.

"Go ahead," Grace urged. "Eat here."

When Moussa finally reached her hand into the pot and settled down to eat her share, Grace made her way back to where she sat with Ikem and Cabeto. Sinking down between them, she asked, "How could Moussa know the Ga people touch food only with their right hands? How could she know she offended them because her ways are so different from theirs?"

"Not-alike people have not-alike ways," Ikem observed. "To other eyes, not alike can look wrong."

"We must not have fights that come from misunderstandings," Cabeto stated. "These walls have already seen too much fighting and too much pain."

"It is because too many people are coming out of the cells too fast," said Gamka.

Now that Antonio and Tungo had gone through the fortress's maze of corridors and passageways and released captives cell by cell, things were indeed growing more crowded and confusing. And more and more difficult, as Gamka continually pointed out.

"We can't just leave them chained up to starve or to die of thirst!" Grace told him.

In many rooms, Antonio and Tungo found nothing but empty manacles and piles of chains. But then they would throw another latch and push open another door, and once again they would be face-to-face with absolute horror. In one room, more than a dozen people lay piled together in chains, in their own filth. Most were too weak to do more than moan in misery. But one poor soul managed to lift his head and groan, "*N nin saasaa le mu.*"

"*Estan enfermos,*" Antonio said.

"They got the flux!" Tungo cried out. Quickly, he backed away. "Close the door! Lock it!"

Antonio hesitated. The poor wretches cried out, pleading for help.

"Lock it!" Tungo insisted. "You want us all to die?"

Antonio knew the disease all too well. Tungo was right—it was a killer.

Tungo kicked the door shut and slipped the bolt into place.

Antonio shook his head sadly and closed his ears to the pitiful pleas of the dying captives. He forced himself to turn the key and move on to the next cell. To leave them locked in to die alone was horrible. To think of the flux sweeping through the entire ragtag group of survivors was unthinkable.

Just down a dark, narrow hallway they discovered a red clay slave house with twenty-one people chained inside. At first, when Antonio and Tungo began to free them from their chains, the captives were confused about what was happening.

Antonio urged them toward the door.

"*Didhte waw?*" one man asked. "Where are we going?"

"To freedom," Tungo said.

As quickly as Antonio and Tungo unshackled captives, Sunba gathered them together and guided them through the winding passageways. The newly released slaves winced and shaded their eyes as they emerged from the darkness into the large corner room bathed in sunlight. This was where Joseph Winslow and the white sailors had spent so many hours drinking, carousing, and gambling away their gold at fast hands of lanterloo.

When Grace heard the released Africans speaking in their different tongues, she smiled broadly and greeted them, each in his or her own language.

"*Assalamou!*" she said to the three whom Sunba just led up. "Peace be to you!"

"*Bakham!*" they answered, their broad faces beaming. "Thank you! Oh, thank you!"

"Come," Grace said. She walked over to another clutch of Wolof sitting together. "You will be welcome here. You are one people."

Grace did her best to help all who came up from the chains below to find others who understood their tongues and knew their ways. Already groups from the Yoruba and Fanti tribes had come together, and some from the Hausa and Ga people had found each other as well.

All at once, angry voices rang through the corridor, followed by what sounded like rocks crashing. Cabeto sprang up and ran to the door.

"What's going on?" Grace called after him.

A group of three men and two women ran past them. All five dashed over the rubble and on toward a jagged opening at the far end of the corridor. The door to the outside had been blown apart.

"Stop!" the guard called out to them. He held a musket, but he wasn't certain what to do with it. The weapon was never intended to keep the captives in. "If you go out, you be killed!" the guard warned.

"We not stay in this place!" one of the men called out.

Cabeto sprinted after them. "No!" he pleaded. "Please! You must not go out there!"

"We not captives to you!" the man yelled back. "We be free!"

The first man squeezed through the opening and jumped. A woman followed right behind. Just as the next man began to push his way through, gunshots exploded outside, and the man caught in the opening froze. Then another shot rang out. The man fell forward, through the doorway, and out of view.

Silence enveloped the corridor. Even so, a fourth man sprang up and he, too, jumped through the opening.

Immediately, another shot sounded. The last woman in the group backed away from the door in horror.

When the four went through the doorway to their deaths, the sun was at its zenith. By nightfall, several more had jumped through, each followed by gunfire from outside. In the fortress, one argument after another erupted. Several people attacked others. Then a knife fight left one man dead.

"Set up armed guards around the food and water," a grim Cabeto instructed Antonio.

"If it's this bad in the daylight," Grace said, "what will happen when darkness falls?"

"I cannot think about it," Cabeto answered.

It was Grace who first suggested moving apart.

"We have the entire fortress," she reasoned. "Let's encourage those who speak alike and have the same ways to move out into some of the empty cells. They can settle their own arguments and solve their own difficulties according to their customs."

"It be a good idea," Ikem agreed. "Each people can mark out their own place."

"And over each, we can set up a leader who will have final say about any disputes," Cabeto said.

"Tomorrow we do it," Ikem said. "Tonight we stay awake. Tonight we stand guard."

As newly released captives arrived from the dungeons and cells, Grace searched their faces for a straight nose and a strong chin with a tuft of dark hair, and she looked at the sides of their heads for half an ear. But she never found such a face.

"Antonio," Grace said as she came up behind him. "You once said you had seen a man named Yao who had my father's brand burned into his shoulder. Do you remember?"

"*Lo siento mucho,*" Antonio told her. "He is locked in a cell alone on the other side of the fortress. The part we did not release. I am sorry."

Grace couldn't trust herself to speak lest in her disappointment she dissolve into tears.

"We will still try to make a way over so we can unlock those cells too," Antonio said.

"When?" Grace asked. "Maybe tomorrow? Or the next day?"

"When will the lioness attack us again?" Antonio asked anxiously.

Grace stared at him. Fear etched his face; terror brimmed in his strong, black eyes. *How totally amazing,* Grace thought. *So much fear at the mention of my mother!*

Grace longed to say something comforting, something reassuring. Instead she told Antonio the truth: "I don't know when she will come. I only know she will. Antonio, if you can remember exactly where it was that you saw Yao, maybe—"

"When she comes back, it will be *ultimo vez,*" Antonio said flatly. "It will be the end, no?"

"Tomorrow, Antonio?" Grace pressed impatiently. "Will you release the other side of the fortress tomorrow? The side where Yao is?"

Antonio stared blankly.

"When the lioness returns," he repeated, "then it will be the end."

40

Only a white man would confuse the beat of a dancing drum with the words of *ntumpane*. A dancing drum was meant for a single village alone. Its sound did not catch on the wind and fly far and wide. But the *ntumpane* were made from the tweneboa tree with the hide of an elephant's ear stretched taut over the end so that each word would sound clear and sharp. Every drummer searched out his own forked branches of ema wood, and from them he made drumsticks that could carry the talking drums' messages up and down the coast. The words even traveled across to the inland, flying from one *brono* to another.

Porcupine of Africa . . .

. . . beat a thousand to death . . .

. . . a thousand will rise anew.

The wind grabbed up the words of the drums and sent them soaring in every direction. When the words blew in through the open window of the London house, Lingongo heard them and she smiled.

Finally, her father's warriors were on the way. With them in the fight by her side—with them giving her strength from the ancestors—she could not lose, no matter what the white men did.

Lingongo knew the language of the royal drums perfectly. But she didn't know everything.

Prince Obei reclined in his private residence in the most powerful chiefdom in the Kingdom of Gold. He was so busy admiring the carved stool with which his father had gifted him that he didn't immediately pay attention to the words of the *ntumpane*—not until he stopped running his hands over the smoothness of the pounded gold long enough to cock his head to listen to the message of the drums. They were calling the warriors to fight! So the Great and Powerful One had listened to his wise words after all. Already, warriors were on their way to help the rebels.

Proudly, and with a great show of importance, Obei went to the throne room to inform his father that he desired permission to approach him. The king was extremely busy, the prince was told. All day Obei waited for an invitation, and the longer he waited, the more irritated he grew. Finally, as the sun sank into the grasslands, Obei decided he had waited long enough. He was a prince, and he would not be barred from the king's presence. So he pushed his way past his father's guards.

When Obei burst into his father's royal presence, he stopped and stared. It was true, the king was busy. He was busy laying out plans with Tutu, Obei's younger brother.

"You gave a carved stool to me!" Obei accused.

"I gave a more powerful one to your brother," the king replied.

"The *ntumpane*," Obei said. "They say our warriors are on their way to the fortress to fight alongside Africans. They say we are going to do battle against the white man."

"Is that what they say?" the king responded. "Perhaps that is what you hear only because that is what you want them to say. Perhaps you do not like the message their king has ordered them to speak."

Obei also knew the language of the royal drums perfectly. But even he, the firstborn of the Great and Powerful King, did not know everything.

"Your brother does not fight against me, Obei," the king said. "He sees the wisdom of working with the white men, of taking the muskets and gunpowder they offer us. He understands that unpleasant compromises are necessary if we are to remain the most powerful and respected kingdom on the coast of Africa."

Obei looked at his brother and asked, "Tutu, who do you back in this battle?"

"Even now our warriors fight with Lingongo alongside the white men," Tutu said.

"No!" Obei shouted. "The ancestors would never permit such a thing!"

Only because he was desperate did Obei dare to steal into the sacred *nkonnwafieso* in the dark of the night to seek out the blackened stools of death. But he was not the first one there. Already calabash halves lay open, filled with special food and drink, offerings for the ancestors.

Obei boiled with anger. What did Tutu think? That his older brother would give up without a fight simply because the king refused to stand beside him? Hah! Obei was like a porcupine that cannot be harmed. He could defend himself against the white man's guns, and he could defend himself against the attacks of his own brother. When his spines were shot off, they would grow back again, and they would be stronger than ever. Just like the porcupine, that was Prince Obei.

41

Cabeto searched all morning for his brother. Finally, he found him sitting alone in a far cell, watching three children laugh and play. Quietly, Cabeto moved over and folded himself up next to Sunba.

After a long silence, Sunba said, "It frightens me to hear children laugh. I wonder what will happen to them."

"Perhaps they will walk free with the rest of us," Cabeto answered. "Or perhaps we will all die like heroes."

Cabeto waited for his brother to speak again. After a few moments, Sunba asked, "Do you wonder, my brother, if I am the traitor?"

"No," Cabeto said. "It cannot be you."

"How can you be certain?" Sunba asked.

"Do you not remember our father's proverb? He would tell us that even if a log soaks a long time in water, it will never become a crocodile. Much has happened, my brother. But all the horror cannot change you into something you are not. The traitor is not you."

Again they fell into a long silence.

Finally, Sunba said, "I do not want to be chief, Cabeto. You are the leader. If more trouble comes or if we see times of celebration and power, I will be by your side to help you."

"I thank you," Cabeto said.

"Do we need to speak of Tungo?" Sunba asked.

"When two brothers fight, a stranger reaps the harvest," Cabeto answered. "Tungo looks out only for Tungo."

How long the brothers would have sat together and enjoyed the calm of one another's presence is hard to say. Certainly, they had not had nearly enough time when Grace burst in upon them.

"Cabeto! Sunba! Tungo stirs up trouble with his talk of war," she cried. "He frightens the new people."

With a sigh of resignation, Cabeto stood up.

"Yes, my brother," Sunba repeated with the trace of a grin. "You can be the leader."

As the three entered the dungeon, Tungo jabbed his musket toward them and accused, "And where is this leader you talk about? He conspires with the daughter of the lioness and the slave trader!"

"We do not conspire, Tungo," Cabeto said wearily. "Please. Unless we stay together, we will all share the same end."

"No, not all of us," Tungo shot back. "Not the traitor."

His eyes brimmed with hatred, and he fixed them on Grace.

Now Gamka jumped up beside him. "Tungo and I will not listen to a leader who harbors a traitor!"

"I am not—" Grace protested.

"Gamka says what we all know!" Tungo yelled. "I say, throw her out and let her crawl back to her own people. Let her crawl back to where she belongs!"

Both Cabeto and Grace tried to speak, but the confusion in the room fast changed to anger, and no one would listen.

"No!" Ikem bellowed. He stood up in front of Tungo, his scarred face transformed into fierce anger. "It not be her. The traitor not be Grace."

The room fell silent.

"How do you know, old man?" Tungo asked sharply.

"Trustees, men of Africa—the white man brought them to attack us," Ikem said. "When they see us fight in ways of their fathers, with hands and knives and wits, some drop white man's guns and pick up knives to join us. And some hold their guns but shoot white man attackers."

"Yes, yes," Tungo said impatiently. "We all know that, and it was good. But that tells us nothing about the traitor!"

"One trustee who put gun down and took up knife to fight beside me was with the lioness when she see the traitor leave the tunnel," Ikem said. "The lioness made the traitor very afraid. He said he would give the Dutchman in trade for his freedom."

"So you knew all the time and you did not tell us!" Tungo accused. "Well, who is this traitor you protect?"

Ikem searched over the crowd. Then he pointed to one man and said, "Him!"

In the stillness of the dungeon, where not even a child moved, Gamka suddenly jumped up and bolted for the entrance. But Grace leaped in front of him and blocked his path. As Gamka faltered, men piled onto him and pinned him to the floor.

"It was not me," Gamka cried. "I am a warrior, not a traitor!"

Tungo strode over to him. "Let him up!" he ordered.

Slowly, hesitantly, the others loosened their grip and backed off.

"Thank you, Tungo," Gamka said. Tears of relief filled his eyes and ran down his cheeks. "I knew you would believe me. We are the real warriors here, you and me. We—"

Tungo pulled out his knife.

Gamka started to sob. "I can still do much to help us, Tungo
. . . all of us. I'll talk to the lioness. When you went to look for
the Dutchman and Antonio, I stepped out of the tunnel and
she saw me! Tungo, the only one she really wants is her daughter. All we have to do is hand Grace over to her, and she will
let us go. Please, Tungo, it is what you wanted! Trade Grace for
our freedom! Please!"

Tungo grabbed Gamka's hair, jerked his head back, and
raised his knife.

42

From the library, silent and empty without Grace, to the dining room where no one ate anymore, then across the inside kitchen and out to the ridiculous parlor, Lingongo paced through the London house. Up the stairs to the bedchambers and back down again. Out into the courtyard and back inside, and then once again to the library to start all over. Lingongo must have made the round a hundred times, pacing long into the night. Each time she turned back to the library, her frustration grew. How was it that those miserable rebels managed to turn everything around to their advantage? To always make her look the fool? Well, this must not continue. It *would* not continue! She would see to that.

As Lingongo passed the parlor window, she caught the rustle of movement outside. But when she looked out, she could see only darkness. Quietly . . . ever so carefully . . . she made her way outside and over toward the mango trees. That's where she saw Joseph. He had rounded up his favorites from among the compound's slaves and chained them together. Lingongo stifled her amazement—not at the gathered slaves or even at her husband's unexplained actions at this strange hour, but at the unaccustomed look of determination etched across his pasty face. Many years had passed since she had seen Joseph Winslow wear that look.

"Move!" Joseph ordered the column of slaves.

Lingongo ran around to the outside and positioned herself in front of her husband. "What are you doing?" she demanded. "Are you taking them up to the fortress? In the middle of the night?"

Joseph ignored her.

"They will only join the rebels!" Lingongo insisted. "More slaves will only make them stronger."

Without so much as a glance, Joseph stepped around her.

"Does your foolishness know no bounds?" Lingongo cried in exasperation. "Is there no end to your idiocy?"

But something in Joseph had changed. For the first time, he seemed immune to his wife's stinging words. Grasping a whip in one hand and a pistol in the other, he prodded his bound slaves past her and out across the freshly dug sweet potato field. With a flick of the whip, Joseph forced the men to jog out to the stone wall. He opened the gate, and they disappeared through it.

Joseph rushed the men along the dark pathway, down in the direction of the baobab tree. The occasional person on the road stepped aside to let the chained column pass, then stood and gaped after it. Without pausing at the great tree to show even the slightest reverence to the ancestors, Joseph turned to the narrow road on the left and marched the slaves up toward Zulina. He didn't slow his pace until he arrived at the fortress gates. Suddenly exhausted, he paused, but only long enough to catch his breath and mop the perspiration that dripped from his mottled face. Then he set about unchaining his column of slaves.

"They's brush yonder. And twigs down below too," he said

as he swept his arms around him. "'Eap 'em all up 'round the fortress door over there!"

The slaves set to work. Yet even as they gathered the brush and piled it up, Joseph barked out commands. "More! 'Eap it up round 'em windas too. Pile it 'igh, I say! More! More!"

He punctuated every command with a snap of his whip, and each snap landed across the back of whichever slave was unlucky enough to be within range.

Finally, in exasperation, the slave Joseph called Tuke threw his arms wide and exclaimed, "Please, Master, look 'round. There be no more for us to gather."

Tuke's words seemed to yank Joseph out of his frenzied daze. He looked around him and blinked. As best he could tell, the ground had indeed been picked clean—although with only the hint of first light, it was difficult to tell for certain.

"They's still the gunpowder," Joseph said.

Over to one side, two trustees stood guard over four barrels.

"Put 'em in amongst the brush!" Joseph ordered. "Next to the wall. Space 'em out a bit now, but make it powerful right there." He motioned to the outer wall above the dungeon.

When the job was done, Joseph ordered, "Now roll up 'em barrels o' palm oil we brought from the storeroom." Motioning to the heaps of brush, he shouted, "Soak 'em piles down till no oil be left! Not one drop!"

Lingongo had watched her husband take off across the sweet potato field, and she had done nothing. She understood him in his weakness. She was used to that, and she worked it to her advantage. But his sudden show of strength confused her. She waited and waited for him to regain his senses and come creeping back, but as the time wore on and he didn't return, she grew increasingly uneasy. So with nothing but the waning stars of early morning to guide her, she turned her steps toward Zulina.

Lingongo topped the road just in time to hear the first explosion and see a wall of flames roar across the front of the fortress. Outlined by the light of the leaping fire, she saw the slaves huddle together and cringe as far back as they possibly could.

But where was Joseph?

Finally, as she moved closer, she spied her husband, standing alone. With no other sound but the thunder of fire she heard him pour out his mournful lament, "Me slave fortress! 'Tis ruined! 'Tis ruined!"

A second explosion rocked the ground. Then a sudden flurry of wind snatched at the blaze and sent a shower of sparks soaring into the dawn sky. For many minutes, Lingongo contemplated the scene that flared before her, and she weighed her options. Carefully . . . deliberately . . . the shock disappeared from her face. In its place—triumph.

Carrying herself regally, Lingongo glided over to stand beside Joseph.

"We have done it, Husband!" she announced. "The fire will burn the vulnerable parts of the fortress and smoke out the slaves. My father's warriors are on their way, and they will destroy the survivors. Soon the rebellion will be completely crushed. Soon everyone will know we are the winners—you and I!"

But there was no sign of victory on Joseph's face.

"All me slaves wi' be dead," he said bitterly. "Even me prize breeders, burned to a crisp. Wot kind o' win is that, I asks ye?"

Lingongo reached over and laid her hand lightly on Joseph's arm. Then in a voice as sweet and smooth as Ikoma honey, she said, "Must I remind you about the wars of which my father spoke, Joseph? Or that we have a storeroom filled with firearms and gunpowder ready for trade?"

Joseph's countenance lightened immediately.

"We can get all the slaves we want, my husband," Lingongo purred. "Fresh ones who fear their masters and do not dare think of rebellion."

The slightest smile tugged at the corners of Joseph's mouth.

"And we will set those fresh slaves to work cleaning up Zulina. Very soon our compound will again work as it should. And it will be far better and far more prosperous than ever before."

Prosperity and success. And vindication. The very thought of all of it brought the ruddiness flushing back to Joseph's cheeks.

Lingongo smiled. Oh, she knew her husband well.

43

Before the first glimmer of light had made its way into the dungeon, a soft thump awakened Grace. It could have been anything, of course—maybe a stone tumbling from a damaged wall or even someone knocking into someone else in the dark. But then the whoosh had followed so quickly. Perhaps it was because everyone had already been through so much that they rolled over and slept on—but not Grace. And not Cabeto.

"It's started!" Grace said under her breath.

Grace awakened Antonio and Ikem, and Cabeto roused Sunba and Tungo. Then Grace touched Safya and Oyo.

"Get ready," Grace whispered. "Something is about to happen."

"Gather up guns," Cabeto told the others. "Whatever comes to us, we will be ready." He knew the language of the talking drums. Although he did not speak of it to Grace, he knew the king's warriors would be there, and that they would fight alongside Princess Lingongo.

As dawn stretched across the parched savanna, that first thump had exploded and rocked the dungeon. Even as the original captives spread out among the sleepy men and women and calmly but urgently roused each person, shouts bellowed from outside. Then a guard stuck his head through the door and screamed, "Flames! All around us! Flames reaching to the sky!"

"Stay at peace," Cabeto called out. "We must use our heads. We cannot allow our fear to take over."

"What is it?" Hola mumbled as he rubbed the sleep from his eyes. There was terror in his voice, and he clung tightly to Ikem. "What's happening?"

"We do not know," Ikem told the boy. "But whatever comes to us, we will stand together." His voice was tender, and he made no attempt to push Hola away.

Another guard cried though the door: "Fire is everywhere!"

Amid a fresh wave of panicked screams, Grace said, "But rock will not burn, and this fortress is nothing but rock."

"Rock all around us, yes," Cabeto said soberly. "But the supports for the rocks, they are all of wood."

Yes! Now Grace could see that timber beams did indeed anchor the four corners of the room. The doors were solid slabs of wood—the door frames too. There was enough wood in the dungeon alone to smother all of them in smoke.

Another explosion rocked Zulina—this one so strong that part of the outer wall collapsed.

"We have to get everyone out of here!" Grace cried in a hoarse whisper. Immediately, the irony of her words struck her, and she moaned, "But get them to where? Where can we go?"

"*¡Puedo demostrarte adonde ir!*" Antonio said. "I can show you where! *Es grande*, a storage room in the center of the fortress where fire and smoke cannot reach us. Follow me and I will take you there! *¡Vamanos!*"

Cabeto jumped up on top of a water barrel. "Listen!" he called out. "The lioness and the slave trader attack us with smoking fire! There is only one place of safety—deep inside the fortress. We must go there now, and we must move quickly!"

"If we go deep inside the fortress, we will be trapped by flames and smoke!"

Tungo yelled.

"No," Cabeto pleaded. "We will go to a place where fire and smoke cannot reach us."

Another explosion rocked the room, so strong it knocked ceiling beams loose. The wind blew billows of smoke through gaping holes. Coughing turned to choking, and choking to desperate gasps. A loud wail rose from the back of the crowded room. Off to one side, someone screamed and pushed forward toward the door, the only way out of the dungeon.

"Grace and Antonio will be outside the door," Cabeto said with a calm that belied the urgency grabbing at his voice. "Move out quickly so you can go with them. Now!"

As one, the entire crowd swarmed toward the door.

Across the room, Tungo leaped on top of an empty water keg. "Cabeto leads you to your death!" he yelled. "Stay here with me, where you can see the outside! The stone walls protect us here."

A fourth boom rocked the room, and part of the ceiling fell in.

"Go! Now!" Cabeto cried. "Quickly!"

"No! Stay!" yelled Tungo. His eyes flashed in angry defiance. "From now on, I am your leader!"

As beams around the tunnel door burst into flames and smoke poured down the corridor, shrieks echoed through the dungeon. People surged forward, every one frantically pushing the one ahead.

"Come with me to the heart of the fortress," Cabeto called through the rising panic. "No wood is there to burn—no gunpowder to explode. Come, I beg you. Come to where you will be safe!"

Cabeto moved up behind the agitated procession that pushed its way toward the door.

"Go and you will die!" Tungo cried. "Follow me! I will be your new leader! I will be your chief!"

Hola, paralyzed by fear and confusion, stood rooted to one spot. Cabeto hastened over to the boy and grabbed his hand. "This way," he said. "Come with me."

"I can't find Safya!" the boy cried frantically.

"She searches for you," Cabeto said. "Come along. We will find her."

A loud blast sprayed shards of rock down on them, and then a ball of flame exploded in the center of the dungeon. With smoke-muffled screams, terrified people hit and pushed and stomped anyone between them and the way out.

"Do not let your fear control you!" Cabeto pleaded. "Be calm or no one will get out!"

From the doorway, a voice beckoned—strong, confident, and with comforting assurance. It was Grace. "Come this way," she called. "Step through carefully. Give me your hand. Next person now. Quick, but with care. No, no, you must not push. Good, good. We will all make it. Not many people left now. Come along. Come along."

Cabeto took Hola's hand. Flooded with hope, he threw back his head and laughed out loud. Together the man and the boy lifted up those who had fallen and helped them back to their feet. They urged on those too overcome with fear to move. Those who could not walk, they picked up and carried up the stairs and out the door.

With Grace's help and encouragement, the roomful of people moved quickly through the doorway. Even so, smoke closed in on them and flames licked at the door.

Cabeto gave Hola a push. "Go on, boy," he said. "Get out now."

"No," Hola insisted. "I want to stay and help you."

Cabeto picked up the boy and lifted him through the door. Then he turned back to get one more woman who lay injured. Just as he reached her, another explosion rocked the dungeon. A blazing beam overhead cracked and toppled. Cabeto jumped aside, but the beam crashed down too quickly for him to get out of its way.

"Cabeto!" Grace screamed as she darted toward him.

Sunba shouted, "Antonio has already gone, Grace. You go after him. The people will follow you! I'll get Cabeto and meet you in Antonio's storeroom!"

"But—" Grace protested.

"Go!" Sunba ordered. "Lead the people or they will all die with Tungo!"

Fighting back tears, Grace grabbed Hola's hand and dragged him alongside her as she rushed to the head of the crowd.

"I don't want to go without Cabeto!" Hola sobbed.

"Neither do I," Grace said. "But we will go anyway. Cabeto is in the hands of God. We all are."

Explosion after explosion rained down so fast it felt as though the earth would split open. Flames licked through gaps in the stone, igniting wooden beams and doorframes.

"Look!" Hola gasped. He pointed to a small opening in the stone wall and ran over to peer through. Grace was right behind him. From that vantage point, they could see the front of the fortress. Everything was ablaze—the huge doors, the wooden bridges and walkways, the scaffoldings and facades—all a wall of roaring flames.

"Come!" Grace ordered hoarsely. "Hurry!" She ran blindly, pulling Hola along with her.

Up ahead, Grace heard the ragged panting of people held too long in chains. As they struggled to keep up with Antonio's long strides, the slap, slap, slap of their bare feet on the stone floor mixed with weary gasps. Behind them, screams and shrieks from those who chose to stay behind with Tungo stabbed the air.

"In here!" Antonio called.

Only after everyone else was safely inside did Grace duck into the windowless room.

"*¿Esta cada uno aqui?*" Antonio asked. "If everyone is in, shut the door!"

"But Cabeto and Sunba aren't here!" Hola cried, his voice rising in panic. "They won't be able to find us with the door shut!"

"*Sí,*" Antonio answered gently. "They will find us . . . and very soon."

In utter exhaustion, Grace gasped and choked like everyone else. She sank to the floor and leaned back against the wall. How could these stones dare to be so cool and damp when the rest of the fortress raged in flames? Shaking her head as if to clear her thoughts, Grace allowed her aching eyes to drift closed.

"Cabeto," she said softly. "Oh, poor, poor Cabeto."

If he didn't come, how could everyone go on? What would they do without a leader? If Cabeto didn't come, what was *Grace* to do? How could *she* go on?

Oh, and what of all the others? The ones who stayed behind with Tungo? At least they had a chance. But what of all those who never made it out of their cells? What about Yao? Poor Yao, who so longed to be free! What about him?

44

As the harmattan winds whipped up the inferno at Zulina fortress, the ground rocked with blasts more powerful than any thunder. Terrified villagers fell prostrate before the sacred baobab tree and beseeched friendly spirits to beg the ancestors to have mercy. On the roads that went both ways from the tree, men and women trembled and sank to the ground, moaning as they waited for their lives to end. The angry winds carried no words of hope, for the talking drums had fallen silent.

At the compound where Grace had lived all but the past ten days of her life, fiery shadows danced through the London house, although no one was there to see them but Mama Muco.

As soon as Joseph Winslow started gathering the slaves together, Muco had hidden herself in the shadows to watch. She heard Lingongo's blistering words to him, but to Muco's astonishment, her master paid his wife absolutely no mind. He went his own way and did exactly as he pleased. Joseph drove the slaves right past her, across the fields, and off toward the gate. Lingongo had paced through the night, and just before the first light of dawn, she stomped off too—after him, Mama supposed. Yes, Mama Muco had seen it all. And the entire time, neither Joseph Winslow nor Lingongo had ever once mentioned their daughter.

As soon as Lingongo was out of sight, Muco started her vigil. "Oh, Lord God, help us," she breathed. "Whatever is happening up there is not good for anybody, especially not for Grace. Please, please, help Grace!"

Then the dark room lit up like morning. Muco, silenced in the middle of her prayer, had opened her eyes to the horrible sight of the sky on fire. With a cry of dismay, she hurried from the house and out to the courtyard, then across the garden. Flames danced in the pink-streaked sky. They seemed to engulf the entire fortress. Mama Muco fell to her knees and clamped her eyes shut against the awful scene. She threw her apron over her head and bellowed out in a flood of tears, "Oh, God! Oh, God! Save my Grace! Please, please, save my Grace!"

That's when the explosions had started. Louder and louder they thundered. What could it mean?

At long last, when the sun hung hazy and red in the sky and the thunder-noise had finally stilled, Mama shaded her eyes and stared hard into the distance. Could that be someone coming across the sweet potato field? She squinted hard. Yes! Definitely, three men were headed her way. As they got closer, she recognized them as three of the slaves Joseph Winslow had bound and taken to the fortress with him.

"Tuke!" Muco called out. "Tuke, is that you? You wait right there for me!"

Muco hitched up her skirts above her plump knees and hurried toward the men, yelling the entire way. Lingongo would whip her to death for such foolishness. Well, just let her try!

"Stop!" Muco cried. "You wait for me, Tuke!"

Tuke turned and stared uncomprehendingly at this strange

sight that tore across the field toward him. The other two men did the same.

Muco rushed up to them, completely out of breath. "Please . . . ," Muco gasped, "did you . . . see . . . Miss Grace?"

"Miss Grace?" Tuke asked. He looked confused, as though he couldn't quite understand the question.

"Up there!" Mama demanded in irritation. She gestured toward the flaming fortress. But then her tone melted into pleading. "Please, Tuke, please, tell me. Is Miss Grace all right?"

"We didn't see Miss Grace," another man said. "We don't know anything about her."

All three men stared blankly, stupefied.

"We didn't see any one of 'em," the second man continued.

Tuke's eyes suddenly welled with tears. "The fire burnin' everything, and gunpowder and all . . . and them trapped inside."

"What of Grace?" Mama demanded.

"We had to do what we done!" Tuke implored. "Mister Joseph, he be the master over us. We's nothin' but his slaves. It ain't our fault. None of it! We had to do it!"

"But did you see Grace?!"

"The king's warriors come," Tuke said. "That's when we got our chance to run. We couldn't watch no more. Even if the master kills us, we couldn't watch no more!"

Abruptly, Tuke turned his back on Muco and started to run in the opposite direction. The second man followed him. The third man hesitated. He looked at Muco as though he wanted to say something more, but after a moment's hesitation, he too turned and ran.

For several minutes Mama Muco stared after the three men. But there was no time to lose. Already, thick smoke shrouded Zulina.

"Grace!" Mama Muco called. "I will see you again!"

45

"I can't stand it any longer!" Grace whispered to Antonio. She was careful to speak in a soft tone so as not to encourage those already complaining of their dreadful thirst and their growing hunger and the stuffy air in the storeroom. Such discomforts Grace could endure. What were hunger and thirst and close quarters at a time like this? Hadn't every one of them been dragged to Zulina in chains and forced to live worse than animals? No, she couldn't abide the endless wait and not knowing.

Antonio had climbed up and unlocked a small vent high in the wall that opened out to the ocean, so now they had fresh air. They could also see the daylight pass into night and then night pass back to day. Already they had been in the storeroom for one entire day and night. Soon a new day would dawn, and still Cabeto and Sunba had not come.

"I'm going to look for them," Grace whispered to Antonio.

"*Por favor, no,*" Antonio pleaded. "If you leave, everyone will want to go."

"We cannot hide in here forever. At some time someone will have to venture out and see what happened."

Grace was right, of course. The people couldn't stay locked

in the room much longer. Somehow they had to find food and water. What neither Antonio nor Grace dared say was that food and water were unlikely to be available anywhere in the fortress. It could be that some water barrels survived the attack, though that was unlikely. As for food, though, that was all but gone, even before the fire.

Reluctantly, Antonio nodded his agreement. "Then go now, before daylight," he said. "And Grace . . . *vaya con Dios.*"

Moving as quickly and quietly as a caracal on the prowl, Grace reached the door. She pushed it open just wide enough to squeeze through and silently pulled the door closed behind her.

With one hand on either side of the narrow passageway, Grace cautiously felt her way along in the dark. The acrid stench of smoke filled her nostrils and made it difficult to breathe without coughing. Grace paused and ripped one of the sleeves off her dress and held it over her face.

As the smoke grew thicker, Grace dropped to her hands and knees and crawled along the stone walkway. It was strewn with chunks of broken rock. The sharp, jagged pieces ripped into her palms and sliced through her white petticoat to gouge into her knees. Billowing smoke blinded her. Other than her own choking gasps, she couldn't hear a sound. With a panicky dread, a terrible thought leaped into her mind. *Could it be that I'm the only person still alive outside the storeroom?*

Grace couldn't tell how far she had gone, but her knees had ripped away part of the flounce of her petticoat, and the rough stone walk had rubbed her hands completely raw. Her lungs felt as though they would burst from all the smoke. Grace could not go any farther. She eased herself low against the wall

"Cabeto!" she whispered hoarsely. Then louder she called, "Cabeto! Can you hear me?"

No sound returned but her own raspy breath.

Grace gathered all her strength and shouted, "Ca . . . be . . . to!" Then she collapsed into a fit of coughing.

When she finally regained control of her breathing, Grace listened hard—nothing but silence. She was alone. In despair, she turned around to start the long, painful crawl back to the storeroom. What would she tell the others? That it was too soon to venture out? Perhaps that they should wait until the sun was high in the sky and then someone else should try? Antonio maybe? Or would it do any harm to extend the false hope that by now Lingongo might be appeased, and—

A strong arm grabbed hold of Grace.

"What?" Grace exclaimed. Then bursting with excitement, she called out, "Cabeto! Is that you?"

"No, not Cabeto," came the answer. "It's me, Tungo."

Tungo! Grace's heart sank.

"Come with me," Tungo ordered.

"No!" Grace cried. She struggled to pull free of his grasp. "Leave me alone. I'll never call you leader! I'd rather die right here!"

"Come with me, Grace." Tungo's voice was urgent, and the sharp edge was gone. "I'll never ask you to call me leader."

When Grace stopped struggling, Tungo released his grip. He moved forward and then pushed his way under a collapsed wall. Grace slid under after him. She rubbed her eyes and blinked hard. They were in a room with a hole blown in the far wall. Early morning light streamed through—bright light and fresh air.

"Over here," Tungo called.

Grace caught her breath, ran over to the battered wall, and fell to her knees. It was Cabeto, lying on a makeshift bed. The muscles of his leg were exposed where his flesh had been scorched away. Beside him lay Sunba, his shoulder shattered.

"Did everyone make it to the storeroom?" Cabeto asked in a strained voice.

"Yes," Grace said. "Antonio was right. The fires and smoke didn't reach us there." Then she looked around in confusion. "But . . . just you three? Where are the others?"

"There are no others," Tungo answered with a heavy voice. "The ones who followed me are no more."

Grace stared at him in stunned silence.

"They are dead? All of them? Then how did . . . you . . . ?"

"Because he came back for us," said Cabeto in a weak voice.

The fire was gone from Tungo's eyes. "I thought I led them to safety. But when I came back for them, the whole room was rubble," he said sadly.

Grace buried her face in her hands and wept.

"What should we do, Cabeto?" Grace implored. "The people must have a leader. Tell me what we should do."

But Cabeto had already drifted into unconsciousness. He would not lead this day or the next.

Tungo yanked at Grace's arm and motioned toward the door. Voices out in the passageway. Grace reached for Tungo's musket, and Tungo let her take it. He pulled a knife from the sheath at his waist.

"We showed 'em, we did. Not a one's left livin'!" It was Joseph Winslow's crowing voice, and he was just outside their room.

"I want to see her body." It was another familiar voice. "Only then will I be satisfied."

Tungo would not look at Grace. There was no mistaking Lingongo's voice, nor was there any question about whom she demanded to see.

Grace tightened her grip on the musket. "Tungo," she whispered, "you are leader now."

"No," Tungo answered. "The people will never trust me. I cannot be their leader."

"Then," said Grace, "until Cabeto can again stand before the people, I will lead them. Come!"

Grace eased out from under the fallen wall just as Lingongo stepped toward it. The two stood face-to-face. Instinctively, Lingongo flipped forward the hand in which she held her whip. But Grace was ready. She raised her musket and pointed it in warning at her mother.

"If'n we finds that 'er—" Joseph's patter stopped abruptly when Tungo pressed a knife against his throat.

"No," Grace said. "You did not kill everyone."

Lingongo stared at Grace. In an even voice, she said, "Then our work is not yet complete."

Joseph was not nearly so calm. First, the color drained from his face, and his eyes rolled back in his head for just an instant. Then he immediately began to squeal in a most pitiful way. "Grace, me darlin'! I's so 'appy to see ye alive and well! Now we kin work t'gether, on the same side. Us, Grace . . . ye and yer pap."

"Tungo," Grace said without taking her eyes from her mother, "bring *Admiral* Joseph Winslow inside."

Tungo pressed the knife more firmly against Joseph's throat and pushed him toward the room where Cabeto and Sunba lay injured.

To her mother, Grace said, "Move, Lioness."

46

"*Buenos días.*"

Pieter DeGroot jerked his head up, opened his eyes, and stared at the form that floated before him—a tall black man, free of shackles. It could only be another of his hallucinations.

"It is good to see that you still live, *mi amigo*," Antonio said.

And yet, this apparition certainly looked and sounded real. Pieter opened his mouth, and then he shut it. Again he opened it, but all he could think of to say was, "Lingongo. Is she here?"

"*No, señor,*" Antonio said with a grin. "Only me . . . and I brought this." He held up a ring of keys. Only then did Pieter allow himself to attempt a crooked smile . . . and release a spark of hope.

First, Antonio loosened the bonds that secured Pieter's swollen wrists. Henry Taylor had done his job well. Then Antonio slipped in the key and removed the manacles Lingongo had clamped on his lanky legs, now worn raw. His arms, weak from the beatings and his captivity, fell useless at his sides. Antonio gently took the Dutchman's right arm, and ever so slowly and carefully he moved it up and down and all around. At each movement, Pieter cried out in pain. Antonio took his left arm, and he did the same thing. But this time, Pieter's cries mixed with shouts of joy. His laughter boomed out loud. It was like being reborn!

"What happened?" Pieter asked.

"*Mucho, mi amigo,*" Antonio said. "Too much to tell you now. I will leave it to others to explain."

He lifted Pieter's legs and began to move them, first the left one and then the right.

"I heard such tremendous explosions that I thought the fortress would fall down," Pieter said. "It sounded like a cannon attack."

"*Sí,*" Antonio acknowledged. "And fire, *también*. And gunpowder. You can thank God the lioness left you in this far place, or you would not be alive."

Antonio helped Pieter to his feet. When Pieter's legs crumpled beneath him, Antonio asked, "Can you walk?"

"Yes," Pieter said. "Oh, yes! Just give me a minute."

"*Señor,*" Antonio said, "you can wait here or you can come with me. There is another I must set free. *Uno más.*"

"I'll come with you!" Pieter said without a moment's hesitation. "I don't want to spend one more second of my life in this hole."

At first it was all Pieter could do to hobble painfully along. Although Antonio took great care to walk slowly, Pieter struggled to keep up with him. But after several minutes, Pieter's wobbly legs reaccustomed to holding him up, and then they remembered how to move him forward. With each new step, his walking became easier and easier, and steadier and steadier.

Halfway down the corridor, Antonio stopped abruptly. It wasn't until he pushed his key into what appeared to be nothing more than a cracked stone that Pieter noticed a tiny cell recessed into the wall. One twist of the key, then a shove, and a hidden door scraped open.

In the tiny cell, a single man sat propped up against the far wall. He was secured only by a chain attached to a manacle bolted around his neck and locked to a stud in the wall. The man stared blankly at Antonio and Pieter. Reaching out to them, he struggled to get to his feet.

"Yao," Antonio said. "*Su amiga* Grace sends you greetings."

Yao opened his mouth, but so starved was he for water that when he tried to form words, little came out but a strained croak. In the far corner—too far for Yao to reach—stood a bucket of stagnant water and a filthy cup. Pieter grabbed the cup, dipped it in the bucket, and brought it to Yao. Yao snatched the cup and gulped greedily.

Antonio loosened the shackle on Yao's neck. "Come along! Follow us!" he urged. "Many others in here are also newly freed. Soon no more slaves will be shackled in Zulina."

No longer was the hallway quiet. With both Grace and Antonio gone, others had also started to venture forth from the stuffy storeroom. Now almost everyone had left. Many wandered around the passageways. A few had gone off in search of loved ones, but most headed back toward the sunny corner room.

Antonio put his hand on Pieter's shoulder. "Now I will say *adiós, señor*," he said.

"*Adiós?*" Pieter looked at him in confusion. "Why do you say good-bye? I'm coming with you, Antonio."

"Not *adiós* to you, *señor*. *Adiós* from me," Antonio said. "I shall leave you. Capitán Carrillo sets sail tonight with the tides, and he offered to take me back on the ship as a crewman. Not as a slave, *no*. But as a free man."

"Do the others know this?" Pieter asked.

"No," Antonio said. "They would think me a traitor to sail with a white man who fought alongside our enemies. But I don't belong in Africa, *señor*. My father and all his ancestors before him were born here, but I am a stranger to this land. I do not understand the African tongues, and I do not know the African ways. I have no one here and no place to go. All I know is the white man's world."

"Antonio," Pieter asked, "how can you be sure you will truly be free?"

Antonio's dark eyes clouded. "No black man can ever be sure of the truth of a white man's words. *¿No?*"

"Perhaps you should—"

"But I will go with him anyway," Antonio said, "because I have no choice. And I will pray to God for protection." Antonio grasped Pieter firmly by the hand and said, "*Gracias, señor,* for all you did for us. *Muchas gracias, mi amigo.*"

Antonio handed Pieter the ring of keys. "Here," he said. "For all the cells, and all the chains and locks inside—for anyone who remains a slave."

Antonio turned and walked down the passageway toward the sea. Toward the door of no return.

"*¡Vaya con Dios!*" Pieter called after him. "Go with God, my friend!"

Antonio did not look back.

47

"O thers 'll come fer us, they will," Joseph said to his wife. "They'll undo these chains an'—"

"No one will come," Lingongo snapped. "Everyone has fled this disaster."

"Them cannons is still out there, Woman, standin' ready fer the other white men to use. When Stevens and the Spaniard come—"

"Joseph! Can you understand nothing?" Lingongo cried in exasperation. "The white men have left! The last few were willing to fight as long as my father's warriors stayed between them and the rebels. But when Obei turned the warriors against us and they refused to hunt down the rebels—when they turned on us—then your brave white men turned and ran like the cowards they are!"

"But they will—"

"They will do nothing!" said Lingongo. "They do not care about you, Joseph. They do not care what happens to Zulina. All they care about is their own hold of slaves."

"Yer father, then," Joseph said hopefully. "'E will send more warriors to fight again' them wot turned traitors—"

"No! He will not. My father does not send his warriors out

to fight on the side of those who lose wars. If we are to get out of this place alive, we have to do it ourselves."

"An' jist 'ow are we to do that?" demanded Joseph with rising impatience. "Looks to me like ye is ever bit as chained up as I is."

"By thinking," Lingongo said. "By being smarter than slaves."

Chained wrist and ankle, husband and wife sat together in one corner of a room guarded by a couple of African men they had never seen before. The men spoke no English. Lingongo knew this by the blank stares she and Joseph got from the guards as she talked openly to him in English.

Lingongo, dirty and disheveled, slumped back in the corner and gazed up into the faces of the men who held their guns at the ready. She sighed deeply, and in the language of her father she said, "Am I the only daughter of Africa still held as a slave in this fortress?"

The guards stared blankly at her. They glanced at each other and shook their heads in confusion.

"We do not understand your talk," the shorter one answered in Tungo's tongue.

In the man's own language, Lingongo asked again, "Am I the only daughter of Africa still held as a slave in this fortress?"

"You are not a slave," the short man answered. "You are a prisoner."

"A prisoner?" Lingongo asked, her eyes wide and her face stricken with fright. "How can that be? This white man . . . ," here she looked at Joseph, "this slave trader who looks at us Africans and sees only gold, he dragged me here in chains. Why am I now a prisoner of my own people?"

The short man paused and looked questioningly at the tall man. The tall man shrugged. "Tungo says she is a prisoner," the tall man said in answer to the short one's unspoken question.

"You are a prisoner," the short man repeated.

Joseph looked from one to the other, unable to comprehend a single word. "What ye sayin' to 'em?" he demanded of Lingongo.

"They say you are a coward because you let a woman fight your battles," Lingongo told him. "I tried to defend your honor."

Strange, Joseph thought. *Lingongo's cowering tone didn't fit her words. And, anyway, if the guards were to say such a thing, why wouldn't she join in the attack? That's what she usually did.*

"They say if you had the courage to fight for yourself, they would respect you and let you go," Lingongo added.

Well, Joseph thought, *perhaps it did make some sense after all. A man should act like a man.* So he jumped to his feet. But since the chain that bound him to Lingongo was wrapped tightly around both of them, his quick action immediately jerked her arms painfully to one side and up over her head. Joseph didn't even notice.

"Ye bloody 'eathen devils!" he bellowed to the guards. "I'll show ye I ain't no coward!"

Lingongo whimpered pitifully, and a look of pained terror washed over her face. Joseph, who did his best to assume an appropriate fighting stance despite the restriction of chains, paid her not the least notice.

"Ye wants a fight, does ye?" he challenged the guards. "Jist loosen me chains and give me a chance. I'll show ye wot I kin do!"

The guards jumped to their feet and both pointed their muskets at Joseph.

"Put down 'em guns and gi' me a chance at a fair fight!" Joseph ordered belligerently. "I'll give both o' ye a good throttlin', I will! One ye ain't soon to fergit, neither!"

The guards looked questioningly from Joseph to Lingongo.

"He said he will kill me, and then he will kill both of you," Lingongo sobbed out to them in Tungo's tongue. "Please . . . can you loose the chain that binds me to him? Then you can do whatever you want with me."

The short guard hesitated.

"I will still be your prisoner," Lingongo said. "But I will be a prisoner *alive*. If I am to die, should it not be at your hands instead of his?" She looked up at Joseph, who glared from one to the other in angry confusion. Lingongo cringed and shuddered. Another tear spilled from her eye and rolled down her cheek.

The short guard said to the tall guard, "I told you they were not together—not such a beautiful one with an ugly white slave trader."

"Tungo told us—" the tall guard began, but the short guard waved him off.

"Tungo did not have time to tell us anything. We must be certain to protect her from the white killer of Africans."

The short guard laid down his gun and cautiously approached Lingongo. He gazed at her face—so lovely, so vulnerable. He paused only a moment, took the key from around his neck, and unfastened the chain that connected her to her husband.

"It is working," Lingongo mouthed to Joseph. "See? They have removed the first chain. Now is the time to show them what you can do!"

Encouraged, Joseph lunged at the guard. But since the chain was not yet untangled from Lingongo, it again jerked against her arms, this time even more violently than before. Lingongo screamed in pain. The tall guard charged forward and cracked Joseph across the head with the butt of his musket.

Lingongo lay her head back and let her eyes flutter closed.

Her moans continued ever so piteously, even though the corners of her mouth tilted just the tiniest bit upward.

Never could Lingongo's people have risen to the respected stature of the most powerful chiefdom in the Kingdom of Gold had they not understood the importance of stealth in conquest. Her father never could have earned the right to rest his feet on the *sika'gua*, the Golden Stool of Power, had he not mastered the secrets of silent subjugation that took so many of his enemies in their sleep. As darkness overtook the room, Lingongo began to work a piece loose from the finely woven cloth she wore wrapped around her. Slowly, painstakingly, she picked at the weave until she had a strip just the right length and width. Then she rolled it and rolled it until it was long and tight and strong. Only then did she lay back to wait.

No longer were moans and wails the sounds of Zulina. New hope sprang up from the ashes and rubble and diffused a happy clamor throughout the fortress. Old threats crumbled under the promise of a new beginning. Hope and possibility floated on the breeze. So as the darkness deepened, the tall guard smiled and lay down his musket. He settled himself as comfortably as he could on the roughly hewn stone and allowed his eyes to close. Soon he was snoring loudly.

As silently as a python slithering through the trees, Lingongo edged away from Joseph. Through the slit openings of her eyes, she watched the short guard as he tried to get comfortable.

"Hunnnh," Lingongo moaned softly.

When nothing happened, she tried again, only this time a little bit louder: "*Hunnnh!*"

The short guard turned his eyes to her, and Lingongo twisted her lovely face into a grimace of pain.

The short guard crept over to where she lay. "Does something cause you pain?" he whispered.

"My arm."

Lingongo's words were barely audible, little more than a wispy breath. The short guard had to come closer to hear her. He bent down and inclined his ear to her silky smooth face, just to make certain he didn't miss a single word.

"What?" he asked.

"The white man," she breathed. "He may have broken my arm."

The guard lay his gun down and reached out toward her smooth chocolate arm.

In the flash of an eye, Lingongo's arm shot upward. Before the short guard had time to cry out, the chain between her wrists caught him across his windpipe and he fell into her lap. Lingongo pulled out the cloth rope she had made and jerked it around the man's throat, squeezing it tighter and tighter, just as a python would do to its victim, until with the faintest gurgle, the guard stopped breathing. Quickly, Lingongo pulled the key from the string tied around his neck, and with it she unlocked the chains from her wrists and ankles. Just before she slipped through the door, she turned to admire her escape. Without so much as a twitch, the tall guard and Joseph Winslow continued to snore in their sleep.

Much later, when the tall guard finally sounded the alarm, Tungo was furious. He wanted to tie the tall guard up by his neck and leave him to hang in the scorching sun until he was dead. Just to be certain no one misunderstood the message, he wanted the body of the short guard to hang beside him upside down.

"What is the good in that?" Cabeto asked. "The lioness is safely back in her compound. It will not drive her out, nor will it bring her back to us. Nothing will do that."

But Tungo would not be placated.

"She laughs at us!" he said bitterly.

"But we will walk free," Cabeto pointed out. "So why is it not we who laugh?"

"It is a plot," Tungo said. "Lingongo will be back for us."

Grace said nothing. Cabeto was right; they were now free to go. This was what they had fought for. And yet . . . she knew her mother. Grace glanced over at Yao, who at long last stood at her side.

Yao stared straight at her. "Please, may I speak?" he asked. The others nodded, so he looked over at Tungo and continued, "You speak well. Grace knows the truth in what you say, but how can she speak against her own mother?"

"As long as the lioness lives, she will hunt us," Tungo insisted. "She must be stopped. Today is the day."

Tungo fixed Yao in a hard stare. Yao returned his stare, just as steady and just as hard.

Without another word, Tungo grabbed up the flint box Pieter had brought them with their supplies, turned, and strode from the room. Without a word, Yao followed—out of the room, through the corridors, and out of the charred fortress.

The truth was, Tungo knew what he needed to do, but he couldn't do it alone. He needed Yao. Tungo didn't know his way around the lioness's lair. Only once had he been in her compound, and that was in the dark of the night with Antonio and Joseph Winslow. Up at the fortress, Joseph had directed the two trustees to load up a horsedrawn wagon with guns and gunpowder and to hide the load under sacks of millet. When night had fallen, Antonio took Tungo and the wagon down to the London house. Joseph Winslow met them at the gate and led them to the storeroom. There they unloaded the crates of munitions, stacking them one box on top of the other until the storeroom was filled. Nervous and agitated, Joseph had continually pressed and threatened them to work faster: "'Urry now, if'n ye 'opes to see tomorrow!" Almost before the last crate was unloaded, Joseph himself had turned the wagon around. On the way back to Zulina, he had hissed, "One word 'bout this to anyone an' I'll put a bullet 'twixt yer eyes, I will!"

But Yao . . . it was different for him. Yao knew every clod of dirt on the compound grounds. He knew how to get over the wall, he knew the number of steps between the mango grove and the cashew grove, and he knew how to steal silently through the sweet potato fields and the kitchen garden. Like Antonio, he could creep right up to the front door.

As soon as Tungo told Yao about the gunpowder stacked up in the storage shed behind the house, Yao knew exactly what they must do.

As Yao left the fortress, he paused to pick up a long piece of tightly twisted fabric rope from the ground. Perhaps it was the bright colors that caught his eye. Or maybe it was the sparkle of gold thread that ran through it. All the way to the London house he worked and twisted the fabric so that by the time he and Tungo got to the kitchen garden, it was as hard and stiff as a stick. He found the palm oil on the other side of the house—just what he needed to soak his new rope.

Grace was in the fortress kitchen with Safya and Oyo and other women, boiling millet and stirring in pieces of the fish that Ikem and his men brought up from the sea, when the sky suddenly roared to life and rained fire. The room whirled and tossed like a ship on a stormy sea.

"The end is upon us!" Oyo screamed as she flung herself to the floor. Cooking pots crashed down around her.

"Hola!" Safya cried in alarm. Frantically, she stumbled from the room, calling out for the boy. "Hola! Where are you, child? Where are you?" Safya had come to think of him as her own, and she could not abide the thought of losing him. Certainly not like this!

Grace was only vaguely aware of the screams and terror around her. She had been hanging cloths out the window, and from there she had a good view of the flat grassland below, including part of the compound wall. When the explosion rocked the fortress, she saw pillars of flame shoot high into the air, and they came from inside the wall. Grace bolted for the doorway. She pushed past Safya and ran down the passageway, out to the scorched front of the fortress, and on to the road that led down to the baobab tree.

When she caught sight of the cataclysm that stretched out before her, Grace shrieked in horror. Much of her father's stone wall lay in ruins, and the entire London house was ablaze.

"Mama Muco!" Grace screamed.

She fell to her knees, buried her face in her hands, and sobbed.

48

"I was wrong about you," Yao said when he saw Grace again. "You did not stay a slave." He bowed his head before her in respect.

"No," Grace answered. "And neither did you." But there was no triumph in her voice, only profound weariness.

"It will do no good to talk of what is past," Cabeto said from his resting place beside the window. "Good or bad, right or wrong, it is over. All is behind us."

"All is not behind us!" Tungo declared. "We have one prisoner left. Slice his throat and throw him into the sea, I say. Only then will all be behind us!"

Grace sprang to her feet. "No!" she protested. "You will not murder my father too!"

"Not murder," Tungo answered. "Justice. Remember the hundreds and hundreds he sent to their deaths. Give to him what he deserves."

Grace looked around at the others assembled in the room—the same room that less than two weeks earlier had been her father's favorite place in Zulina, and her mother's most hated. Somehow, it had come through the attack with little damage. Her eyes settled on Pieter. With an entirely new authority, she said to him, "Bring in my father, Captain. We all fought this battle together. Together we will decide his fate."

Pieter left with Ikem right behind. Tungo sat in stony silence.

"He is your father," Cabeto said to Grace. "It was to you he did the greatest injustice."

Grace didn't answer. She turned her attention to the corner window and looked down at the remains of her father's stone wall and the still-smoldering ruins within it. Imagine! All this time Joseph Winslow could sit in this awful fortress, its walls echoing with agony and horror, and he could see her entire world.

The door opened and Joseph, shackled in chains, hobbled into the room. Grace mustered every effort to force herself to turn around and look her father straight in the face.

Joseph blinked and gazed around him, first at the desk, then at the maps piled on the side table. He seemed confused, uncertain of what was happening.

"Me ol' office!" he said with the trace of a smile. "Thank God in 'eaven it ain't burnt down!" He looked around and said with a conspirator's wink and a chuckle, "Used to throw dice in 'ere wi' any man wot had a big enough stake, I did."

Grace's eyes never wavered from her father's face, yet Joseph didn't seem to be aware of her presence.

"Where's 'Tonio?" Joseph asked suddenly. "Where's me ol' *juju*? Could use 'im 'bout now, is wot."

"Father . . . ," Grace said softly as she moved toward him.

Joseph's face suddenly twisted, and he struggled against his chains. Still, he refused to look at his daughter.

"This fortress be *mine*!" Joseph shouted in defiance. "'Ow dare the likes o' ye truss me up like a dirty slave? An' in me own castle at that!"

Although he couldn't understand a word Joseph said, Tungo ordered in the tongue of his own people, "Silence! You lost the battle, white man! This is the day you die!"

Joseph glared back at Tungo. He might not understand the African language, but he couldn't miss the tone of voice.

"Ye 'eathen murderer!" Joseph spat. "Ye thinks ye kin git away wi' killin' a white man? Kill me an' ye will die. Me mates will slice ye open an' leave ye so's all kin see yer black 'eart!"

Suddenly, Joseph spied Pieter DeGroot at the back of the room. "An' ye, ye dirty, rotten traitor!" he bellowed. "Yer soul be damned fer turnin' yer back on yer own kind!"

"And may God have mercy on yours . . . Admiral," Pieter replied softly.

Tungo moved forward, his knife pointed toward Joseph's throat. Joseph let out a sharp cry. His bluster gone, he began to sob.

Grace positioned herself between her father and the blade of Tungo's knife.

"No!" she ordered. "He does not have to die. We are not murderers, Tungo. We can put him on his ship, and he can sail back to England where he belongs. He will be gone from us forever."

"Let him go?" Tungo roared. "After what he did to all of us? And to our villages and our kin?"

"Please!" Grace pleaded. "How can it hurt us? If he's gone from Africa, he can never again do harm to anyone here."

"No!" Tungo insisted. "The slave trader dies today. Right here! Right now! He will leave this earth crying and begging like the despicable coward he is!"

"I will not allow it!" Grace moved over and resolutely placed herself in front of her cowering, whimpering father.

Cabeto grabbed up the crutch Pieter had made for him from

a tree branch and struggled to lift himself to his feet. "Listen to me, Tungo!" he said. "This man caused terrible things to happen to my village, to my kinsmen and my friends. He allowed evil things to happen to us here in this wretched place, things too horrible to speak about. Every one of us has a right to hate him. Grace has more of a right than any of us. But what Grace says is true—to kill him now would be to murder him. And we are not murderers."

Tungo glared at Cabeto. His face contorted in anger. "Do you justify this white man's actions? If there is any true defense, speak it quickly! I ask to hear it now."

"I cannot say one word in his defense," Cabeto replied. "There is no way to justify his actions. And so I do not ask for justice. Instead, I plead for mercy . . . for Grace's sake."

Sunba stepped forward. "I do not wish to disagree, my brother, nor do I wish to dishonor Grace. But there can be no mercy for this man. Too much evil stains him. Such a one requires justice."

Joseph's whimpers turned to wild sobs and then disintegrated into blubbering. "Ye is me daughter, Grace, me darlin' girl. 'Twas always me what pertected ye from yer mother's whip. Me what bought ye dresses from London and taught ye to be a lady. Don't ye remember, Grace? Don't ye remember yer pap?"

Grace's face was set. She showed no emotion for her distraught father, yet neither would she move from her position as his shield.

"He has nothing left," she stated. "Isn't that punishment enough?"

Tungo turned on Grace. "No!" he exclaimed. "It is not enough! How can you even suggest such a thing? You of all people. He deserted you into our hands! He gave you up to die!"

Joseph heard the angry tone, and he saw the threatening gestures, yet he could not understand a word being said. In frustration, he yelled, "Stop yer 'eathen blabber! Cain't any of ye talk like 'uman bein's?"

"Grace argues on your behalf, Joseph Winslow," Pieter said. "Even though you left her to die, and then you tried to burn her to death in the dungeon. Despite all that, she argues for mercy."

Lunging toward Grace, Joseph cried out, "No, me darlin'! 'Twern't me wot done them thin's, I swear it! 'Twas yer 'eathen mother! Not me, darlin'! I wouldn't a let ye die 'ere! I would've saved ye, is wot!"

Grace ignored her father and said to the Africans, "From the beginning, your desire was to go back to your homes and live in freedom. Now you can do that. Now we all are free to go where we want and live as we wish."

Joseph's eyes darted frantically from one face to the other as he struggled to understand. Suddenly, he spied Yao, and new excitement rose up in him.

"Ye tell 'em!" he exclaimed. "Tell 'em how I risked me 'ide to save ye from me woman's whip. Ye done me wrong, boy, tryin' to escape and causin' all kinds o' trouble wi' 'er. Yit I kep' 'er from beatin' ye clean to death. An' when she turned murderous toward ye, I brought ye up 'ere to Zulina to 'ide ye away fer yer pertection, I did. Tell 'em that, boy!"

"Yes, I will tell them—Father!" Yao said in English.

Joseph recoiled as though Yao had slapped him across the face. He opened his mouth, but no sound did he utter.

"I will tell them how you took your son, born in the African village to a woman you stole from another man and forced to be your own, branded him with your brand, and kept him in bondage as your slave. I will tell them how you never dared to let your African wife know your blood ran in his veins because she was your master as surely as you were master of the slave boy and his mother."

"Now see 'ere!" Joseph sputtered.

But Yao wasn't finished: "I'll tell them that you so feared Lingongo that you chained and shackled your son and bolted a yoke around his neck. That you forced him into this slave fortress and locked him away with the rats. Yes, Father, I will tell them how you left me—your own son—with no food to eat and no water to drink. I will tell them how you deserted me to die alone."

Yao paused, and in the moment of silence that followed, Grace breathed in wonder, "Yao! My brother?"

"And so you agree," Tungo pressed impatiently. "He deserves to die!"

"Yet you did not deprive me of life when I was first born as you could have done," Yao continued. "You let me live. And you did not sell me to a slave ship. And it was by watching you in your weakness that I grew strong."

Yao turned to Tungo and said, "Everything you say is true, Tungo. Joseph Winslow is a white slave trader who deserves to die. But I say, listen to Grace. Send him back where he came from and let him live. Let him forever be haunted by his memories and his deeds."

"The offspring have spoken," said Ikem. "There be no more killing."

"So be it," Cabeto decreed.

The next day, Pieter DeGroot rowed Joseph Winslow out to the double-masted *Mourning Dove*, which Pieter himself had stocked and made ready to sail. Only after they were on board the ship did Pieter unlock Joseph's chains.

"I cain't sail th' bloody ship by me'sef!" Joseph protested angrily.

"You best thank the good Lord above that you get a chance to try," Pieter said. "And thank your daughter that she was willing to place herself between you and the sharp side of the knife."

Joseph glared at Pieter and spat in his face.

"May God have mercy on your soul!" Pieter called out as he rowed back toward shore.

As Joseph Winslow went about the work of setting sails, Grace stood alone on the rocky bluff that overlooked the harbor. Billowing wind dusted her face and whipped at her clothes as she kept silent vigil. Joseph was well aware that she was watching him, yet he refused to acknowledge her. Finally, he hoisted the anchor and brought the *Mourning Dove* about.

As he sailed out of Zulina harbor, Joseph refused to give so much as a backward glance at his daughter who stood alone, dirty and ragged in the remains of her once exquisite bird-wing blue day dress. Instead, he raised his clenched fist high in the air, and turning just enough so that Grace would not miss a single word, he bellowed in angry defiance, "Good riddance to this God-forsaken continent o' devils an' demons. May it an' ever'one on it burn in everlastin' damnation!"

49

The harmattan winds, which at long last had calmed into a cooling breeze, pushed an entirely new drumbeat through the air. "I wish I could understand the talking drums," Grace said to Yao. "Their beat almost sounds like singing."

"Ivory horns—that is what you hear," Yao told her. "They call everyone to listen carefully because the drums have a very important message to tell." Yao paused and lifted his head high to listen. Then he said, "The talking drums tell of a parade in honor of a new ruler for Lingongo's people. Even now the men carry him through the kingdom on his golden chair. And the drums say a *kyinie* waves over him so that heaven cannot see the crown on his head."

"Oh," said Grace. She had heard her mother speak of those enormous parasols—beautiful, they were, woven of the finest silk and intricately embroidered with thread spun from gold. "He rides between heaven and earth. The new ruler must be very great indeed."

Grace closed her eyes and lifted her face to the gentle wind.

"Come, Grace," Yao said. "Our father is gone. All that was inside the stone wall is no more. Everything is different now—for both of us."

The sun that had shone gigantic and golden red as Joseph Winslow sailed from the harbor had all but sunk into the sea, yet still Grace gazed out across the endless ocean. For a long time Yao had watched her from the charred balcony above, but finally, he came down to keep silent vigil at her side.

"The London house is gone," Grace murmured.

"Yes," Yao said.

"My mother was in it."

"Surely she was," Yao said without emotion.

Grace could not bring herself to speak of her pain over Mama Muco.

"What you and Tungo did—I don't know anymore what is wrong or what is right," Grace said. "If I was truly African, perhaps I would hate Joseph Winslow and want him dead. And maybe I would detest Lingongo and call her a traitor. If I was truly English, perhaps I would look at you and call you a murdering savage. But I am neither African nor English, Yao, so I just don't know."

"What you are is a free woman," Yao said. "Leave this place and live in freedom."

Yao reached out his hand, and Grace took it. Together they made their way around the blackened stones of the fortress, struggling and stumbling over piles of strewn rubble.

As Grace and Yao rounded the far corner—Grace doing her best to avoid the charred remains of piled-up brush and bushes—they stepped into a joyful celebration. In the fiery sunset, the entire front of Zulina rang with shouts of jubilation. Around the scorched remains of the gate and spilling out across the face of the fortress, people laughed and chattered happily in many different tongues. Grace watched as strangers discovered others who spoke their language and knew their ways, as they found familiar faces from neighboring villages. She broke out laughing. She couldn't help herself. Slowly at first, then more quickly, people gathered into small bands to laugh and dance and celebrate together, and then to start back home.

"What will you do now?" Grace asked Yao.

"Go back to my village," Yao said. Then he paused and touched Grace's arm. "And you? Will you come with me?"

Hot tears filled Grace's eyes. She shook her head. "I don't know the ways of Africans," she said. "I only know the ways of the London house."

"But there is no London house anymore," Yao said.

Grace nodded. "Still, it's all I've ever known."

"I will show you the ways of Africa," Yao said. "My mother and sisters will teach you. They will welcome you, my sister."

"No, Yao," Grace said. "You go to your village. You go home."

"And you?"

"I must make a new way."

Yao argued and he reasoned and he pleaded, but all to no avail. And so at last he turned away from Grace and set his face toward his village. Grace stood silently and watched him go. Long after he had disappeared around the bend, she stared down the road after him.

Cabeto, leaning heavily on his crutch, limped up behind Grace. He, too, looked out over the scorched savanna, now blacker in the setting sun, and he shook his head sadly. Group after group of jubilant people wound their way down the road, unwilling to wait any longer to begin their trek back home.

"What do you see when you look down there, Grace?" Cabeto asked.

"The end of my world," Grace said. "I'm happy for all those who can go back to their villages. And I wouldn't want to go back to my old life even if I could. Still . . ." Her voice trailed off, and tears filled her eyes.

"Do not be so quick to envy these people," Cabeto said. "Many of them will also find that everything they knew has come to an end. Even in the best times, things do not stay the same. And the best times are no more."

"What about you?" Grace asked. "When will you leave?"

Cabeto shook his head. "I cannot walk that far. Nor can Sunba, with his arm and shoulder wrapped up. We will have to stay here for a while."

That night, Grace found it impossible to sleep. Early the next morning, as she made her way out of the fortress, Pieter DeGroot called out, "Grace! Come with me. I have something to show you."

Pieter led Grace through the winding passageways and off to a remote cluster of rooms deep in the heart of Zulina. "These were your parents' private quarters," he said. "Anything you find here is yours."

"No!" Grace exclaimed. "I don't want any of it! I will never be anything like either of them."

"Of course you will," Pieter said, "because they are the ones who made you who you are. Lingongo made you strong and independent and decisive. Joseph Winslow made you adventurous and curious about the world. It doesn't have to be the weak and wicked parts of them you follow, Grace. It can be what was strong and successful and determined and beautiful. It's up to you to put aside the evil and find the good."

And so, in the golden beams of morning, Grace wandered alone through the private rooms, captivated by the excitement of discovery. High on a shelf she found a folded garment made of brightly colored fabric. She pulled it down and carefully unfolded it across the floor. The long fabric strip was pieced together out of thin bands of the finest imported silk. Each band had small designs woven into it with strands of pure spun gold—cubes in one, triangles in another, diamonds in another, birds in yet another.

"An *asasia*!" Grace gasped. "A real *asasia*!"

Reverently, she ran her hand over the intricacies of the silk fabric. She couldn't read the writing woven in it in gold thread, but she knew that each design recounted a different proverb. Her mother would have been able to identify each one of them.

Such garments could be worn only by kings or princes, or occasionally by the most honored of princesses. Grace shut her eyes and tried to picture her own ancestors proudly parading in this royal rainbow-colored raiment.

Glancing down at herself, Grace realized for the first time that she was wearing nothing but a ripped-up piece of her dress top, a linen chemise, and her flounced petticoat with a tear in the front. She was dressed mostly in her underclothing! Of course, they were so grimy, shredded, and covered with ashes that few people were likely to recognize them for what they were. Quickly, she pulled off the filthy garments. She grabbed up the beautiful cloth and swung it over her left shoulder the way she had so often seen her mother do and then she tied it securely in place. Just the feel of the luxurious royal robe against her body made her feel like a different person.

Already the road that led down to the scorched grasslands was empty of all but a few indecisive stragglers. Almost everyone who intended to leave Zulina had already gone. At Cabeto's command, Hola—who was still there—had run through the fortress rooms and called for anyone who remained to come and be counted.

In all, sixteen people sat together. Grace and Cabeto and Sunba were there, and Hola and Safya. Ikem stayed. Three other men and two women were also there, and five little children who were left unclaimed.

"Maybe we could all go to your village," Grace suggested to Cabeto.

Cabeto looked around at the old and the young, the men and the women. At the dark faces and the light, the broad and the narrow. He also listened to the different tongues being spoken.

"No," he said. "The people would not all feel at home there. No, we have a new village right here."

"Well, you can't stay at the fortress," Pieter DeGroot said. He was still with them, although he had already signed onboard a French ship and would be sailing before the new moon. "This is a valuable harbor here. Already it's being eyed by several men who jostle with each other to see who will take it over. The wisest thing would be to leave here as soon as you possibly can."

"Then we will go," Cabeto said, ". . . somewhere."

As the others drifted away, Grace wandered around to the back of the fortress—back to the rocks over the harbor. Again, she stood alone and stared out to sea. What was it like on the other side of the ocean? In England, the land of her father—the land of the other half of herself? Were there others somewhere like her, with skin that wasn't black and wasn't white? Hair that wasn't black and wasn't red? Who didn't know how to be either African or English?

"Are there others out there who do not fit in anywhere?" Grace said out loud.

"Yes. There be others."

Grace gave a start and jerked around to see Ikem standing behind her. "Oh, I didn't see you!" she said, flushing with embarrassment.

For several minutes, the two stood in awkward silence.

"You want to know why I did not at once tell about the traitor," Ikem said.

"Everyone thought it was me," Grace said.

"I did not tell because people change. I changed. The Dutchman changed. I did not tell because the traitor should also have a chance to change."

Grace was silent for several minutes. Then she said, "I hoped my father would change. And my mother too. But now it is too late."

Ikem said, "Who can say what time is too late?"

50

"Someone's coming! Someone's coming!" It was the excited call of little Tawia, who never just talked, but danced and sang everything she had to tell.

"Who's coming?" Grace asked with a laugh.

"Up the road! Up the road!" Tawia sang out.

Grace followed the little girl as she danced out the doorway and over the baked ground. Sure enough, if she squinted against the sun, Grace could see a stocky figure trudging up the path, balancing a good-sized head load.

"Who's there?" Grace commanded.

"Good Lord, Child, who you think it is?" came the weary reply.

"Mama?" Grace gasped. "Mama Muco?"

Grace broke into a run.

"Mama!" she cried. She threw herself into the strong, familiar arms with such force that she knocked the head load clear off Mama's head. "I thought . . . I was so afraid . . . that you had . . . that you were . . ."

"Not me, Child!" Mama said. "When I saw Yao outside the wall, I went into your father's room and got his key and unlocked the gate. He would not tell me anything except that you were alive and there would be trouble so to get out. I quick grabbed me some things and I ran for the village."

Tears streamed down Grace's face.

"Look at you!" Mama exclaimed. She stepped back and gazed at Grace, who was again draped in the beautiful royal *asasia*. "A princess, you are, Grace! More beautiful than your mother ever was."

"Thank you," Grace said, although she felt a little ashamed of herself for being presumptuous enough to have donned the royal apparel.

When Grace helped Mama Muco heft the head load back onto her head, a packet of millet fell out.

"Oh, Mama! You brought us food!" Grace gasped.

"It is a gift from a friend of yours," Mama said.

Grace looked at her in confusion. What a thing to say!

"You know I have no friends," Grace told her.

"A gift of more food than I could carry," Mama said. "Milled flour and millet and sweet potatoes and cassavas and groundnuts—"

"We have barely eaten for three days!" Grace laughed. "Who could have known?"

When they got up to the fortress, Mama reached into her head load, pulled out a note beautifully written on fine paper, and handed it to Grace.

"Open it," Mama urged.

Grace unfolded the linen sheet and read:

How marvelous it must be to actually do something that matters! This may be my only chance to act in a daring way and do something of worth. I do not ask for a wedding gift. Instead, I give a gift to you. Live and be happy, Grace.

Sincerely Yours,
Charlotte Stevens

"Charlotte?" Grace asked incredulously. But how—?"

"She came to me," Mama said. That was all.

By the time the sun reached its height, the hungry group sat together to eat vegetable stew and share their experiences. "We have to leave Zulina," Grace told Mama. "We don't know where to go. We need someplace where we can start over again, but where?"

"I want to show you something," Mama Muco said. She went over to her pile of belongings and rummaged through. She pulled out her old missionary Bible and leafed through it until she found the place she wanted and then pushed the Bible over to Grace. She pointed to chapter 61 in the book of Isaiah. "Read what the sacred words say," Mama instructed.

Grace read aloud:

The Lord has sent me to bind up the brokenhearted,
to proclaim liberty to the captives,
and the opening of the prison to them that are bound . . .
to give unto them garlands of beauty instead of ashes,
the oil of joy instead of mourning,
and a garment of praise instead of a spirit of despair.

Grace looked up from the Bible. "*Opening of the prison . . .* ," she repeated slowly. "We did that, Mama! *Joy instead of mourning . . . praise instead of despair.* We saw that right here! Everyone dancing and laughing with joy. *Beauty instead of ashes*," Grace repeated slowly. Then more of a question than a statement, she said, "The compound?"

"Plenty of land there that didn't burn," Mama Muco said. "Sweet potatoes still lay in the far field. And coconuts, mangoes, and cashews hang on the trees. There's millet and groundnuts and cassavas and beetles aplenty to roast in the fire. The London house is gone, but there's mud and stone and sticks to build round huts, and more than enough palm fronds to thatch the roofs."

Grace looked questioningly at Pieter DeGroot, and he nodded slowly.

"Yes," he said. "It is the harbor and the land overlooking it that the men fight over, not that scorched parcel of earth. That land is yours, Grace. You would be as safe there as anywhere."

Grace looked around her. Safya sat tall, looking calm and relaxed with her eyes half closed. Hola leaned against her, and Tawia snuggled on her lap, the little girl's lips making high bird noises. Ikem was there, his face creased by a smile—how could she ever have feared so kind a face? Sunba stood next to Ikem—so like Cabeto, yet so different. Oh, and Cabeto, of course. Dear Cabeto.

Even Mama Muco was here.

And now a place for them all.

"Yes, a new beginning," Grace said as a smile spread across her face. "All of us together, but each one individual. A new village where we can each one be. A new beginning for us right here, right now. Beauty instead of ashes."

Lexicon

By the late 1700s, slavers who had long gone up and down the coast of West Africa to find captives for the slave trade were pressing further inland. Little wonder, then, that the slave houses were such a jigsaw of languages and peoples. The words, names, and peoples in this book represent many tribes of the area, including Dogon, Wolof, Ga, Hausa, and Yoruba.

AH KEEN: "Strong warrior."

ASASIA: Prized and valuable clothing reserved for royalty.

ASE: The power possessed by a witch doctor or diviner.

ASKARI: Soldiers of an African king.

ASSALAMOU: "Peace be to you."

BAKHAM: "Thank you."

BRONO: One section of a tribal village.

BUBUANHUNU: Impossible to calculate.

CAN TON: A Dogon village built around a water hole.

COFFLE: A group of slaves chained together in a line.

DASHIKI: African buttonless shirt.

DIDHTE WAW?: "Where are we going?"

DURBAR: Celebration ceremony.

FOUFOU: Traditional African dish eaten from a common pot.

HARMATTAN WINDS: Seasonal winds that blow sand from the Sahara Desert across West Africa. Many believe that in the midst of such a wind, things suddenly become what they were not.

JOAM: A slave at the lowest level of Wolof society.

JUJU: A magic amulet.

KENTE CLOTH: Wraplike royal attire made of fine imported silk, or of cotton with silk threads woven through. The usual design is made up of small geometric patterns, such as diamonds, cubes, triangles, and so forth. Each design is linked to an African proverb.

KYINIE: Brightly colored parasol that symbolizes the sovereignty of African kings.

LANTERLOO: An old gambling game played with cards and dice.

MAAFA: The term used by Africans to refer to the slave trade. It means "the great disaster."

NJADENGA: "The Big One in the Sky"; God of the heavens.

NKONNWAFIESO: The house where the stools of power are kept on a wood or clay bench and covered with a blanket.

NTUMPANE: "Talking drums" specifically constructed to carry messages far and wide.

OBEAH: Witchcraft.

OHEMMEA: A high-ranking royal woman granted unusual power and great prestige.

OHLA: Honorable leader.

OKYEAME: A speaker who conducted negotiations and held court in the name of the king.

SAMANKA: A medicine formulated to ward off harmful powers.

SIKA'GUA: The Golden Stool that was the political-ritual symbol of unity and power and was believed to embody the spirit of the nation.

SLATTEES: African kings who permitted Europeans to compete for African slaves.

SOFO: A priest who entreats the ancestors for wisdom and guidance.

STAD: African village.

THILA: A guardian sent by the ancestors to stand beside people and protect them.

TOGBUI: Prophets and prophetesses, avatars and sages who speak the words of the ancestors.

Discussion Questions

1. In *The Call of Zulina*, the first book in the Grace in Africa series, Grace Winslow straddles two worlds. Do you see her as more African or more English? On what do you base your opinion?

2. We meet three decisive women in this book: Grace, Lingongo, and Mama Muco. What are the strengths of each? How would the story have been different had any one of them lacked such strength?

3. Why do you think Joseph Winslow raised Grace the way he did? Do you see conflicting motives?

4. In what ways were Grace's actions bold? In what ways were they foolish? Could she have accomplished her goal any other way?

5. For more than two hundred years, people have debated who should bear the blame for the slave trade. How did each of the following groups contribute to that horrible period of history: Europeans? Colonials? Africans? Could the slave trade have survived without the help of any one of these? Why or why not?

6. What do you see as the significance of the wind that blows throughout the book?

7. It is always easy to look back at periods and events in history and judge them through 21st-century eyes. Two examples are attitudes toward marriage in the 18th century and the practice of primogeniture (the gifting of all the family land to the eldest son). What

were the pros and cons of the marriage "deals" made on behalf of Lingongo? Of Grace? Of Charlotte? Pieter De Groote explains the reasoning behind primogeniture. Do these reasons seem valid? What were the drawbacks of such an arrangement? Why do you suppose it is no longer followed in most of the Western world?

8. John Newton, slave ship captain turned abolitionist and author of the hymn *Amazing Grace*, claimed that an additional great evil of the slave trade was the way it "debased" everyone who participated in it. How did the slave trade affect Joseph Winslow? Jasper Hathaway? Pieter De Groot?

9. How did Grace change by the end of the book? Do you think this change would have taken place without the trigger of her impending marriage to Jasper Hathaway?

10. By the final chapters, was Grace more African or more English? Why?

Clash of Worlds

~ ~ ~

1

West Africa, 1792

The African sky sizzled a deep orange as a blistering sun sank over the far side of the village wall. All day long one *griot* after another had stood up in the village, each storyteller taking his turn at weaving together a piece of the tale of how a few African captives outsmarted and outfought the powerful white slave man in his very own slave fortress to win freedom for many. Each did his best to make his piece of the story the most dramatic, the most spectacular, the most breathtaking of all. Each one decorated his tale with songs and poems and gorgeously crafted words, so that when the entire story tapestry was complete, his part would shine out more brightly than the others. Each storyteller's efforts were rewarded with energetic cheers from the crowd.

Grace, settled comfortably between Mama Muco and Safya, grabbed at her little son who was once again doing his best to wriggle away from her.

"Stay close, Kwate," she warned. Grace tried to be stern with him, but a smile tugged at the edges of her voice. Never in her life had she been as happy as she was at that moment.

As the sun pitched low on the stifling evening, as the feast goats crackled in the roasting pit, as children threw beetles in the fire to toast and then dig out and pop in their mouths, drums beat the celebration into a fever pitch. People had poured in from villages far and near to join the celebration and bring offerings for the ancestors, for the great rebellion was a part of their lives too.

Their *griots* came along and jostled for a chance to stand before the people and weave in their own village's piece of the story. And because it is in the nature of a storyteller to be a bit of a gossip, each one tried to outdo the others in telling the latest news about the restoration of the Zulina slave fortress. A new white man ran it now, one announced. He was called by the name Hathaway, and he was a harder man than Joseph Winslow ever was.

Grace caught her breath. Jasper Hathaway? The man her parents had tried to force her to marry?

Another storyteller jumped to his feet. "The beautiful Princess Lingongo," he said. "Even now she sits on the throne of her people beside her brother. I know this truth from one who just saw it with his own eyes."

At this, Grace gripped Mama Muco's arm and caught her breath. "Mother is alive!" she gasped. "How can it be?"

Mama Muco kept her attention fixed on the *griot*. Thinking Mama had not heard her, Grace shook Mama's arm and said, "Did you hear that? Did you?" Only when Mama Muco refused to look at her did Grace understand; this came as no surprise to Mama.

"Does Cabeto know?" Grace asked. When Mama Muco still did not answer, Grace demanded, "What else is everyone keeping from me?"

"We cannot control what is happening around us anymore than we can change what happened to us," Mama Muco said to Grace. "All we can do is decide how we will live our lives. Our life here is good. Let us be happy and give thanks to God for today."

Far down the village's stone wall, out beside the rusty gate that still stood open, Hola shuffled impatiently, his musket propped against the wall.

"I want to hear the stories too," he complained to Tetteh, who stood guard with him. "And I want a fistful of that goat meat before the good part is all gone!"

"You have heard those same stories every year for the last five years," Tetteh said.

"But every year the *griots* have more tasty bits to tell us," Hola answered. "Besides, every one of the last five years I have had to stand guard, even though no one has ever tried to do us harm. So what would it hurt for you and me to take turns at the gate tonight?

I'll go listen to the stories for a while, then I'll come back and you can go listen."

Tetteh shrugged. "We should not disobey our elders, but if you are not gone too long, I suppose—" Hola was out of sight before Tetteh had a chance to finish.

Just as Hola slid noiselessly in behind a clutch of other young men, the last storyteller finished weaving his tale and the drums pounded out *durbar!* Celebrate!

Mama Muco, full of wisdom and years, stood up and danced her way over to the fire. Safya, with her gentle ways and the look of sleep forever on her eyes, got up and joined Mama, clapping her hands and shuffling in time to the drums. Ama, who had only recently come to the village with her two brothers, followed. Then, one by one, other women shuffled up and joined the growing dance line.

"Come on, Grace!" Mama called out. But Grace hugged little Kwate to herself and shook her head. Actually, she was glad to have an excuse to stay out of the dance. She enjoyed watching, but the fact was, even after five years, she didn't understand African dances. Whenever she tried to participate, she looked every bit as awkward and out of place as she felt.

There is no African in your hands and feet, Grace, her mother used to tell her. Evidently her mother was right.

Tawnia, who was almost twelve, leapt to her feet and pranced toward the end of the line, but Mama caught the girl by the shoulder and gave her a gentle shove back.

"Child, you are not yet a woman," Mama scolded. But as Tawnia stomped away, Mama rumbled a soft chuckle.

The men sat together in small groups and watched the women dance. Suddenly, Cabeto jumped up. As Grace laughed out loud and little Kwate clapped his hands, Cabeto waved his arms and danced with an awkward gait toward another group of men who had just helped themselves to roasted goat meat. He tore off his shirt and threw it down in front of an older man with graying hair and a sturdy round face.

"You, Tuke!" Cabeto called. "Will you be brave enough to dance?"

Tuke jumped to his feet. His arms flying wildly, he kept right on chewing as he danced over to a group of young men and threw his shirt down in front of them. Everyone roared with laughter as

Hola answered the challenge. He jumped up, tore off his shirt, and danced more outrageously than the others.

"Dance, Hola!" Tawnia yelled, and everyone else took up the chant.

Tetteh, alone at the gate, struggled to see what was going on. Why was everyone calling Hola's name? Tetteh had to admit that Hola was right in his opinion that standing guard was the same as doing nothing. He was also right that there never had been a threat to the village. Maybe Tetteh would also go and watch the celebration . . . for just a few minutes, perhaps.

When the dancing finally stopped, Chief Ikem, his walking stick grasped tightly in his wizened arm, stood up in front of the fire. Shadows of dancing flame reflected on his midnight-black face. They seemed to bring to life the intricate tattoos etched across his forehead and down both his cheeks. When the chief raised his staff over his head, the drums stopped and flames shot up, sending a shower of sparks flying into the darkened sky.

"Five years past, in this season when all sweet potatoes be dug, we be a small band of survivors with no hope in us," Chief Ikem said. "Five years past, when all sweet potatoes be dug, we work together to raise a village out of ashes left by the slave trader and the killer lioness. But now, those years lie with the ancestors. Tonight, with all sweet potatoes dug, we celebrate a happy village of peace and love."

Had the dream of peace and love not come so persuasively from the wise lips of Chief Ikem, someone might have noticed that an owl had soared through the firelight and perched in the highest branches of the ghariti tree that brings life to the people, then that person would have recognized the harbinger of calamity. Had Hola and Tetteh had enough years to understand that just because something had not yet happened, that didn't mean it never would happen, they might have closed the gate in the wall, slipped the bolt into place, and stood fast at their post. Had the fire not roared so brightly that it blinded the villagers' eyes to everything else, at least one person in the crowd might have noticed that not all the trees were still, as trees should be on a breathlessly still night.

But that was not to be. It was a night of *durbar*. The fire crackled, the drums called for celebration, and everyone laughed out loud and clapped their hands and rejoiced together in the happy village of peace and love.

Want to learn more about author
Kay Strom and check out other great
fiction from Abingdon Press?

Sign up for our fiction newletter at
www.AbingdonPress.com
to read interviews with your favorite
authors, find tips for starting a reading
group, and stay posted on what new titles
are on the horizon. It's the place to connect
with other fiction readers or to post a
comment about this book.

Be sure to visit www.KayStrom.com!